Hello, Sunshine

**Center Point
Large Print**

Also by Laura Dave and available from Center Point Large Print:

Eight Hundred Grapes

This Large Print Book carries the Seal of Approval of N.A.V.H.

Hello, Sunshine

Laura Dave

CENTER POINT LARGE PRINT
THORNDIKE, MAINE

This Center Point Large Print edition
is published in the year 2017 by arrangement with
Simon & Schuster, Inc.

The text of this Large Print edition is unabridged.
In other aspects, this book may vary
from the original edition.
Printed in the United States of America
on permanent paper.
Set in 16-point Times New Roman type.

ISBN: 978-1-68324-497-4

Library of Congress Cataloging-in-Publication Data

Names: Dave, Laura, author.
Title: Hello, sunshine / Laura Dave.
Description: Center Point Large Print edition. | Thorndike, Maine :
    Center Point Large Print, 2017.
Identifiers: LCCN 2017025762 | ISBN 9781683244974
    (hardcover : alk. paper)
Subjects: LCSH: Large type books.
Classification: LCC PS3604.A938 H45 2017b | DDC 813/.6—dc23
LC record available at https://lccn.loc.gov/2017025762

My Js.

The secret of life is honesty and fair dealing.
If you can fake that, you've got it made.

—*Groucho Marx*

June

1

You should probably know two things up front. And the first is this: On my thirty-fifth birthday—the day I lost my career and my husband and my home in one uncompromising swoop—I woke up to one of my favorite songs playing on the radio alarm clock. I woke up to "Moonlight Mile" playing on the radio (where it is almost never played) and actually thought, as you only would think if you're a total fool (or, perhaps, if you were about to lose your career and your husband and your home in one uncompromising swoop): The world, my world, is good.

I stayed in bed, in my fresh Frette sheets (a birthday present to myself), the sunlight drifting through the windows, the air chilly and light. And I listened to the entire song, crooning assuredly through my apartment.

Are you familiar with the song "Moonlight Mile"? It's a Rolling Stones song—not nearly as popular as their ubiquitous "You Can't Always Get What You Want" or as wedding-song-sticky as "Wild Horses." "Moonlight Mile" is just the most honest rock song ever recorded. I don't offer that as my personal opinion. I share that as fact: an inarguable fact, which you should twist into your brain and heart so that when someone argues the virtues of a different song as the epitome of greatness (prepare for the Beatles, who naturally arise as a challenge to the Stones), you can smile and quietly think, *I know better*. It's nice to know better. It's nice to know that when you hear the closing guitar riff of "Moonlight Mile," what you're actually hearing is a piece of music so soft and difficult, so dangerous and quiet, so full of life and death and love, that just below its surface, the song is telling you a secret—a secret that I was just starting to understand—about everything that matters in this world, everything that grounds us and eventually leaves us, all at once.

The tricky part is that the song was the product of an all night jam session between Mick Jagger and the Rolling Stones guitarist Mick Taylor. It was Taylor who had taken a short guitar piece recorded by Keith Richards and reworked it for the session. And it was Taylor's idea to add a string arrangement to the final song. The legend goes that Taylor, for good reason, was promised a songwriting credit. But "Moonlight Mile" was officially credited to Jagger/Richards. Keith Richards would later deny Taylor's involvement at all, and say that Mick Jagger delivered the song to the band all on his own.

Normally, if you were to ask me about this, I'd

say: Who cares? The credit didn't matter, what mattered was the song. Taylor kept playing with the band, so he'd let it go.

Except on the morning in question—the morning of my thirty-fifth birthday, the morning of my crisp Frette sheets, of rightness in the world—the injustice of Mick Taylor's omission was at the forefront of my mind, and I looked him up on my phone.

Considering what was about to happen to my world, it was odd that this was the moment I focused on Taylor. Call it foreshadowing, call it intuition. For the first time, I found myself sympathizing with him. Even though, in my particular story, I'm not the guy you root for. I'm not Mick Taylor. I'm not even Mick Jagger.

I'm Keith Richards, getting credit and telling lies from outside the room.

I heard a groan next to me. "Didn't you make a rule about phones in bed?"

I turned to see my husband, waking up, yawning for effect. Danny Walker: Iowa raised, strong chin, fearless. His eyes were still closed, his long eyelashes (thick lashes, like someone had tinted them, slathered them with rich mascara) clasped tightly together.

"You can't even see my phone," I said.

"I don't have to, I can *feel* it," he said.

He opened his eyes, stunning green eyes, those lashes surrounding them like a web. I resented those lashes, those eyes. Danny was more naturally beautiful than any woman would ever figure out how to be. Especially his wife. And while some women might have been okay with that, proud even, or so blissfully in love they didn't keep score, I was not one of those women. I kept score. I hadn't always, but somewhere along the way I started to. Which maybe was part of the problem. But I'm getting ahead of myself.

"It's *your* rule," he said, pointing at the phone. "Shut it off."

"That's the first thing you want to say to me today?" I said.

"Happy birthday." He smiled, his great smile. "Shut it off."

He moved his hand down my stomach, his touch ice cold. Our apartment was an old converted loft in Tribeca (recently photographed for *Architectural Digest*), a few blocks off the Hudson River, and freezing in the morning. No matter the season, no matter June's gnarly heat. It was freezing. It was also oddly loud, the noises from the highway and the river comingling to remind you there was nowhere else in the world in quite the same identity crisis. It was by far the nicest place we'd lived together—a large step up from the first place we'd shared at the University of Oregon. A garden apartment, the landlord had called it. He was right in that you could see the garden from the basement windows that looked up toward it.

There were three apartments after that, but none of them had the loft's corner windows—with views of the Hudson River and Battery Park—making everything in New York look beautiful.

I tossed my phone to the side of the bed, tossed Mick Taylor to the side.

"Good. Let's start again, then. Happy birthday, baby," he said. And, for a second, I wondered if he'd been thinking the same thing about our real estate past, our shared history.

He started to kiss me, and I stopped thinking. All these years in, I could still get lost in it. Lost in Danny. How many people, fourteen years in, could say that? And, yes, I'm glossing over the other part—the part where that took a hit. But I had vowed to change all that. And, at this particular moment, I was dedicated to changing all that. Very dedicated.

Danny moved on top of me, his hands working their way down my thighs, when I heard it. My phone beeped from the side of the bed, a bright and shiny email notification coming across its screen.

I flinched, instinctively wanting to grab it. It could have been important. A hundred and fifty people worked on my show; it usually was.

Danny peered at the phone out of the corner of his eye. "How is that putting your phone away?"

"I'll be really quick," I said. "Promise."

He forced a smile, moving away. "No, you won't," he said.

I flipped to my inbox screen, and there was the email.

The subject line was simple enough.

Hello, Sunshine

I didn't recognize the sender's email address. So I almost didn't open it. I like to tell myself that if I hadn't, I could have stopped everything that came next.

Door one: Sunshine Mackenzie ignores the email, has birthday sex with her husband, and life goes on as usual. Door two: Sunshine pushes her husband aside and opens an email from someone called Aintnosunshine, and life as she knows it ends.

Let's guess which door I took.

Do you know who this is? Here's a hint: I'm about to ruin you.

I laughed, a little loudly. After all, it was such a ridiculous email. So incredibly over-the-top, like the spam you get from Nigeria asking you to send your bank account information.

"What's so funny?" Danny said.

I shook my head. "Nothing. Just a silly email."

"They usually are."

This was a point of friction between us. Whereas my entire career existed online, Danny was an architect and sometimes didn't even check

14

his email more than a couple times a day. He'd learned how to contain it, disregarding ridiculous emails from difficult clients, who were obsessed with their Gramercy Park brownstones, their Bowery rooftops. He'd learned how to contain it, so he could get the work done for *them*. It was a skill that his wife, apparently, had yet to learn.

I turned back to my phone.

"All right. You've chosen," he said.

Then he pulled the blankets back, got out of bed.

"No!" I said. And I reached to pull him back down. "Danny! Please come back. That's a birthday order."

He laughed. "Nope, too late."

Then the next email came in.

Do you think I was kidding? I'm not the kidding type.

Some would even say humorless: www.twitter .com/sunshinecooks

This stopped me cold. Why did he choose the word *humorless?* (At that moment in time, knowing nothing, I thought the hacker was a he.) It was a specific word. It was also a word I used often.

So I clicked on the link.

And there was my verified Twitter account staring back at me.

There was my profile complete with a photograph of me in my studio kitchen—wearing

15

a peasant blouse and strategically distressed jeans, my blond hair swept off my face in a loose bun.

@SunshineCooks

Cooking for a New Generation. Host of #alittlesunshine. NY Times bestselling Author: #afarmersdaughter, #farmtothenewyorktable & (coming soon!) #sunkissed

And a new tweet to my 2.7 million followers.

Apparently from me.

I'm a fraud. #aintnosunshine

I must have let out a gasp, because Danny turned. "What?"

"I think I was hacked," I said.

"What are you talking about?"

He walked back over to the bed to see for himself. I quickly pulled the phone away. Even in the chaos, I still had an instinct to control it, keep it close. And, of course, to keep it away from him.

"You know what? It's nothing."

"Sunny . . ."

"Danny, I'm forwarding it to Ryan now. He'll deal with it. It's his job."

Danny looked unconvinced. Fourteen years. He knew things. "Are you sure?"

I forced a smile and repeated that all was well. So he nodded, walked away.

First, though, he leaned down to kiss me. A sweet kiss. A birthday kiss. Not the sex that we'd been close to, but something. Something lovely.

Which was when the phone's bright light shined again, another tweet coming in.

Let me stop there, though.

Before we got the next tweet, the next hack, before we got to what it said. The thing that led to the demise of my career, my home, my marriage.

You remember how I told you that there were two things you should know right up front?

The first was how it happened. On the morning of my thirty-fifth birthday, "Moonlight Mile" welcomed me to my day, my husband still loved me, and then the email came in. The start of something I couldn't stop.

The second thing you should know? I was not (certainly at that moment in time) a good person. Some would even say I was a *bad* person. And everything this emailer—the hacker, the imploder of my perfect life—had to say about me was the truth.

See how I told you how it happened first? Garnering sympathy. Take that as proof of the second.

2

I sat in my living room, my laptop open in front of me, tweet number two burning up.

Luckily, Danny had a consultation for a project on Central Park West so it wasn't hard to get him out of the apartment quickly, leaving me alone to sit there in my egg chair—a mid-century purple swivel seat that I purchased for too much money shortly after *A Little Sunshine* was picked up to series. I normally loved sitting in my chair. I was oddly attached to it, considering it was as ugly as it had been pricey. Though, at that moment, even my favorite chair was giving me hives. Well, it probably wasn't the chair. It probably was the tweets.

To elucidate on the "I'm a fraud thing," here's Exhibit 1: #aintnosunshine

And there was a photograph. It was a photograph of a splashy tear sheet from my first cookbook—*A Little Sunshine: Recipes from a Farmer's Daughter*. A tear sheet with my signature recipe. Tomato pie. A modern take on the Southern classic: a cracker-thin crust strewn with juicy heirloom tomatoes, balsamic vinegar, fresh basil, pine nuts, and layers of creamy mozzarella cheese. It had garden fresh herbs, cracked pepper, and my trademark: citrus in place of salt.

Except my name was crossed out on the top and, in thick black marker, the name Meredith Landy was written instead.

Meredith Landy was my executive producer Ryan's wife. She was a former sous-chef at Babbo who had long ago traded in her thankless restaurant hours to move to Scarsdale, where she spent too many hours redesigning her thousand-square-foot home kitchen—first to mirror Diane Keaton's kitchen in *Something's Gotta Give*, then to mirror Ina Garten's barn-kitchen.

She was also, as I thought only two other people in the world knew, the recipe's actual creator. Two to 2.7 million in the blink of an eye. I had to fight to keep my balance.

"I'm trying to get Twitter on the phone!"

I turned in my chair as Violet, my assistant, walked into the apartment, carrying two Starbucks coffees, her cell phone glued to her ear.

"Fucking West Coast hours," she said. "I've been on hold *forever.* Is Ryan here yet?"

"Do you see him?" I said.

Violet handed me a coffee, plopping down onto the sofa, unfazed by the harsh tone. She was twenty-four, five foot eleven, with wild red hair, a gorgeous smile, and a detailed plan to build her own empire (*Once Upon a Vegan*) by the time she was twenty-eight. She loved to say that when she did, she would be a lot rougher on her Violet than I was.

"Ryan called from the car. He's sending out Meredith's statement," she said. "She had nothing to do with your signature tomato pie or any of your recipes . . . Sunshine has been hacked, yada, yada . . ."

"Who do you think wrote it?"

She stood up. "Hello?" she said into the phone. She paused. "Who are you?"

She started pacing the length of the loft— the open kitchen to the living room—floor-to-ceiling steel windows lining her way. Danny had designed the apartment around those steel windows, their clean lines framing the brick building across the street, an eighteenth-century tea distributor, the etched white LAPPIN TEA on the front still announcing itself.

"No! I need Craig . . ." she said, screaming at the person on the phone.

I turned back to my computer, read the most recent replies to the Meredith Landy tweet.

@sunshinecooks Is this true? #Whatthefuck

@sunshinecooks Thought u were too skinny. #realchefseat

@sunshinecooks Dear Sunshine, you're a monster.

The monster bit felt like a serious overreaction, and for the first time, I was glad to be locked out of my system so I didn't say something to

20

@kittymom99 that I later regretted. I closed the Twitter window and went back to crafting responses for the rest of my social media avatars. I had a staffer who ran each of these. But I was not about to trust a twenty-five-year-old Holyoke grad to deliver a message to my 1.5 million Facebook friends.

"They're shutting it down!" Violet yelled out. "Craig is shutting it down!"

I looked up to see Violet doing the moonwalk over the Persian rug, dancing her way past the windows—as Ryan walked in the front door, arriving, as he always did, just in time to take credit.

"They're shutting it down," he said, like Violet hadn't just reported as much.

Ryan Landy. Columbia Law *and* Business School, newly forty, and chiseled everywhere: jaw, chin, shoulders. He was in his uniform of jeans and a sports coat, his shirt one-button-too-open. Since turning forty, he had adopted the forced-casual addition of hipster sneakers, which added to his perfect mix of little-boy good-looking, sleazy, and something (charming, deceitful) that made pretty much every woman he'd encountered putty in his hands—including his wife, Meredith, who seemed unable to do anything except forgive him for those other women.

Violet, still on the phone, put her hand over the

receiver. "I've got Craig," she said. "Should be down in thirty seconds."

"Should've been down THIRTY SECONDS AGO, Craig," Ryan said, loud enough for Craig to hear.

Violet plugged her ears. "What was that, Craig?" she said, scurrying away.

Ryan headed toward my egg chair, twirled me around, and offered his half-smile. Charming.

"Are you hungry?" he said.

"Am I hungry? Ah . . . no."

He headed toward the kitchen. "Well, you better have something to eat in this place . . . 'Cause I'm starving," he said.

Ryan reached into my refrigerator and pulled out a green juice, a hard-boiled egg. Then he jumped up onto the countertop, taking a seat. My gorgeous gray slate countertop: stunning beside the glass refrigerator, the eight-burner stove, and stainless steel ovens.

It was a chef's kitchen in every way, even if I was a true chef in none.

He popped the entire egg into his mouth. "Don't look so nervous," he said.

"I'm not nervous, Ryan. I'm pissed. How did this happen?"

"Kevin let it happen. But Jack spent the morning securing your other accounts with a firewall," he said, his mouth full. "New passwords, new security codes. Nobody outside this room will have them. Nobody outside Jack, that is."

"Who is Jack?"

"The new Kevin."

I frowned. "It's out there now, though. People are going to think—"

"People are going to think exactly what we tell them to think," he said. "I mean, listen to Meredith's statement," he said as he pulled out his phone and started reading. *"My husband, the esteemed producer Ryan Landy, has worked with Sunshine Mackenzie since he discovered her first video on YouTube, making this very recipe. With the exception of being a fan (and I like to think a valued early taster), I have no claim to any of Sunshine's scrumptious creations."*

"Why is everyone talking to me like I wasn't the one who wrote that?" I said.

He smiled. "I'm just praising your good work."

I nodded, but there was no relief sinking in. It had all gotten a little close. And neither of us was saying the truth out loud. Meredith was the real chef. They were her recipes. Her vision. Or, rather, Ryan's vision, and her execution.

"You don't think Meredith is behind this, do you?"

Ryan laughed, the thought of his wife betraying him apparently hilarious. "No fucking way!"

"What if she—"

"She didn't. It would destroy us financially. She would never do that."

"So, who?" I said.

Ryan shook his head. "A hacker, someone who got into your email . . ."

His nonchalance was really starting to irritate me. "How would a random get so close to the truth?"

He shrugged. "I told you, the bigger you get, the more people come after you. And someone is apparently after you. Probably with the Food Network deal, they're excited . . ."

The Food Network deal. I hadn't wanted to mention it. I was slated to be a cohost of a new farm-to-table cooking show. Competition shows were now the Holy Grail on the network. No one was offered a straight cooking show unless they were a movie star turned culinary star. But that's how popular *A Little Sunshine* had become. The show was premiering in September—at least it was supposed to. Unless this hacker ruined everything.

Ryan jumped down off the countertop. "The point is I cut off his access. There's nothing he can do now."

He. Ryan said *he.* "You think it's a he? That's interesting. That's my gut too."

He walked up to me, so we were face-to-face, his palm gently cupping my neck. "Can we be done with this already? I have other things to discuss, okay?"

I looked away, not wanting to engage with any of his *other things*. "Like what?"

"Tonight. The party."

I closed my eyes. In the chaos, I had forgotten. Danny had planned a surprise party in the back room of Locanda Verde for fifty of our closest friends.

"We should cancel it," I said.

"Cancel it? No!"

I already knew where he was going. He was going to use my party to fix this.

"You're going to spin the story."

"I've trained you well, young Sunshine."

I drilled him with a dirty look. But he wasn't wrong. He had.

"I'm inviting the press. *People, Us Weekly.* Great opportunity to put these rumors to bed."

Ordinarily, I would have rolled with it. But I hesitated. The hack, the day, *the song*—some of it, all of it, had gotten to me. And I was feeling . . . something.

"Danny doesn't want publicity tonight. He specifically said."

"And I care about what Danny wants, why?"

I shot Ryan a look. I wasn't in the mood to stroke his ego—to pretend he'd won the latest battle of work husband versus real husband.

And I didn't want to upset Danny, especially when birthdays were a big deal around here. We'd been together since we were twenty-one, college sweethearts. And every year, we tried to top the year before for each other. Danny was already irritated that I'd peeked at his email and seen the details, asked him to make a few changes to all that planning (to the guest list and the menu and the time—I did keep the venue).

"Look, you can pretend you had no idea," Ryan said.

That was the last thing I wanted to do. While I had become somewhat of a seasoned liar over the years—a job requirement—I used to be a very honest person. And that was the person Danny knew—the one he had fallen in love with. Whenever I tried to *stretch* the truth with him, he would often see through it. And I didn't want to fight.

"Handle it however you want," Ryan said. "But we have to do this, okay?"

"Fine, whatever, just keep it under control."

"When don't I?" He paused, considering. "This morning notwithstanding."

"Ryan, we have to deal with him."

"Danny?" he said, confused.

"The hacker."

He rolled his eyes. "I'm dealing with him! Five people at the studio are devoting all their time to figuring out which weirdo living with his mother in Idaho who jerked off to your videos one too many times did this thing."

"Gross."

Ryan sucked down the juice. "I aim to please."

"Uh . . . guys?" Violet waltzed into the kitchen. "Amber is weighing in . . ."

Amber was Amber Rucci, aka *Toast of the Town*. A fellow culinary YouTube star. All of her dishes used toast as their base. Thick, old-fashioned brioche; salted, grainy rye. Some of her recipes were as simple as homemade almond butter on burnt brioche. Did that even count as a recipe? It counted enough that she was beloved. She was also young and attractive—and the host of the second-most popular YouTube cooking show, tracking only behind *A Little Sunshine*. Years ago, she had reached out and sent me an array of kitchen utensils *(Let's get cooking!!)* to cement something like a friendship between us. I was more than happy to play nice too and sent her back a knife set *(Your stove or mine?)*. Our "friendship" led to joint appearances on each other's shows and a *New York Times* "Night Out" piece. On the menu was my tomato pie, accompanied by her avocado and mint toast.

Now, apparently, she wanted the world to know she wasn't a fair-weather friend.

Believe in the power of Sunshine! #chefsunite #loveandpepper

She linked to a photograph of us on Instagram, preparing dinner in her kitchen.

Violet put her phone away. "That's nice, right?" she said. "Why didn't she email personally, though?"

"What good would that do?" Ryan said. "No one would have seen it!"

"I hate toast," I said.

Ryan smiled. "There's my girl!" he said.

"Violet, I need you to get a few tweets out in the next fifteen minutes," I said. "Something like . . . *'Hello, guys, this is Sunshine (the real Sunshine), what a morning!'* You understand."

She headed toward the living room. "Already on it."

Ryan called out after her. "Use one of those inspirational quotes on Instagram about how scary it is to have someone else speaking for you, pretending to be you. How strong you feel using your own voice again. Something."

Violet turned around. "Ooh! I have a great one from Maya Angelou!" she said.

"Did I ask you for the details?" Ryan said, waving her off. "Use a yellow background!"

Then Ryan turned to me.

"Yellow makes people think of truth," he said.

Had I read that somewhere? Or was Ryan just so convincing when he spewed his bullshit that I not only believed it, I believed I had always believed it?

28

I reached for my coffee. "Good to know."

"I could do without the sarcasm."

"So fix it, Ryan," I said. "What if someone starts digging around? The Food Network will pull the plug. Everyone will pull the plug!"

"Not going to happen," Ryan said.

I looked at him, uncertain.

"We have Meredith saying it's not true. What kind of digging makes sense after that? Besides, no one wants to open that can of worms. There are two people who have released cookbooks in the last decade who had anything to do with the actual recipes in those books. At the most, you have a celebrity who created the *dishes*. The recipes are worked out in a test kitchen by some ghostwriter who actually knows what he's doing."

"A ghostwriter who received credit," I said.

"So you want to tell the world now that Meredith is the ghostwriter? It's a little late to give her credit."

I thought of what I wasn't saying out loud—the stuff that would surely sink our little empire if it got out. "We know it's not just the recipes," I said.

"Sunny . . ."

Ryan's eyes softened, and for a second, it stopped feeling like he was producing me. It felt like he was being my friend.

"We also are the only ones who know. Trust me. We are safe," he said.

He nodded with absolute conviction.

I felt myself sinking into his assured tone. And it was enough for me to push it aside.

"We good here?" he said.

"We are," I said, almost meaning it.

It's amazing, after all, what you'll ignore when you want something to be right, isn't it? Like in this case, the truth.

3

If I haven't made it abundantly clear yet, Ryan had always had something of a loose hold on the truth. One of the first things he told me, in fact, was that he hated the words *lies* and *truth*. He said they were needlessly categorical. He liked to say instead: *the story*.

And the story, as far as the world knew, was a familiar one. It was a story that a lot of women could relate to. I was a small-town girl who, after college, decided to move to New York City. I was young, newly engaged, and struggling to make a name for myself as a journalist. I was working terrible hours at a sports magazine. (We settled on a sports magazine because Ryan thought a woman's magazine was too clichéd.) The point was, I had moved far from where I'd come from—but instead of feeling great about this, I felt a strange pull toward my roots. So, the Sunday I turned twenty-six, I headed to the farmer's market in Park Slope and made a family favorite—tomato pie—walking Danny through the various ingredients with stories of growing them on the farm. At some point, Danny picked up the video camera and filmed me putting the pie in the oven—later revealing the decadent finished treat.

We had enjoyed the night so much—far more than the sticky sesame chicken we treated ourselves to on Sunday nights—that the next Sunday, I did the same thing. And the Sunday after that.

And so it started a tradition. Every Sunday night, I cooked a new farm-fresh meal, recipes developed to highlight in-season produce, local farmers. Everything was easy to make (every chef loved promising ease), but also fun: Danny on the other side of the camera, laughing at the embarrassing anecdotes I shared about growing up on the farm, how they related to the recipe, how they related to our life together now. From the first video, I wasn't just promising a farm-fresh meal: I promised something else. Friendship. Honesty. Someone saying it was okay to embrace wherever you came from as a part of where you wanted to go.

Danny started posting the videos to YouTube to share with our family and friends. He called them, "A Little Bit of Sunshine: Sunday Night with a Farmer's Daughter."

He, of course, had no idea they would go viral.

Well, viral is an exaggeration. But fifty thousand people did tune in for the first one. And after we posted about five of them, they caught the eye of a Food Network producer, Ryan Landy, who saw in this unabashed small-town girl the opportunity to bring cooking to a new generation. It wasn't just my recipes he liked, he would later say in the first profile of *A Little Sunshine* in *New York* magazine, it was the feeling. Small-town girl turning into city woman. My East Village apartment was rustic and homey. My fiancé in his jeans and button-down was handsome without trying. And while I was just wearing a T-shirt and jeans, my hair swept into a bun, I looked like you'd want to look with your hair swept into a bun: friendly, sincere, girl you wanted to be friends with pretty.

A Little Sunshine, he said, was aspirational for young, ambitious New Yorkers: twenty-somethings and thirty-somethings who didn't shop for clothes anymore, who bought *pieces;* who turned 800-square-foot apartments into glamorous, mid-century homes; who through sheer force of will (and eighty-hour workweeks) turned relationships and jobs into the family and career they wanted. But these women, in their efforts to become the women they thought they should be, sometimes lost sight of the women they used to be—the women they truly were. Here was someone being who she truly was. And being embraced for it.

My grainy videos made people feel like I was their most authentic friend. And, from day one, the fans (how weird, at first, to think of *fans*) craved that authenticity. They wrote emails, they wrote letters, they wrote in the comments: *Who knew that in the kitchen I would rediscover a piece of myself? #justadentistsdaughter.* (She was a hedge fund manager who'd won two Midas Awards and lived in a ten-million-dollar loft on Hubert Street.) We put her testimonial on the top of the webpage.

This woman, all these women, who had their fifty-dollar blow-outs and Pilates lessons and green juice in the morning, now, every Sunday, instead of takeout, they had *A Little Sunshine*. It was cooking as a way of escape, cooking as a way of joy. Cooking as a way to make their boyfriends and husbands feel wanted and make them feel like they were more than their busy jobs. It was cooking as a way to spend time with Sunshine Mackenzie—a pretty (but not too pretty) girl who, just like them, was taking a little time away from trying to be everything to everyone to stay true to herself.

It was a great story, right?

If only any of it were true.

The day I turned twenty-six, I wasn't uploading anything to YouTube. I was working at a bar and grill in Red Hook. At the time, it was one of the only bar and grills in Red Hook—a small community at the tip of Brooklyn, named after the hook at its end that stuck out into Upper New York Bay. Nowadays, it was nearly as hip and pricey as the more convenient and yuppied-out Brooklyn neighborhoods near it—but at the time, it was still fighting its gentrification—an IKEA going in, artists purchasing town houses, a Michelin-starred chef setting up shop in an abandoned Chevron station. Most important, while completely inconvenient to everything in Manhattan, Red Hook was relatively convenient to the graduate school where Danny was getting his master's in architecture.

Of course, over time, Red Hook had become more than just convenient. It had become a plan. There was a brownstone off Pioneer Street that we couldn't begin to afford. It needed a gut renovation, landscaping, indoor plumbing (no joke). But we loved it all the same—its small backyard, an exposed brick wall that ran the length of the living room. Danny had become friendly with the owner, who had several equally dilapidated properties around the neighborhood. He was considering selling to us, if, in exchange, Danny would renovate the brownstone as a show property: an example of how the other properties could be lovingly refurbished. Danny agreed that he would build out those properties as well, if buyers were interested.

So, in theory, it was to everyone's benefit. I loved the idea of having a home—a real home that I wanted to come home to (something I'd never had). Danny needed clients. The owner wanted to cash in on Red Hook's burgeoning popularity.

I was tending bar to pay our rent, and Danny was moonlighting at an architecture firm in Tribeca on the weekends to pay for everything else, including our down payment. We weren't going to be able to celebrate my birthday together that night. We weren't going to be able to celebrate my birthday until we each had a corresponding day off—which looked like it was going to be sometime in August.

Ryan walked in around 10 P.M. I'm sure of the time because a drunk couple—two regulars, Austin and Carla—were arguing at the bar. Right as the front door opened, Carla poured their pitcher of beer over Austin's head.

"Sorry!" Austin said. I didn't know if he was talking to me or to his girlfriend. I knew he didn't mean it.

I perched on the floor, wiping up the sticky, yeasty mess, staring at the clock, counting the minutes until closing. So I didn't quit. So I didn't fill another pitcher of beer and throw it right back at them.

"You've certainly gone and made a mess of things now," Ryan said.

This was the first thing he said to me, sitting on the corner barstool, wearing a pinstriped suit. I looked up at him, taking a final swipe at the floor.

"Not my mess," I said.

He shrugged. "If you're the one cleaning it up, what's the difference?"

I smirked, preparing to ignore him. Sometimes they ended up here—smarmy guys in fancy suits, their wives asleep in their Park Slope town houses. They usually arrived with a woman they didn't want to be seen with anywhere else. I looked toward the door, half expecting someone to join him.

"It's just me," he said, as if reading the thought. Then he flashed me his smile.

Ryan would later say that I smiled back at him, welcoming him, but I doubt that's true. I don't remember having any interest in even serving him a drink—this guy talking to me from his height of the bar stool, my low of the floor.

"Guess I'm a little overdressed for this place," he said.

I shrugged. "All the same to me."

"Well, I didn't feel like heading home just yet. I just lost my job."

"Oh . . ."

"Yeah, well, officially, I resigned to pursue a secret project."

"And you thought you'd find it here?"

I worked on tips. You would have thought I'd try to keep the sarcasm in check. But I had beer on my knees and I didn't feel particularly badly for a guy who could sell his suit and make more than I was paid in a month.

He laughed. "No, I thought I'd get drunk here. And I'll start looking tomorrow."

"So what can I get you?"

"Do you make martinis?"

"Not well."

"Just a beer, then."

I filled up a pint and put it in front of him. "Five dollars," I said.

"Five dollars?"

He shook his head, taking out a ten, motioning for me to join him in a beer. It was an offer I had to accept, pouring myself a pint, so I could pocket the other five.

"Maybe you should learn how to make a martini," he said. "Increase that profit margin."

"I don't intend to be here long enough for it to matter."

"Where do you intend to be?"

"Anywhere else."

He tilted his head, taking me in, his phony smile disappearing, a different look appearing on his face. Like all of a sudden I interested him.

"To anywhere else," he said, lifting his glass, tipping it toward mine.

I heard a glass shatter on the ground and turned in time to see Austin stand up, Carla slamming him in the chest.

"I'm out of here!" he screamed, throwing the front door open, heading outside. Then Carla started crying hysterically.

Ryan nodded in their direction. "Lovely couple," he said.

"They're here almost as much as I am."

He motioned toward the front door. "I was just eating at the new French-Korean restaurant around the corner. Have you been there?"

I shook my head.

"The CEO wanted me to check it out with him."

"Before he fired you?"

"We're doing this new show, restaurants off the beaten path. Or, I should say, the Food Network is doing a show on off-the-beaten-path restaurants," he corrected himself. "Though I'm taking it you're not a regular viewer."

"Not exactly."

"Do you like to cook?"

"Does grilled cheese count?"

"But you like to eat?"

Truthfully, I loved to eat. My favorite activity since moving to New York (and one I couldn't really afford) was scoping out delicious restaurants and dragging Danny to them on a day off. With our schedules, the scoping had subsided, as had the eating out. But I still kept notes of places I wanted to try, and of the most appealing foods—for whenever we had more time to seek them out.

But I didn't have an opportunity to say any of that.

Ryan looked me up and down, the extra padding in my hips all the answer he seemed to need.

"Obviously you eat."

"Are you getting to a point?"

"I'm interested in the grilled cheese," he said. "Your grilled cheese."

"Why?"

"Would like to hear how you make it."

He put another twenty down on the counter, motioning for a refill.

"Humor me."

I started to say that I used American cheese and Wonder Bread, to shut him up. Though the combination of the twenty sitting on the bar and how little I wanted to do the requisite comforting of Carla encouraged a truthful answer.

"I grew up in Montauk, and there is this great bakery a few towns over . . . It opened a couple of years before I left for college, freshest bread you've ever tasted . . ."

"Levain."

I was a little impressed. Most people mentioned the Barefoot Contessa, which had since closed. I must have shown it, because Ryan smiled a little wider, proud of himself.

"I do this for a living," he said. "Did it for a living. So you use a bread like theirs? What kind of cheese?"

"Swiss. And I add tomatoes and avocado, and mayonnaise."

"Mayonnaise? That sounds kind of disgusting."

"Softens the bread in a way butter alone won't."

"Makes it closer to Montauk?" Ryan looked impressed. "Levain has a location on the Upper West Side. They're pretty famous for their cookies."

"They should be famous for the bread."

"And you grill your bread and cheese in Red Hook these days." It wasn't a question—it was like he was working through something. "That's exotic."

"People may think it's exotic, but . . ."

"What people *think* is all that matters."

He nodded as the front door swung open, the drunken Austin returning, Carla jumping into his arms. They started kissing, happily together again, their fight already forgotten.

"And boyfriend, I take it?"

"Fiancé."

He took a sip of his beer. "*Fiancé.* And what does fiancé do?"

"He's an architect." I paused. At this point, I still valued the truth. I still always tried to be accurate. "He's actually studying to be an architect."

"And what do you want to do when you grow up?"

I didn't want to answer that. Mostly because I didn't have a great answer. The plan had been for me to go back to school after Danny finished, but I was feeling tired at the notion. Maybe I was just feeling tired.

"You know, the spitfire questions are starting to make me uncomfortable."

"Fair enough, let me ask you just one more." He motioned toward the stool beside him. "Could you sit for a minute?"

"Is that the question? 'Cause the answer is no. I have customers."

He looked around at the mostly empty bar, Austin and Carla now making out with each other in the corner.

"Not many," he said. And he smiled, licked his lips. Mr. Drunk Pinstripe. He thought he was so charming. Looking for something from me that I wasn't willing to give him.

"Well, I also have a fiancé," I said.

"The famous architect. I got it." He pointed at his wedding ring. "I just want to talk to you."

"About what?"

"Your optics."

"My . . . what?"

"Red Hook. Young and pretty . . ."

He tilted his head like he was convincing himself.

Was this guy kidding me? I pushed my hair behind my ears, defensive. It was the Danny effect. I'd historically never paid too much attention to my looks (maybe it was growing up without a mother), but Danny made me feel like I was stunning: my long blond hair suddenly sexy, my uniform of tank tops and cargo pants,

42

effortlessly stylish in his eyes. Who was this guy to downgrade me?

"The right amount of pretty," he said, like the issue was settled. "I can definitely work with this. Girls won't feel threatened, especially because you're an outsider. Born and raised in the South. Farm country."

"I'm from Montauk."

He shook his head. "Nah, makes you sound rich. Can't start off rich. We'll pick somewhere in Florida or Texas. We'll make your dad a tomato farmer."

I looked at him, confused.

"What's your name?" he said.

"Sunny," I said.

"Short for . . ."

"Sunshine."

He laughed, thrilled. "Seriously? That's *too* perfect. I can definitely, definitely work with this. Sunshine Mackenzie. A farmer's daughter! Keeping it real in the Big Apple."

"That's not my last name."

"It's a star's name. A food critic eating at the restaurant tonight had that name. She had a way about her. That's what we're going with. You'll be my Justin Bieber. For the cooking world."

He was, at this point, talking to himself. I looked at him. "Who?"

"People love the discovery narrative. That's how we'll play it." He paused. "A chef for the next generation. That's what they don't get. That's what they never fucking got. How to do fucking modern."

I pointed toward Carla and Austin, who looked dangerously close to undressing each other. "I'm going to check on those guys."

Then I started to walk away.

He called out after me. "I'll give you a month's salary if you'll have a cup of coffee with me tomorrow."

I stopped walking. "Why would you do that?"

"The job opportunity I'm telling you about."

"You just told me you were fired. You don't have a job to offer."

He smiled. "I think I just might."

I leaned across the countertop. Did he not understand? "I make a pretty good grilled cheese," I said. "That's it."

"A certain TV personality who just opened his fifth Tex-Mex restaurant made a SPAM taco when I found him. Nothing to do with any-thing."

I stared at him in disbelief, slightly confused by what he was asking me to do: pretend to be a kind of cooking show host? "Look, I know you're having a tough night, but . . ."

"Three months' salary. Double the number of what they pay you here. Really, how would I know?"

We had no money, no heat. Danny was taking

a second job moonlighting at a botanical garden. We had seen each other for five hours in the last week. "Are you insane?"

"Bring your fiancé tomorrow," he said. "Then decide."

Ryan reached out his hand to shake on the deal. It wasn't slimy or cold. It was warm at the very moment that I needed warmth.

"I'm just saying yes to the coffee."

"I got it. No promises."

But he kept holding on to my hand, like a promise. And in that moment, I think I decided to do it. Not just the meeting, but the job.

Of course I never thought it would become what it became. No one did. Except Ryan; I guess Ryan did.

I sound like I'm making excuses. But why should I make excuses? There was a guy sitting before me telling me that he was giving me a way to stop waitressing, to earn a ton of money, to grow up. And I was going to do what? Pretend to cook a meal?

Even Danny, my gauge of what was good and bad in the world, just thought the whole thing was kind of funny. He didn't seem concerned during that first coffee the next day. It wasn't really a big deal—the first lie. After all, the stakes were low. It was just a recipe. It was just a video. Until the video became a hundred videos. And a produced YouTube show. And a cookbook that hit the bestseller list. And a second cookbook that also did. And an empire.

And the lie stopped being about what you cooked and how you cooked it. It was about everything in your life. Where you came from. Who you were. Where you were going.

How do you stop the train then? Even if you wanted to? And I wasn't saying I wanted to.

It's easy to pretend I'd made a deal with the devil. But Ryan genuinely didn't think we were doing anything wrong. And somewhere inside, I think I knew we were.

So which one of us was the devil?

4

Danny came home at 5 P.M.

I flinched when I heard the front door open, not anxious to do the rundown of the day—not anxious to see the look Danny got on his face when the conversation turned to my work. I cranked up the record player, hoping Bob Dylan would mitigate an argument. But, surprisingly, Danny walked into the kitchen with a huge smile and a bouquet of Gerber daisies in hand.

"A little Dylan?" he said. "That's certainly a nice way to come home."

"A bouquet of flowers is even nicer."

He pointed at the daisies. "Oh, these? They're not for you."

"Shut up," I said.

He walked over, kissed me hello. "Something told me that you could use them. Are you hanging in okay?" he asked.

I waved off his concern. "Great."

"Really?"

He tilted his head, not buying it, wanting to hear the truth in all its dirty matter. I used to love this about him, but recently I found it tiresome. I just wasn't in the mood for too much honesty. And Danny was the one person who demanded it, who didn't want me to perform for him—which, often, felt like the hardest performance of all.

"Meredith's statement was just picked up by the *Huffington Post*," he said, and started to read it aloud.

I nodded, not interrupting him, even though I wanted to correct him. The statement had posted to *Huff Post* hours ago.

Thanks to Meredith, the noise had quieted down. Everyone assumed (why wouldn't they?) that I had been hacked: my followers sending out much kinder tweets.

@sunshinecooks Still my favorite chef in the world #sunshineforever

@sunshinecooks Tomato Pie doesn't know how to lie #apoetwhodidntevenknowit

"So you and Ryan pulled it all the way back?" he said.

I held the flowers to my nose, breathed them in. "Looks that way."

"Congratulations," he said.

I heard the slight edge in his tone. Danny's relationship to this—to all of this—was complicated. He didn't like that there was a fake story behind *A Little Sunshine*, that there were lies he had to remember about where I came from, about how the show had started. Somewhere along the line, though, he thought that the lie had become the truth. I let him believe that many of the recipes Meredith had developed over the years were my recipes. I let him believe

I was actually doing my job. I let him believe a lot of things.

Danny reached into the cabinet and pulled out a bottle of wine. "No one seems to be blogging about it anymore," he said. "And I read that one of the Real Housewives got pregnant by another housewife's husband. So that certainly is more exciting than who really came up with your sweet potato hash."

I rolled my eyes, though I couldn't help but smile at the effort—given how much I knew it must have pained Danny to look up that headline on TMZ. "So . . . how did Central Park West go?" I said.

Danny uncorked the wine, shrugged nonchalantly. "Pretty good."

"What does that mean?" I said.

He smiled proudly. "I got the job," he said.

I threw my arms around him. This wasn't just another job. It was a game changer for Danny: a five-thousand-square-foot dream apartment overlooking the park. The type of project that not only ended up in *Architectural Digest*, it ended up on the cover.

"That's so great!" I said.

"There is a small downside. The job starts right away. So . . ." His smile disappeared. "No Italy."

Italy. We were supposed to spend July there—a long-overdue vacation as soon as *A Little Sunshine* wrapped. We'd eat linguine with clam sauce for every meal, great wine. We'd have proper time away together, to enjoy each other again. And to make the baby Danny desperately wanted. Time we apparently needed—the baby not coming on its own, not coming without a conscious attempt to try.

"So we'll postpone," I said.

"That's okay?"

I waved him off, secretly happy to postpone the baby-making a little longer, and very happy it was his work that was causing us to cancel: Danny disappointing me, as opposed to the other way around.

"Are you sure?" he said.

"Ah, Italy's terrible this time of year any-way."

He laughed, his great laugh. It was kind and open, pulling me into the present moment, and toward him.

He clocked it. "Thank you."

"I wish it was just the two of us tonight, though, so we could celebrate properly."

He looked at me, probably hearing it in my voice—something close to the truth. "So let's cancel the party."

I laughed. "We can't."

"Sure we can. Fuck the fake surprise party. I'm serious. We'll kick it old-style. Order in takeout? Dealer's choice."

I smiled. "Don't tempt me."

He moved in close, our faces practically touching. "Let me try and tempt you."

He looked serious all of a sudden, a little too serious, hoping that I would agree to play hooky: the two of us camped out in front of the television with a little sushi, a terrible movie playing.

"If you don't want the party, let's forget it," he said.

I paused. "Well, it's not about what I want."

"Ah." He pulled back. "So what? Ryan wants to do some damage control?"

Danny's expression changed, almost hardened. Danny used to tolerate Ryan, but the toleration had taken a downturn. He could barely stand to be in the same room with him. And he certainly didn't care what he thought about anything.

"What do you think?" he said.

"A performance is probably mandated."

"A performance is probably mandated . . ." he said.

And he laughed, clearly irritated by that response.

I stared at him, annoyed. How had this conversation taken this turn? Was he seriously angry about a party? I almost brought up Italy again. If anyone was choosing their job over marriage in this conversation, shouldn't Danny be the one on the hook? And why should I apologize for choosing to protect *A Little*

Sunshine? Which pretty much had purchased the apartment we were arguing in.

Danny rubbed his hands together, seeing the look in my eye. "Forget I asked," he said. "If you've got to do this tonight, we'll do it. We'll have our alone celebration tomorrow."

I followed his lead, playing nice. "You promise?" I said.

"Of course." He corked the bottle, gave me his winning smile, the one he reserved for just me. "Consider this saved for tomorrow," he said.

And we walked toward the bedroom to get ready, a small thing to do together, except when it turns out it's for the last time.

5

L ocanda Verde had one of the best private rooms in New York—dark and rustic, with a fireplace and long farm tables. It was a great place to park a party of fifty in, especially this fifty, who would already be on their second martinis, grazing on the passed plates of duck confit and cheese, on the small bowls of fruit, quietly whispering about the drama *A Little Sunshine* faced that day, pretending they had no doubts in my authenticity.

Danny and I were perched in the hallway outside, listening, Danny's hand on the doorknob.

I took a last look at my outfit, straightening my dress. It was a simple print dress over thick tights, my hair swept up off my face. Understated. Presentable. Considering what kind of day I'd had, I decided that was no small miracle.

"Ready?" Danny said.

"Is it too late for sushi and *Notting Hill*?" I asked.

" 'Fraid so," he said, but he hesitated, his hand still on the doorknob.

On the other side of the door at my intimate surprise party, Sarah Michaels, a society reporter for *Vogue*, would be mingling with our college friends Derek and Michelle. Kelly Specter would be snapping a few photographs for *Food & Wine*. Someone from the *New York Post* would be talking to my cookbook publisher confirming that the Twitter hack was indeed a fluke. The evening was no longer purely celebratory. It was business.

"Let's just get this done," Danny said. "And get back to the wine waiting for us at home."

Then Danny smiled, and I relaxed in spite of myself. And maybe this was my first mistake. As soon as I took a breath, my phone vibrated in my purse.

I went to grab for it, but Danny was already turning the doorknob, people already shouting *surprise!* as he opened the door.

My eyes ticked around the room at everyone in attendance, a blur of smiles and applause and raised champagne flutes. Maggie, who designed our apartment (and who arguably had the most influential design blog in the business), ran over and gave Danny a hug. She had been a longtime friend of his and I was happy to see her. I was also happy to see that she had come alone. Maggie was as notorious for her terrible taste in men as she was for her great design style.

I was about to reach in and give her a hug when Louis Leonard, the head of my publishing company, walked over to me with two martinis in hand—one of them with extra olives.

Louis was in his early sixties, and a handsome

guy, whom everyone liked. Even Danny had gotten close to him over the years. Ordinarily, I would've happily taken a drink from him and sat in the corner listening to him fill me in on everything interesting that had happened at the party before we arrived. Except my phone vibrated again, a message waiting.

"Uh-oh," he said. "That's a bad face."

"Impressive that you still recognize the difference," I said.

Louis laughed and turned to Danny, whose arm was wrapped around Maggie. "How are you, my friend?" Danny asked him.

"Doing great," Louis said.

Danny patted his shoulder. Then he followed Maggie into the room and toward the small contingent of our friends.

Louis tilted his head and took me in. "Don't think about it for one more minute. We all know who you really are."

I felt a twinge in my chest, but I pushed it down as he handed the drink over.

Then he leaned down and whispered, "A woman who clearly knew about her surprise party."

I laughed and he tipped his glass in my direction.

"Come and find me, but not until you've had at least one of those," he said.

He looked me up and down.

"Maybe two."

I smiled as he headed off, and I turned to check out the crowd. How could I casually slip away now? And where on earth was Violet? I looked around the room at the guests—Derek and Michelle; Kelly Specter; Ryan and Meredith; Christopher, who photographed my cookbooks, and Christopher's new fiancée, Julie Diaz. Julie was a partner at The Agency. She repped a lot of talent in the culinary world, and had made a play to be my agent, though Ryan (with his law degree) said there was no reason to bring someone else into the mix. What he meant was he didn't want to hand over any of the money.

I was about to lose it when I spotted Violet making her way toward me, a slider in her hand.

"What's going on here?" she said in a singsongy voice. "Why do you look like someone just gave you a bad oyster?"

"My phone won't stop buzzing," I whispered.

"How many emails do you get a day on average? Not to sound like Ryan, but you're going to have to pull it together."

She was right. But I pulled my phone out, and I saw a familiar subject line.

Hello, Sunshine

I clenched my teeth. This was starting to get irritating.

Did you think you'd get rid of me so quickly? #exhibit2 #comingsoon

Violet, who was reading over my shoulder, laughed a little too hard, trying to suggest that it didn't matter. "This freak can send all the emails he wants. Your Twitter feed is secure! No one is getting in there!"

She pulled out her phone and showed me, like proof. No Tweets, not from me, not from the fake me.

"What's going on, ladies? Why are we standing in the doorway?"

I looked up to see Ryan walking over, Meredith coming up behind him. She was dressed elegantly in knee-high boots and thin black pants, her long, honey-blond hair appropriately straightened. Her arms and thighs not revealing the three children she'd pushed out.

"Aintnosunshine just wrote again," Violet said, holding up my phone to show him.

Meredith smiled tightly. "Our friendly neighborhood truth-teller?"

It was loaded, and why wouldn't it be? Meredith had been okay with this pact originally. It had paid for her McMansion, and she got to stay home and raise the kids. But, like Danny, like all of us, Meredith had never thought Sunshine Mackenzie would be such a star. And, well, who doesn't want their share of the spotlight? Nobody.

I took Meredith's hand, looking her in the eye. "I can't tell you how much I appreciate you backing us up on all this today."

"It was a lovely statement, wasn't it? I honestly thought it was pretty close to what I would have written. You're a real pro."

Another loaded smile.

"Let's everyone play nice." Ryan stepped in. "And let's try to put the events of the day in the rearview, shall we?"

I held up my phone, the new email. "How exactly should I do that?"

"Block his email address."

"That's what you have to say?"

Ryan grabbed the phone from Violet, shoved it back into my pocket. "No, what I have to say is there is press everywhere, so happy faces, people. And get out of the doorway. It makes you look short."

"Ryan, I thought this was handled."

"It was!" Violet said. "It is."

"This bastard can email all he wants, that's all he can do at this point," Ryan said. "We've cut him off at the knees."

The word *knees* was not even out of his mouth when my phone started to buzz again—when everyone's phone started to buzz, that universal buzz letting you know you had an update on your Twitter feed.

Ryan pulled his phone out as Violet looked at hers, confused. "Ah . . . guys."

Ryan's face turned bright red.

Violet opened the door, motioned for me to

step outside. She clearly didn't want me to read whatever it was in that room. "You've been hacked again."

"I don't fucking believe this," Ryan said.

I reached for my phone, my heart pounding. "What happened to 'No one is getting in there'?"

Ryan shook his head. "Violet?"

"I don't know how they got back in," she said. "I mean, Jack put up the firewalls . . ."

"Well, Jack is fired," Ryan said.

I stopped listening, looking down at my Twitter feed.

What I was doing while Meredith Landy was cooking. #herhusband

There was a link to my Instagram account, where there were two new photographs posted. They were outtakes from a photo shoot for my new cookbook—a day a film crew had come in to do a "behind the scenes" feature.

The first photograph was of Ryan and me laughing in a corner, Ryan feeding me a brownie. Not exactly innocent, but not convincing, either. The next photo was a little worse. Ryan and I were leaning against the chef's table, a little too close together. My hand was on his chest. His mouth was moving right up to mine.

We should have stepped outside. Instead, we found ourselves in the front of the room as everyone looked up, as if in unison, eyes darting between Ryan and me—and Meredith.

Ryan let out a laugh. "Guys, this was the photo shoot for Sunny's new cookbook," he said. "Outtakes. Further proof that anything can be taken out of context to appear a certain way."

"It was." Violet pointed to a spot in the photograph's corner. "That's me in the background. I was *there*."

The ease and strength with which they lied was astounding.

But that was the key to lying, wasn't it? Believing it yourself? Or finding something in the lie that you could believe? We had done a photo shoot that day. Violet had been there. This was just long after she went home.

I looked at Danny, who was standing in the back of the room with our college friends, looking down at Derek's phone. It was my great luck we were separated—if only by a few feet. If we hadn't been, if he had been right next to me, he would have known immediately what I had done. Now I had a chance to convince him, to convince everyone.

Meredith, bless her heart, put her hand on Ryan's shoulder and helped do just that.

"So someone wants to turn this into an eventful evening!" she said.

Violet jumped in. "Spoiler alert! Sunny will *inhale* any brownie someone puts in front of her."

I laughed. It was such a perfect thing for her to say, defusing the moment. If I didn't know better, I'd believe her. And something about my laughter—truthful, real—furthered that cause. People started to put their phones away, wanting to be on the inside of a joke, the inside of a story, that they could talk about later. What a start to Sunny's birthday party! She got hacked *again,* and it was hilarious.

Even Danny, who now was looking up at me, didn't seem fazed. I didn't dare smile at him, though. I shrugged as if to say, *I have no idea.* I shrugged because it was the only thing I could do that wouldn't give away my guilt.

Ryan gently wrapped his arm around Meredith's shoulders. And luckily, she was looking back at him with love in her eyes, totally convinced.

"When we throw a party, we really throw a party!" he said, giving me a wink.

Then he pointed toward the waiters, motioning for them to start dinner service.

"I'm going to step outside with Sunny and Violet to deal with this silliness, if everyone wants to start on their *cacio e pepe.* And please save me some!"

Except then everyone's phones beeped again.

A new tweet.

What I was doing while Meredith Landy was cooking. #part2 #herhusband

This photograph hadn't been taken at the studio. It was taken in a hotel room in Aspen—a naked photograph. I was just out of the shower, looking at myself in the mirror, and if you looked closely you could see a man (visible in the mirror's reflection) taking the photograph from the doorway.

Ryan.

The room went silent. Movie-theater-at-a-good-movie silent, except for the ambient music playing. Which, I swear, got louder.

My face turned bright red. I wouldn't look at Danny—I didn't want to look at anyone—until I figured out something to say so they'd stop looking at me like I was a stranger. Only a stranger, after all, would cheat on her husband—on their friend. And only a stranger would be involved in what was shaping up as fraudulent behavior across the board: recipe-stealing, husband-borrowing, infidelity.

Meredith turned toward her husband, her voice hushed. "What's this, Ryan?"

For a moment, Ryan—yes, Ryan—was speechless. He shook his head, like this was all ridiculous. Then he managed to find his words.

"That isn't me!" He pointed at the photo. He was pretty hard to make out. He motioned in my direction, urging me to jump in. "Sunny, tell them!"

I felt my throat close up. You would think that with all my experience lying, I would easily lie in this moment.

But the day had taken its toll.

I took a breath. And then, I told the truth.

"I'm just going to need a minute," I said. "I'm a little too mortified that there is a naked photograph of me circulating online to defend against a ridiculous story as to how it got there."

I didn't dare look toward Danny still, but everyone else nodded, understanding—their looks moving from accusation to something closer to sympathy. Maybe the truth sounded different.

Ryan latched onto their belief like a life preserver. "Yes! Out of respect, everyone please delete those posts while Violet and I get to the bottom of this terrible exploitation of someone we all adore."

Adore. It was the wrong word to use. Very un-Ryan. And I could see that Ryan knew it. He knew it before he even looked over at Meredith. *Adore* was the one word he shouldn't have used in that moment when he was hiding the fact that he and I had made a mistake. Or at least that's what I called it, that night in Aspen.

"You son of a bitch!" Meredith whispered under her breath.

"Meredith . . ." Ryan said. "Please."

Violet touched Meredith's arm. "Meredith, come outside with me, okay?" she said.

Meredith, rightfully, pushed Violet away. Then

she slammed out of the private room, her knee-highs causing a ruckus on the stairs.

Ryan kept his smile plastered to his face. "Folks, if you'll excuse me!"

He followed Meredith outside, walking quickly out of the private room and breaking into a run, the stairs giving him away.

I looked toward where Danny had been standing, but he was gone. Then I heard him behind me. Rather, I felt him, his hand touching my shoulder.

"Hi, everyone. I can't speak to what is happening right now with Meredith and Ryan, probably one martini too many . . . though, just to be clear with you all, there is nothing about that photograph that is a problem except that it ended up online. I took that photograph of Sunny. It was a private moment between us, which someone has posted without permission."

Everyone looked at Danny mesmerized, partially because he was mesmerizing and partially because he had to be telling the truth.

"And more importantly, tonight's spinning away from what we're all here for. And that's to celebrate Sunny."

I looked at him with such gratitude I thought I was going to cry.

"So you all should sit down, eat, enjoy your evening."

Then he took my hand, really took it, gripping

my fingers in his. And we walked through the restaurant and outside, Greenwich Street uncharacteristically empty.

This was when he turned and looked at me, his eyes no longer kind.

"I probably bought you a day back there to get your story straight."

I didn't want to look at him, so I looked down, cobblestones under my feet, my shoes sinking into each other.

"Was that a hotel bathroom?"

I didn't answer.

"What was he doing with you there?"

My voice came out like a whisper. "Danny, I don't know what to say."

He lifted my face and forced me to meet his eyes.

"Say something," he said. "Say something, or that's the last kind thing I'll ever do for you."

"It isn't what you think. It was just one night."

"*Just* one night?" he repeated.

I nodded. Because, in that moment, I thought my ultimate loyalty was on the line. I believed that on one side of it, my husband of fourteen years and five apartments and all of my love (as flawed as it was) would be able to forgive me for a small transgression. One night, nothing in the scope of things. And on the other side of that line, there was nothing I could say—not *I love you*, not *I'm sorry*—that would make him understand.

He kissed my cheek softly, his skin rough, his lips quick. "I was wrong," Danny whispered into my ear. "You should have said nothing at all," he said.

6

I couldn't bear to go back to the party. And going immediately home felt even worse. So I walked south down Greenwich Street, heading across the West Side Highway to Battery Park. I sat down on a bench, the night wind blowing, and looked out over the Hudson River, the world so beautiful and serene, it seemed impossible that my life had just imploded a few blocks away.

I couldn't begin to touch what had just happened with Danny, which might be why I focused on myself. Damage control. The fifty people at my party, several of them with microphones to the world: How was I going to turn this around before they used them? Was Danny's speech enough to hold them? Those embarrassing photographs—had Violet gotten Craig to pull them yet? How much damage had they done on a Friday night before she did?

I could only hope that, somehow, Ryan had figured out how to make it all salvageable. If he had managed to calm Meredith down, I knew we had a shot. He would go back inside, Violet alerting him to Danny's speech, and he would do the rest. Ryan raising a glass to a birthday gone wrong, but a year ahead that would be full of goodness and friendship, etc.

If their fingers were in the dam, at least for tonight, if the *New York Post* and *Food & Wine* and all the press at the party tweeted our side of the story, we could deal with this tomorrow in some way. Couldn't we?

The truth was, as I asked myself the question, as I tried to breathe in the possibility of the answer being *yes,* I knew it all came down to convincing the world that my relationship with Ryan was platonic. If there was one thing women couldn't forgive each other for—if there was one thing they didn't want to forgive—it was another woman being adulterous. You could abuse drugs (an addict, not your fault) or railroad someone at work (it's business), but if you slept with another woman's husband, it was like you slept with *everyone's* husband. It was like you betrayed all womankind.

Until, of course, it was you who found yourself in the role of adulterous bitch.

And, for whatever it's worth (and if you're even able to believe me), my situation with Ryan was more complicated than the naked bathroom photograph would initially suggest. I only slept with Ryan once. Do I sound like a politician trying to get out on a technicality? Perhaps. So let me be clear. From day one, we flirted. We were more involved than we should have been, spending time together that we should have reserved for our spouses, and sharing pieces of ourselves that they longed for and we too easily gave up to each other instead.

The hotel in the photograph was the St. Regis in Aspen. We had been there for the *Food & Wine* Classic last year, so I could judge a new chef competition. At the party that night, Ryan drank too much champagne and lost his hotel room key and ended up on my floor. And when he got up and climbed into the bed, I let him in.

How had we gotten there? Into that hotel room together? Ryan was the only one who knew— truly knew—all my secrets. Maybe it was a justification, but it didn't feel like a justification. Sometimes you create a world so intricate, so nuanced, that only the two of you can understand it. And that was what we did. It was never about love or anything like love. It was about something that felt completely real.

And the point is, the very next morning, I told Ryan it had been a mistake. Did I confess the transgression to Danny? Why tell him? It would only cause him pain. I guess that's what all cheaters say. But in this case, it was true. Nothing had to change between us. I moved on and, with the exception of a little leftover weirdness, Ryan moved on too.

The hacker apparently had not.

My phone buzzed again, shaking in my pocket, and I looked down at another tweet.

A Farmers Daughter? #idontthinkso

And a link to: *aintnosunshine.nyc*

I clicked the button, an entire website up and running—my yearbook photo from high school, front and center, my real name, Sunshine Stephens, underneath. And all the details too:

"Sunshine Stephens grew up in Montauk, on prestigious Old Montauk Highway, in a cliffside mansion. No small farming town, no home on the range. Her father was a famed composer. She had quite a cushy childhood."

The description was wrong. We'd had no money, it wasn't a mansion, and my childhood was the opposite of cushy—but it didn't matter. Everything I had sold on the air was a bill of goods, and everyone would know it now. It wasn't just strangers who would feel betrayed hearing about who I used to be. It was friends and colleagues—everyone whom I'd never told who I really was. Since Sunshine Mackenzie's inception, I'd kept my past from all of them. As for the people I'd grown up with, I had theories as to why they'd stayed quiet—theories about how my town stopped caring about you as soon as you walked out the door. Ryan dismissed that reasoning though, saying they'd stayed quiet for the reason everyone stayed quiet: People only spoke up about something if it benefited them. I palmed my phone angrily, not sure what to do. If I could find out who was doing this, maybe there was a play to be made. But how on earth was I going to do that?

It was as if the freak had heard me contemplating. My phone buzzed, and I looked down at the alert, a text from a blocked number.

Tough Night? #aintnosunshine

I wrote back quickly. *Who are you?*

I could ask you the same thing.

Pls. What do you want?

The little ellipsis started going like crazy. *What do you think I want?*

I was shaking, completely furious. Whoever this was, he was enjoying it. Enjoying the discomfort I was in. He was punishing me in every way he could think of.

Are you after money here?

Wrong question.

The little ellipsis started going again. Then, suddenly, it stopped. And started again.

How much money?

I thought of what Danny and I had in savings. After the apartment renovation and the money he'd put into his business, it wasn't a lot.

Forget it. Bye 4 now.

I looked down at the phone, horrified that this horrible person had ruined my birthday, my marriage, my career. He wanted to play games? I could play games too.

A little game of telephone, specifically. In which I palmed my phone and hurled it right over the railing and into the Hudson River.

7

When I got back to the loft, I heard someone rummaging around in the kitchen. And for a second, I thought Danny was there. I didn't think he'd forgiven me, but I thought maybe he had forgotten something—that he'd come home to get clothes for the night. That I'd have another chance to win him over. To get him to lie down and talk it through. To get him, for the night, to stay.

"Sunny?" I heard from the kitchen.

It was Ryan.

He walked into the living room, a bottle of scotch in his hand. "Where have you been?" he said.

"Nowhere. Why are you here?"

"It's nice to see you too," he said.

I was gutted and all I wanted to do was get into bed. Wake up, like in *Groundhog Day*, get to start this birthday again. But there was Ryan, a terrible reminder that that wasn't happening.

"I thought you could use some company," he said. "And I was sure I could use a drink."

"What if Danny was here?"

Ryan sat down in my egg chair. "Danny is not coming back here. Tonight took care of that."

"Please get out of my chair."

Ryan moved toward the couch. "So Meredith's a wreck, but after I sent her back to Scarsdale in an Uber, I was able to go back in and calm everybody down. And it actually worked. I mean, Danny helped a lot, I've got to say. Did you propose the idea of that speech?"

"No."

"Well, I'm impressed. Didn't think he had it in him."

"I don't want to talk about Danny."

"Do you think I want to talk about Danny?"

I sat down in my chair, weary and miserable. I wanted Ryan to go, but I was too exhausted to press it.

"Point is, after a little finagling and hand-holding, I got everyone buying that it was a misunderstanding. I even suggested that Meredith was actually angry about something else."

"What'd that be?"

Ryan poured some scotch into a glass. "A woman friend I made upstate."

"Thanks for taking that hit," I said.

"The little hacker fucker is a pain in my ass."

I walked to the cabinet, grabbed a glass, and poured myself a scotch as well. "What are we going to do about the website?"

He took a long pull from his glass. "I was hoping you didn't see that."

Then he shrugged.

"Well," he said, "the stuff with your past, I think I can finagle."

I met his eyes. "Seriously?"

"Who can't relate to someone pretending to be something they're not in order to please other people? It will make *A Little Sunshine* even more popular. Every girl who ever lied about her age on OKCupid will be rooting for you."

"People don't like a fraud."

"*Everyone* is a fraud, Sunshine. Everyone with an Instagram page, a Facebook account. And certainly everyone with a cooking show. How many of these folks are cooking for themselves, really? They're figureheads. All of them. That test kitchen at Cook TV? It's never busy with the real people. It's their cronies. Other people making the recipes. And don't get me started on the Food Network."

"Think we went a step beyond that, Ryan."

He waved me off. "Tomato, *tomahto!* We sell an image of the person in front of the camera. And that's the job. To be the perfect image. You did the job and did it beautifully. So now we just have to change the image."

"To what?"

"Learning, getting real, for real. Self-embrace. It's the latest thing. And it doesn't matter how big the lies are. People forget. They always forget the details."

"It's the internet, Ryan. Naked pictures aren't quickly forgotten."

"Craig's pulled them, my lawyers are all over it, that part is handled. And Meredith will calm down and handle the rest. She wouldn't want to put her children in that position. Outing their father, as it were."

I didn't know if it was the scotch, but I started to think that it could actually work. "So . . . it's your plan to ignore the lies?"

"My plan is to change the story. My plan is to fix this for you. For us."

He leaned forward, holding each side of my egg chair. And he looked into my eyes. Despite everything I knew about him—everything he showed me over and over again about how he felt about the truth, how he felt about doing what was ostensibly right—it was in the moments like this that Ryan amazed me. Because he wasn't playing around when he looked at me like that. He wasn't pretending. He was looking into my eyes, so I would see it: his sincerity. How much he wanted to do right by me.

"Look, the Food Network gig, they're going to put that on hold. Those guys don't like controversy. But we'll get it back. I swear to you. The only thing America loves more than adoring someone is hating her. And then having a new reason to love her all over again. So we pretended a little about where you came from because you were embarrassed about where you came from. Everyone can relate to being embarrassed. Everyone can relate to wanting to change their own story so they're presented in their best possible light."

I nodded, starting to feel calmer.

Ryan had made up the story once, he could make it up again. If anyone could, it was Ryan.

Sensing my quiet praise, he smiled. I smiled back, taking a breath.

This was probably a mistake. He took it as an invitation and kissed me. I pulled away.

"What's wrong?" he said.

I shook my head. "Ryan, we decided not to do this."

"We decided it would get too messy. It's not messy anymore. Danny's out of the picture. And . . ."

"You don't know that."

"Yes, I do."

My heart started to hurt. Fourteen years. He couldn't be. Not just like that.

"It's not about our spouses anymore," he said.

"You think Meredith is going to go along with your plan if you leave her?"

"Yes," he said, totally unfazed, and I realized my error. Ryan didn't operate in the world of self-doubt. He believed he'd get away with anything. And, really, he was probably right.

He pushed my hair behind my ears, leaned in again. "I love you," he said.

Love. Ryan never said he loved me, not like that. The closest he'd gotten was when he hired a crew to film the behind-the-scenes of my photo shoot—the day that was now all over the internet. The camera operator was this really good-looking guy—tall, smart, and studying to be a director at NYU. Ryan thought we were flirting even though it was innocently friendly. And Ryan fired him. When I asked Ryan why later, he begrudgingly admitted to being jealous. *It's hard to see someone you love interested in someone else.* That was what he had said, daring me to argue. I didn't say anything. It hadn't seemed worth the fight.

"I love you and I want to be with you. And I will work it out so ultimately it doesn't hurt us. Look at Joanne Woodward and Paul Newman . . ."

"I don't think they'd like the comparison."

Ryan waited. "I *know* you love me too."

I took a large sip of my scotch, finishing the glass.

Ryan didn't move. "Sunny?"

"I think we should talk about this tomorrow."

"No. I think we should talk about this now. I want this." He motioned between us. "No wives, no husbands. Maybe this is a blessing in disguise."

Ryan didn't say things like that. He'd never said that we should leave our spouses, be together. He wouldn't. Not unless he was certain it would be reciprocated.

"Why are you looking at me like that?" he said.

"Did you do this? So I'd have no choice but to be with you?"

He laughed awkwardly. "No choice? Wow."

"You sure came up with a plan to fix it quickly."

"That's how my brain works. Quickly."

My head was blurry. He had to go, right now.

"If this is about Danny, believe me, he isn't coming back. Not that you belonged with him anyway. I'm proof positive of that."

"Well, I can't do this." I motioned between us. "Sorry."

"Of course you can."

"Then I don't want to."

It came out firmer than I meant it to—but I was angry that he was putting everything on the line, angry he assumed the answer would be yes.

"Well, I don't want to do anything else," he said.

"Ryan, you're not thinking clearly. You're the first person who would say that there is an empire at stake here."

"There are a lot of things at stake here."

My head was spinning. He was putting the entire plan he'd just made on the line? It was now contingent on there also being a plan around us?

He took my face in his hands. "So it's you and me, or I'm going another way."

There was my answer. So I thought about it. I actually thought about pretending. The smart thing would be to pretend that I wanted to give things a shot with him, especially if that was what he needed in order to stay committed.

"Okay, fine."

"Okay, *fine?*"

I looked away. "What do you want from me?"

"A little bit of gratitude, for starters. I made you what you are."

"Please! I just happened to be the girl behind the right bar."

Ryan stood up, his eyes turning cold. "That's only true right now," he said.

Then he took a last sip of his drink and headed toward the door.

"See ya," he said. As though he wasn't saying good-bye. As though he wasn't walking out on a nearly decade-long partnership.

Except he was.

And, like that, he was gone.

8

The next morning, I threw on a pair of jeans and a tank top and headed to my studio, right above Chelsea Market, which housed *A Little Sunshine*'s kitchen, built to look like my Tribeca kitchen: my gray slate countertop, the glass refrigerator.

A plan swirled through my mind. Ryan had jumped ship, yes, but in the light of the morning, I knew that if he could turn this thing around, I could too.

My triage plan: The Food Network was off the table for now, but I would safeguard my contracts still in place, speak to my most important contacts (Evelyn, who was the head of *A Little Sunshine*'s advertising department, Louis at the publisher), assure everyone that Danny's speech had been genuine, that there never had been anything between Ryan and me, and that I already had a new management team ready to jump on board. I made a note to call Julie at The Agency, who would be happy to help pick up the pieces. As soon as I had a few of them in my pocket.

When I walked in, I found Violet barking orders at several production assistants who were on their hands and knees in front of a cabinet, packing files into boxes, organizing all the supplies.

Violet raised her hands in exasperation. "Where have you been? I've called you a thousand times! And your fucking voice mail is full."

"I lost my phone."

"You lost your phone? Of all days!"

I looked around at the chaos, the production assistants moving at double speed. "Why is everyone packing up?"

Violet's eyes went wide. "Do you not know?"

"Clearly not."

"Guys, we are going to need the studio for ten. If you would get the fuck out, thank you . . ." She motioned for the production assistants to go. "But don't go far. There's a lot to do!"

Everyone shuffled out, leaving the two of us alone.

Then Violet motioned for me to have a seat. "*A Little Sunshine*'s cooked," she said.

I looked at her, stunned. "What?"

"Evelyn emailed with a spreadsheet of all the advertisers who have pulled their ads, or who are threatening to pull, or are threatening to *sue,*" Violet said. "No one wants to be in the *A Little Sunshine* business. And the studio wants us out of here by the end of business today. They sent . . . like . . . an official legal email saying you had rented the studio space under false pretenses and they demanded we vacate by the end of the business day."

Violet, who looked seriously afraid I might

throw something, turned away and continued the work of loading files into boxes, of packing up the studio.

I took a breath and focused. Of course advertisers were going to balk. I just had to prove that the fans were loyal to me over any of these rumors. I just needed to stop the hemorrhaging. I would draft a carefully worded email, supportive notes from my fans attached. As long as the fans stayed loyal, I'd have the money folks back in no time.

"And how's the fan base hanging in?" I said.

"About eight hundred thousand on Twitter."

"I lost eight hundred thousand followers?"

"No, you have eight hundred thousand followers left. You lost 1.9 million."

"I can do the math!"

"Do you wanna do it for Facebook, too?"

A nightmare, this was turning into a nightmare. And why would the studio also sting me? It didn't make any sense unless there was another reason. A business reason. A way to turn my loss into their gain. Or someone who had figured out how to.

Ryan. The hit from the studio had Ryan written all over it. He had convinced them to kick me out. He had given them a compelling reason. But what was it, exactly?

"Get Ryan on the phone," I said.

Violet stared up at me, again a deer in

headlights. "I will, but I think you should know first that Ryan and Meredith just issued a joint press release," she murmured.

"Proclaiming my guilt?"

"No, announcing that they are doing their own show."

And there it was. My loss, their gain.

Violet opened the phone and held out the press release, so I could see for myself. "*Putting the Pieces Together*," she said. "A tale of divorce and dessert."

"A show about their divorce?"

"Divorce. And reconciliation," Violet said. "They did a flash poll, and it seems that people want them to work it out, despite his affair. With you."

"It was hardly an affair."

"All the better," she said.

She returned to her file boxes, dumping things inside.

I tried to not explode, to stay proactive. "I'm going to go and check my email."

"Probably a good idea. You have some doozies in there."

I drilled her with a look.

"I'm just saying!"

"Don't."

I headed for the laptop on my kitchen countertop—soon to be Meredith's kitchen countertop—to counteract any additional damage

Ryan had done. Fourteen hours ago, Ryan was professing his love to me. Now he was professing it to his wife. Was any of it real to him? It was all a little real, but the only thing that mattered to Ryan at the end of the day was Ryan. And he was going to do whatever he needed to in order to save his own ship. Including sinking mine in the process.

I opened my email to one hundred new messages. Maybe that sounds like a lot, but it was a pretty typical morning. Maybe even a little light.

I wasn't surprised that there weren't more emails waiting for me. I'd learned early on that people stay away if they think you're struggling. They don't want the stink to fall on them too. It's a strategic error, though. I always emailed the day after someone's show went belly-up, after a failure. So I would be the person they turned to, the person they thought was on their side. That individual could be useful.

Which was why when I first saw that I had an email from Louis, I actually felt a little relief. Dear Louis. He was still on my side! If that was true, the rest of it didn't matter—the rumors, the show cancellation—we would weather this together.

Then I read the subject line:

Notice of Contract Cancellation

I clicked the email open and read the entirety

of the two-page, biting email in which Louis informed *AUTHOR (Sunshine Mackenzie) that PUBLISHER (COOKING WITH GAS) has decided to cancel the contract for SUNKISSED: LOVE FROM THE FARM and the two additional to-be-named future cookbooks in light of author's breech of ethical responsibility.*

We will need the advance repaid by Monday July 1st to avoid legal action.

My heart started to race. After the apartment purchase and renovation, the book advance was pretty much the only liquid money that Danny and I had in the bank.

I wrote him back immediately (and somewhat desperately):

Louis, Pls don't do this! At least let's sit down and talk first?

He wrote back even faster.

I spoke to Ryan. And Danny. There's nothing to discuss. Be well.

Louis was too professional to say anything personal, but I knew from the undertone how hurt he was. After all, he had learned all these things about me yesterday too. I flashed back to a day in his office, telling him stories of my childhood on the farm: picking tomatoes in the field with my father, stewing over strawberry jam. I cringed, thinking of the postcard I'd given him of a little girl making strawberry jam, which he kept on his desk.

Violet came up behind me, the file box in her hands, reading the email over my shoulder. "That's not great."

I sighed.

"What are you going to do?"

I shook my head, anger gathering in my gut. "I'll tell you what I'm not going to do. I'm not giving the advance back."

Violet smiled, impressed. "Really?"

"Without the advance, I'm not liquid anymore. Between the renovation on the apartment, and Danny growing his business . . ."

"So don't! I have a novelist friend who is like ten years late on his book, and he still hasn't given a penny back."

"I doubt you have a friend old enough to have spent ten years working on anything."

"Maybe it was more like five." She heaved the file box higher in her arms. "The point is, what do you think Louis is going to do? Take you to court? Freeze the money?"

I turned back to the computer. I clicked on Danny and my bank account, and it was all still there, safe and untouched.

She was right. Louis would cool down. I would reach out when he'd had a moment to process, and convince him there was a way for us to come out the other end of this. He could publish a different kind of cookbook, with a tinge of true history. Something about how I'd gotten here.

"Should I call the production assistants back in here, get them packing up again?"

I shook my head. "I have a couple of emails to send first."

"Okay, what should I do?"

"Figure out who did this in the next five minutes," I said.

She laughed, but I was completely serious. I knew if we could figure the hacker out, we could figure out how to turn the story. So I was something other than the villain.

"I was able to do a little recon on the aintnosunshine emails," she said. "They definitely originated in the New York area. So it's a New Yorker."

"Great work . . . you narrowed the hacker down to nine million people?"

"At least I narrowed it down!"

I didn't have time for her irritation, or her hurt feelings, so I blew through them. "So you've been trying to figure it out via the tech, right?"

She took a seat, dropping her files on the countertop. "Right."

"Let's go at it another way. Likely offenders."

She nodded. "So . . . like . . . who wants to take you down a peg or two?" she said.

"I think the question is who has the ability."

Something flicked across her face. I hadn't been accusing her. But it was like suddenly she was worried I would put certain pieces together.

I started doing the math. Who had access to all this stuff? Violet and Ryan. And Violet had everything to gain. She wanted her own show. And now, wouldn't there be a hole in the YouTube culinary universe? A hole just right for a five-foot-eleven redheaded vegan to jump in and fill?

She tilted her head. "Why are you looking at me like that?"

"When did Ryan tell you they did a flash poll?"

"Excuse me?" she said.

"You said they ran a flash poll. Ryan would be the only one that could have told you about that."

She paused. "After your kerfuffle, he said he was cooking something up and offered me a job."

"And what did you say?"

She laughed awkwardly. "I said yes. Which is why I'm here now, in your studio, helping clean up files."

"Violet, did you do this?"

"Hack you? I'm going to pretend you didn't say that," she said.

"You know that's not an answer, right? Are you going to work for Ryan?"

"This is unbelievable," she said. "I was going to give you a week. Help you, I don't know, figure out who was behind this, find a place to hide out for a while. Like Tulsa! But I don't need this shit. I'm so out of here."

She reached for the file box.

"So you are going to work for Ryan."

"I'm not going down with this motherfucker of a ship, that's what I'm not doing. Do you know, like five seconds after the photos posted last night, I had several offers in hand? Including from Ryan?"

I stared at her, not letting her hysteria distract me from what she wasn't saying.

Violet headed for the door. "I actually believed that you'd find a way to turn this around. But it looks like I was wrong. You're a sinking ship, Sunny. And while I had nothing to do with the hack, at the moment, as far as I'm concerned, whoever did do this is my fucking hero."

With that, Violet slammed out the door, taking the file box with her.

9

One of the first long articles about my show was in *New York* magazine's Grub Street, which is a food diary of a notable person, following what he or she eats and drinks for a week.

If I'm remembering, they titled the Grub Street piece something like: "Sunshine Mackenzie Pairs a Mint Julep with Sweet Potato Pie." It was a pretty accurate title considering that, one of the nights, I'd written about going with Danny on a mini pub crawl around Brooklyn in which I was searching for New York's best mint julep. Fresh, delicate, a little sweet. The dreamer's drink.

I secretly detested a mint julep. But Ryan liked the sound of *the dreamer's drink,* so mint julep it was, even though I found it sticky and too rich and wholeheartedly believed that bourbon should be drunk with a little ice and nothing else.

After the fight with Violet, and five hours of packing, I left the studio in an Uber full of my files and belongings and proceeded directly to Red Hook—and the old bar and grill where I used to work—to drink my bourbon and ice undisturbed.

While the Uber sat outside, his meter happily running, I sat on the corner stool listening to the only other day drinker, a large tattooed guy named Sidney, who matched me drink for drink, while rattling on in detail about his wedding-planning business.

"I have an Iranian wedding tonight at Chelsea Piers," he said. "Five hundred people."

"You're a wedding planner?" I said.

"I don't seem like the type, right? It was my ex-wife's business and then it was our business together and then I took the business from her in the divorce."

"Why would you do that?"

He shrugged. "I could," he said. "What do you do for work?"

"Nothing anymore."

He took a sip. "What did you do?"

"I lied," I said.

Before I get to this next part, I should make something clear. I don't cry. I'm not one of those weepy-weepies. Hell, I'm not even a subtle sniffler. Danny's father died on the operating table after a six-hour surgery. The doctor came out to tell us, and the whole family lost it. Everyone but me. I loved Danny's father. On some days, more than Danny. But I didn't shed a tear. Instead, I hugged everybody tight, took Danny home, and when he finally fell asleep, I took it out on a long run. Two hours. Staring off into space.

Except sitting there where the whole mess started, I started to cry. Awful, ridiculous tears. Right in front of a mortified Sidney, who motioned for the bartender.

"I'll take a check," he said.

Later that night, I sat on my doorstep in front of my apartment, drunk out of my mind. I was surrounded by the enormous file boxes, the entire remainder of my working life.

I knew I would feel better as soon as I dragged myself upstairs to the comfort of my apartment, but knowing that and actually getting everything upstairs were two different things. The Uber driver had no interest in helping me lug my things inside, which left me where I was: staring at the street, knocking my heels together Dorothy-style, quietly hoping that someone would appear to take me home.

"I don't believe it! Sunny?"

I looked up to see Amber (aka *Toast of the Town*) walking down my block in high heels and a stunning black dress, her makeup smoky and severe, the epitome of New York chic.

As unexcited as I was to see Amber, she looked thrilled to see me.

"I thought that was you," she said. "What are you doing here?"

I drunk-reached for my keys, suddenly

motivated to go upstairs, leaving the files behind if necessary.

"This is my place," I said.

She tilted her head, as if she was trying to remember. "This is your apartment? I should know that, right? I've been here before?"

I nodded, noting Amber's nervousness— her over-explanation of whether she should remember the apartment.

"It's a shame, what's going on with your show and everything," she said. "Did you see my tweet?"

"I did, *thanks*."

"Of course. How's it all going?"

"Not great."

She cringed, full of faux-sympathy. "I just don't know why *anyone* would do this to you! I was talking to Louis earlier, and he was saying, we were both saying, you don't deserve this. I mean, regardless of what you did. To be outed."

That stopped me. "You were talking to Louis?"

"Well, yes. We're putting together a cookbook. *Tender Toast.*"

"You are?"

She shrugged. "They have an unexpected spot in their catalogue. Do you think *Tender Toast* is too soft? We're just rushing to get the book out and I can't tell if it's genius or not. Louis thinks it has a good ring to it, and he's the best there is, but . . . I don't know . . ."

I took Amber in, sobering up, quickly. "Where did you say you're going tonight?"

"I'm just going to get some dinner with my boyfriend."

She pointed down the street, like proof of a restaurant. Except she was pointing toward nothing. My block was small and—at least in New York terms—far away from everything. Restaurants, cabs, stores. There was a world in which you started here to get somewhere, but there was no world in which this was the block where you ended up.

"So are you still in a tizzy trying to figure out who's behind this hack?"

I stared at her, not answering.

"That's why I try to be nice. I'm nice to everyone, so no one would think to fuck me like this."

Which was when it hit me like a sledge-hammer. I had been thinking that it was Violet or Ryan. But Amber had the most to gain from any gap left in *A Little Sunshine*'s wake. That was what she was doing on my street—my quiet, untraveled street in Tribeca. Like a serial killer, returning to the scene of the crime, she couldn't help herself. She had to gloat.

"It's you."

"Excuse me?"

"You're behind the hack," I said.

She laughed in a completely unnatural way:

high-pitched and squeaky, a laugh that was trying too hard. "Have you been drinking? I have nothing to do with this. I mean, what on earth would I have to gain?"

"Seriously?"

"Okay, so I could see how maybe I have a little to gain," she said, trying to hide a smile.

It was the strangest thing—watching her struggle between proclaiming her ignorance and enjoying her victory. Sometimes being drunk can impede your seeing things clearly, though in this case, I thought it was helping me to see how shallow and silly this all was—any issue Amber thought was between us, anything that would lead her to tear so many lives apart.

"But I'm still innocent," she said.

Innocent. If she were really innocent, wouldn't she have said, I have nothing to do with any of this? Innocent was a word chosen when another word was equally weighing on your mind. *Guilty.*

I reached out, grabbed ahold of her arm. It was the most forceful I think I'd ever been with anyone. "Would you just be honest?"

Amber smiled, tightly, removing my hand from her arm. "Honesty is what you want? That's ironic!"

But then her faux-smile gave way to something darker. And I saw it flash in her eyes. The truth of how she felt about me; the competitive fire, the jealousy, and something uglier.

"I haven't *not* enjoyed seeing your fall from grace, considering that you slept your way to where you are now, as I suspected all along." She paused. "And the truth is you give a bad name to us real chefs who are actually trying to make a difference."

"You make toast. You know that, right?"

Her phone rang, an annoying pop song blaring through. "Hold that thought."

She picked up. "Hello?" she said into the phone. "Yeah, on the corner. *Duane.*"

I followed her eyes to a taxi making its way down Greenwich Street. "There's my boyfriend," she said.

The taxi stopped right in front of us, and out stepped a tall, handsome guy in jeans and a T-shirt.

"Hi, A," he said, making his way toward Amber.

"Hi, sweetie."

It took a minute to place him.

It was the cameraman—the one who had filmed the behind-the-scenes shoot for *A Little Sunshine*, the one whom Ryan had been jealous of. The one whom he had fired.

It took him the same minute, his eyes widening, as he looked my way. "Holy shit," he said. "Hey there . . ."

My heart started pounding. I waved hello, not saying anything.

Amber looked back and forth between us, enjoying the moment. "That's right! Don't you two know each other? Charlie worked for you, for a couple of days. Actually, just a day, because you fired him."

Charlie shot Amber a look. "Amber, what are you doing?"

I turned to Amber, keeping my voice low. "Amber, I had no idea he was your boyfriend."

"Well. Now you do."

She leaned into Charlie suggestively and kissed him hello.

"Sunny and I were just talking about how careful you have to be. Who you're nice to, who you fire. Especially when you fire them for trying to stay loyal to their girlfriend."

"Ryan fired him."

"Because you asked him to," Amber said.

I looked at Amber in disbelief. That wasn't at all how that had happened, but she certainly wasn't going to believe it. That was the trouble with being a liar. No one trusted your truth.

Charlie touched her shoulder. "Amber, I want to go," he said.

She kissed his cheek. "We do have a reservation."

"At the restaurant you can't remember the name of? How will you ever find it?"

She smiled. "We'll be okay," she said.

She took Charlie's hand, and they started walking down the street.

Then Amber turned around. "By the way . . . if you asked this person, the person who did this, I'm guessing they'd say it's less about revenge and more about something else."

"And what's that?"

"Loyalty," she said.

And with that she turned off of my block, onto another block going nowhere.

10

Danny's new job site was a gorgeous apartment on Sixty-Fifth and Central Park West. He was redesigning the penthouse: a five-thousand-square-foot stunner complete with a fireplace, floor-to-ceiling windows, and a wraparound balcony. I showed up there at 10 A.M. the next morning in Danny's favorite dress, a yellow twisty number, which I thought made me look like a tulip, but which he seemed to love. At least he had. Whether he'd love it now was a serious question mark.

Did I have a lot of nerve showing up there? Yes. Was it a Hail Mary? Yes. In my defense, he'd had two nights to calm down. He'd had two nights to digest the information that whatever had gone on with Ryan, it wasn't going on anymore. And it couldn't possibly compete with everything that was between the two of us.

The apartment looked like it was more than two days into construction—white oak wood floors already in place, paint slabs lining the walls. Before I had too much time to think about it, though, I spotted Danny.

He stood on the balcony in his hard hat, talking to his contractor, Ralph. The two of them were deep in conversation, which allowed me to sneak outside.

Ralph saw me before Danny did. Sixty-five-year-old Ralph, who looked away quickly, his face turning bright red. He had probably seen the photograph. The naked photograph. Which meant everyone probably had.

Ralph nudged Danny, who looked up and met my eyes. He didn't try to hide how angry he was to see me there.

Ralph was already walking away, not able to get out of there quickly enough.

"Put a hard hat on her, Danny," he called out.

Danny reached under the balcony railing and pulled out a hard hat, handing it over.

"Not that you're going to be staying long enough to need it, but we really don't need to get fined on the first day."

Ordinarily, I would have complained, but I quickly put it on. "I'm sorry to just show up."

"Not sorry enough not to do it, apparently," he said.

So much for a couple of days tempering his anger.

"Did you speak to Sheila?" he said.

My defenses went up. Sheila was our lawyer, our personal lawyer, and she also handled contracts for Danny's work.

"No," I said, a little sharply.

"She's been trying to reach you . . ."

"I'll call her, but I need to talk to you."

Danny looked annoyed. "No, you should probably just talk to Sheila."

I ignored him, pushing through. "It was Amber."

"What was Amber?"

"She was behind the hack. She showed up at our apartment last night to confess. Not confess, exactly, more like gloat."

He looked confused. "Why would she do that?"

"Ruin my life or gloat about it?" I said. "Probably the same reasons. Jealousy. Competition. She already stole my book deal."

I could see him processing this, not sure how to take it. Danny had always disliked Amber, thought she was sneaky and fake. I tried to take comfort in that, until I realized that was probably what he thought of me now too.

"How do you think . . . how did she get access to all your accounts?"

"Her boyfriend worked for the show for a minute. He was there the day they took all those photos. Most of those photos."

Danny's eyes narrowed, as if he were realizing something. "How does he play into this?"

I started to answer him, but he put his hands up, stopping me.

"Never mind. I don't care."

He held my eyes, daring me to ignore what he

was saying. There would be no sympathy for me over what Amber did. Nor about the publisher and the lost book deal, the fight with Violet, what was happening with Meredith and Ryan. He didn't want to hear it. He didn't want anything. Except for me to go away.

His walkie-talkie started going off, someone on the other end needing his attention. He picked it up. "I've got to go," he said.

"Danny, please, if you would just—if you would let me walk you through how we got here."

He stopped. "Walk me through how we got here?"

He shook his head, like this was the last conversation he wanted to have. He couldn't seem to stop himself though.

"I started trying to trace it back these last few nights. What was the last true thing Sunny told me? The last time you felt like you? That's what I've been trying to understand."

This stopped me. "What do you mean?"

"I thought it wasn't a big deal. Some producer guy is going to pay you a little money to be the face on a few recipes. I mean, I didn't give a crap. I never gave a second of thought to whether Lucinda Roy was actually making her recipes."

"That's not her name," I whispered.

"The point is, who cares? It's just a recipe. It's just a lifestyle internet show."

I had a moment of hope. "That's what I'm trying to say! Everything is getting blown out of proportion."

"No, you're not hearing me. It did matter. Because no one becomes terrible all at once. It happens in very small increments. And it paved the way. That little lie. It helped you tell a lot of important lies."

"That's not true. I didn't lie about the important stuff."

"Really? Maybe we should call Ryan in here and hash all that out."

Maybe I should have felt guilty. I was guilty. I'd slept with Ryan. It was a mistake. But I'd known it right away. And I'd immediately known something else, which was how much I loved Danny. So, at this moment, I didn't feel guilty at all. I felt angry. I felt angry because I had chosen Danny. And angry because, at this very moment, he was doing the opposite.

"It must be nice, being so flawless. Can't you appreciate that I'm a victim here?"

"Right. Amber did this to you. Amber made up where you were from, Amber pretended Meredith's recipes were hers, Amber slept with . . ."

He trailed off, too angry to say it. His walkie-talkie started going off again, other people trying to get his attention.

"Leave the hard hat by the elevator," he said.

He started walking away, and I was desperate to stop him—to get him to hear me—which was the last moment you could make someone hear anything. Still, I couldn't seem to stop pushing him.

"I'm still me, you know."

"And who is that, exactly?"

He turned back, the question genuine. For a moment, it felt like there was an opening. Like this might be the start of a conversation, not the end. But before I pushed through that small hole, he shook his head.

"It doesn't matter. It doesn't matter if somewhere deep inside you'd like to believe you're still the woman I fell in love with. That's not who you are now."

"I just—I got a little lost."

He laughed. "Is that what happened?"

"You hate me that much?"

"No. I don't hate you." He met my eyes, almost kindly. "I just don't know you."

Then he kept walking.

11

I walked all the way home. I walked down Central Park West and circled through Columbus Circle, winding down the Hudson River Greenway, all the way to Tribeca. It took me several hours. It wasn't the first time I'd walked the city. But it might have been the first time I walked all that way focusing on the taxi lights twinkling in the circle past the Time Warner Center; the glittering lights of Chelsea Piers; the way Jersey actually looked pretty from across the river. I noticed all of it. It was as if one of those places held the answer to how to turn the last few days around—to get my career back—to find myself walking closer to Danny, as opposed to moving further away.

I walked into the apartment to hear the home phone ringing. No one in the world had the home line except for Danny. I felt a surge of relief run through me. I knew he wasn't calling to say he forgave me, but maybe he was sorry he had been so hard on me. Which felt like an important start.

I picked up. "Danny?"

"No, it's Sheila."

Sheila. Our attorney. Danny's words ran through my head. And the word I didn't want to hear her say. *Divorce.*

I looked at the clock. "Sheila, can I call you tomorrow? It's a little late."

"It's late because I've been trying the cell number I have for you all day but the voice mail is full. And no, it can't wait until tomorrow. It's urgent."

"If by urgent you mean that you're calling to say that Danny is filing for divorce, that's the kind of urgent that definitely can wait until tomorrow."

"He has not."

I breathed a sigh of relief.

"Because in New York State the law mandates a year of legal separation before filing. He has filed for that."

"Great," I said.

"But that's not why I'm calling either," Sheila said. "Are you aware your publisher has demanded that you repay the advance for your cookbook?"

Sheila was our personal attorney, not my business attorney. "How do you know that?"

"The money was deposited into a joint account that you share with Danny, and so we were sent a letter from the publisher that if he touched that money, he would be equally liable."

I laughed. "That's just bluster, Sheila. They'd have to sue to get the money, and Louis is never going to do that. That'll take years and lawyers and he isn't going to want to bother with all that. He is angry right now, but that's not who he is. I'm telling you, he'll calm down."

"Either way, I advised Danny to give the money back."

"Thank you for the loyalty."

She interrupted me, unimpressed. ". . . And he did."

"He did what?"

"We transferred the funds this afternoon."

I felt like I was going to pass out. That was all of our money. As in: Nothing left to pay the mortgage. Or the six-figure bill sitting on my credit card. "What'd you say?"

"I know that impacts your liquid wealth."

"That *was* our liquid wealth."

"Not for long," she said. "There has been an offer on the apartment. And the buyer, who is being quite generous, wants to take possession immediately."

I looked around the apartment—the last bit of solace I had. "That's not possible."

"It's going to have to be," she said. "Danny wants to divide all joint assets as quickly as possible. And the apartment is the largest one."

"He can't just sell our apartment, Sheila."

"Actually, he can, it's his name on the mortgage. As I seem to remember, it was something about protecting *A Little Sunshine*."

She paused, perhaps hearing it in my silence— absolute terror.

"It's a really good offer," she said gently.

"We live on the best street in Tribeca," I said. "Of course it's a really good offer."

She blew past this. "I've been speaking with the buyer's lawyer all day, and in order for the inspections and everything to proceed in a timely manner, the apartment will need to be vacated by the weekend."

"No, Sheila—this is all happening too fast."

"According to the internet, actually, it's been going on for the better part of the decade."

"I'm hanging up on you now," I muttered, trying to muster a last shred of . . . something.

"Look, it's not the end of the world. In sixty days, you'll have your half of the closing and you can get yourself a new apartment in New York."

"And in the meantime?"

"Danny says you are welcome to take any of the furnishings with you. But you will have to vacate by the weekend."

"I literally have nowhere to go."

"Everyone has somewhere to go," she said. Then she hung up.

July

12

There were three calculations that went into how I chose which college to attend. The first was who was willing to pay: University of Oregon, UCLA, and Brown University at the top of the heap. The second consideration was how difficult it would be to get there from where I grew up. Brown was a ferry ride and a relatively short car ride, so it was out from the start. UCLA was a car ride and a long plane ride. But if you made the right Hollywood friends, the ones who summered in the Hamptons and had a propeller plane that let them bypass the Expressway, you could potentially go directly from a cushy flight in Los Angeles to the propeller plane in New York City, and be in my hometown in a fun and reasonably quick way.

But to get to the University of Oregon, you had the car ride, a plane ride, and another lengthy car ride. Fourteen hours, door to door. It was easier to get to Europe. There was safety for me in that. There was safety in thinking there were indefinite obstacles separating me from Montauk. So maybe it's not surprising that it took the destruction of my entire life—losing my husband, my career, my home—for me to return.

And to return at the worst time.

You haven't experienced gridlock until you've been on the Long Island Expressway on the Friday before Independence Day. The traffic has passengers standing outside of their cars, looking out toward the ships and the shoreline—welcoming them like a postcard—and one traveler staring into her rearview in the direction of New York City, trying desperately to believe she can still see it.

I'd had no choice but to drive my car. Leaving it in the garage in New York was insanely expensive—a luxury I didn't have, or I wouldn't have been going to Montauk in the first place. Maybe it wasn't the worst thing, though. All the earthly possessions I cared the most about (including my egg chair) were stuffed into that car, and with everything else that had been lost in the last couple of weeks, I couldn't bear to part with them too.

Besides the egg chair, I hadn't taken any furniture. I'd left it all for Danny, a final gesture I knew he wasn't capable of receiving. He could sell it to the new owners or he could keep it himself. I'd left him a note saying as much and signed (as ineffectually and sincerely as any words I had ever written), *I'm sorry, S.*

It pained me to leave everything for him, not because I wanted any of it (though I did want some of it—the yellow denim couch we had purchased at a flea market in Pasadena, which we had carried up the stairs together). It was more because those things were all that tied us together at that point. If I stayed and fought for the slick leather ottoman we'd purchased at The Future Perfect, it wouldn't earn Danny's forgiveness, but it would keep us in conversation—a fourteen-year conversation that I wasn't ready to stop having. Didn't that count for something that, because I knew he needed to, I stopped anyway?

After five hours of crawling traffic, I weaved off the highway. Fields and farms started coming into view. People opened their convertible tops, stared out at the trees and the green as far as the eye could see—but I couldn't see any of it. I just saw failure.

I was overcome with a feeling that I was going to throw up. I don't mean that as a way to emphasize my incredible discomfort. I mean that literally. I pulled off the road at Stop & Shop, which was jammed with folks stocking up for their holiday barbecues, and parked quickly. I ran toward the grocery store, but felt too dizzy to go inside, so I sat on the ground—on the concrete—in front of the store, trying to catch my breath. Trying to think of anywhere I could go that would send me away from Montauk, away from my childhood home.

I pulled out my phone—my new phone—to see if anyone had called. In a fit of rage, I had almost opted to get a new number. Let any of the traitors even try to reach me! They'd get a disconnected message, a robot's nasally voice telling them they were out of luck. I wasn't able to pull the trigger, though, hoping someone— Danny, Louis—would come to his senses and realize I deserved a second chance.

There were no new messages.

"Why are you on the ground?" I heard.

I looked up, squinting into the sunshine, to see a little girl in a red cover-up, looking down at me.

Behind her, the little girl's mother wrangled two other children into their car seats. She looked up, noticing that her daughter was missing, and I waved as if to say, she's safe over here.

"Are you playing hide-and-seek?" the girl asked.

"You could say that," I said.

"Can I play?" she asked. Then, without waiting for an answer, she sat beside me. "Who are we hiding from?"

I pointed toward a man a few feet away, loading groceries into his car. He was wearing a backward baseball cap, and his jeans were rolled up to his knees. And he was talking two decibels too loudly into his headset, organizing a barbecue that night, telling whoever was on the other end that they should plan on staying over. I seriously thought about asking him if he had room for one more.

"That person?" she said. "That's who we are hiding from?"

I nodded.

She laughed, unimpressed. Then she said the truest thing I'd heard in weeks. "We're going to have to find a better place than this," she said.

13

Summer people in the Hamptons loved naming their houses. And if there was one story that pretty much summed up the difference between growing up there and spending a summer there, it had to do with The Shipwreck— the house next to the house where I grew up on Old Montauk Highway.

The Shipwreck was a large, shingle-style cottage gorgeously restored by the owners—a local architect and his family. The house had been in their family for several generations, his grandfather resurrecting it after the hurricane of 1936. It sat high on a two-acre, seventy-five-foot bluff—with 180-degree views of the Atlantic Ocean.

The architect often rented out his house for parties and weddings. A handful of those, especially in the summer, paid his mortgage for the rest of the year. Most years. But while they were preparing for one August wedding, the bride and groom (a tech mogul and his model wife) decided that the two acres of land weren't enough for their five hundred guests, and so, without the owner's approval, they cut down protected trees behind the house to build a larger dance floor.

The case of cutting down those five trees went

through two lawsuits and eight years. The town sued the architect, the architect in turn sued the tech mogul, the tech mogul countersued everyone. A jury found for the local family and ordered the tech mogul to foot the tree-destroying bill of a hundred thousand dollars. They then ordered the mogul to pay another hundred thousand (and legal expenses) to the local architect for distress.

It was a happy ending, right?

Not so much.

The tech mogul refused to pay. And after eight more years and several more lawsuits, no one had seen a dollar. The architect was forced to sell his home (no longer legally allowed to rent it out for parties). And the kicker? The tech mogul purchased the house under a secret trust.

Which brings me to the difference between growing up in Montauk and summering there. One of you ends up with the house that was never yours. And the rest of you sit there telling the story.

I drove past The Shipwreck—the ocean and dunes glistening just beyond it—and pulled down my family's driveway, up to a house that was never named, a mix of ramshackle and hopeful that defined vintage Montauk. The smaller version of it, a two-room guesthouse, was visible a few yards behind it.

I shut off the ignition and stared at the house through the windshield. It wasn't as grand as

The Shipwreck, or most of the houses that lined this stretch of Old Montauk Highway. I tried to see it as a stranger would, if they had happened upon it, driving along this stretch of the dunes: a traditional Hamptons cottage with a large red door, striking bay windows, a wraparound porch—its charm undeniable. But instead I only wished I was that stranger, that I had driven up to the wrong house. That I could reverse down our dirt driveway to The Shipwreck and hide out in one of their extra wings, where no one would find me.

I didn't have a plan for when I got to the front door. How do you say hello when you've been gone for so long?

So I stayed in the car for a minute too long, maybe five minutes too long, tapping on the steering wheel. I willed someone to open the door so I wouldn't actually have to ring the bell and give them the chance to slam it in my face.

Then I heard sirens in the distance. Except they were getting closer.

I looked in my rearview mirror to see a squad car racing down the driveway, its lights flashing.

A police officer stepped out of his vehicle, screaming into his megaphone, apparently at me.

What was happening? I got out of the car, squinting toward the squad car in the afternoon sun.

"Step out of the car."

"I am out of the car!"

"Step further out of the car. And keep your hands by your sides!" the officer yelled.

I pointed toward the house. "No! See, this is my family's home."

"HANDS BY YOUR SIDES!"

I put my hands down as the officer walked over from his squad car, the sun backlighting him. It took me a second to place him: Zeddy Morgan, fellow graduate of East Hampton High. Fellow native. He'd had a crush on me when I was in sixth grade—or was it seventh?—and left a pack of half-eaten Twizzlers and a love note by the front door. A front door he was now trying to keep me away from.

"Zeddy?" I said.

I gave him a smile, relieved that whatever had started this misunderstanding, it was about to be over.

A look of recognition swept across his face. "Sunny? Sunny Stephens! What are you doing here?"

"Visiting."

"Visiting who?"

I looked at him, confused.

His face turned beet red. "Sorry to do this, but the owners want you to get off the property."

I pointed in the direction of the house— my childhood house. "It's my property," I said.

"Yeah . . . not anymore," he said.

"What are you talking about?"

"The new owners took it over a few years back. Celebrity folk. Very private. They're not here too often." Then he pulled out his notepad and started writing me a ticket. "Though they are here now."

He handed over the ticket. I looked down at it, still trying to process what he'd said about my family's house, no longer in my family. And then trying to process what the ticket said: $500.00. Trespassing.

"Zeddy, you've got to be kidding!" I said. "We used to live here. Would you just explain to the owner?"

He shrugged. "Already did."

"And what did he say?"

"He said you don't live here anymore."

I put the ticket in my pocket. "Nice."

I looked in the direction of the house.

"VERY NICE!" I screamed.

"All right, all right," Zeddy said, motioning toward my car, motioning for me to leave. "Let's not make a scene. I'm going to meet the guys at The Sloppy Tuna. Why don't you come? Five-dollar oysters, two-fifty beers. And they usually just let me drink for free. I can see what I can do. Considering the ticket."

It was a terrible invitation. But it was the only one I had.

I nodded my agreement, and Zeddy opened my car door.

Then I noticed movement on the guesthouse porch. A little girl. At least, I thought it was a little girl. All I could confirm was that whoever it was who raced out of the doorway and back into the house was a blur of blond curls and glasses and skinny, adept legs.

I turned back toward Zeddy.

"So . . . you remember how to get there?" he said. "Just take a left on Old Montauk and—"

"Zeddy, are they living in the guesthouse?"

He looked away. "No."

"Zeddy!"

"They may be living in the guesthouse," he said.

"And you didn't want to mention that?"

He shrugged. "Not my information to share."

I walked down the driveway and toward the small guesthouse, the ocean breeze growing stronger, propelling me forward.

"I wouldn't do that if I were you!" Zeddy called out. "COME BACK! Five-dollar oysters. Two-fifty beers."

I kept moving, taking the front steps two at a time, ringing the doorbell.

"It's my treat!" he said.

She opened the door. She was barefoot in a baby-doll dress (did people still wear baby-doll dresses?) with a ballet slipper in one hand

and a jar of peanut butter in the other. And she had curlers in her hair. At least they looked like curlers until I realized they were sticky balls of the peanut butter.

And yet she looked me up and down, and rolled her eyes. "Of course!" she said.

The first words my sister had said to me in five years.

14

I sat at the kitchen counter, my sister perched over the sink, washing the peanut butter out of her hair. I tried not to make it obvious as I looked around. The guesthouse was more of a guest cottage: a living area with a loft above it, a small kitchen, one bedroom in the back. My sister had decorated it (if you could use that word) with bright throw rugs and sofas, large chairs, my niece's artwork everywhere. Not an empty square foot. It made the house look even smaller.

"I'm leaving for work in five minutes, so you better make this quick," she said.

I looked up at her. She was still tugging ferociously at her hair. "Who did you sell the house to?"

"A celebrity and her husband. Doesn't matter. They're here, like . . . never."

"They're here enough to be assholes," I said.

"Well, I don't see it that way."

She kept pulling at her hair, the kitchen reeking of peanut butter.

"What are you doing?" I asked.

"Is the smell bothering you?" She motioned toward the front door. "Because you're free to go."

"I'm just asking."

"Well, Sammy thinks it's hilarious to put peanut butter in my hair whenever I sleep. And I made the mistake of taking a nap, since I'm on the late shift tonight. So currently I'm in the process of getting it out *and trying not to kill her!*"

She said this last part very loudly, and I noticed movement in the loft above. Sammy.

Samantha. Her daughter. My niece. I put a thousand-dollar check into an education trust fund for her every birthday. I hadn't laid eyes on her since she was two months old. My heart started racing at the sight of her. And, quite honestly, at the thought I couldn't stop myself from having: Could I get that six grand back, if I promised to replace it later? It would be enough for a shitty sublet in New York for the month, it would be enough until I was made whole again.

"We can skip the formalities, I know why you're here. I mean, I said to Thomas, she is definitely going to show up, and he said she would never. But I knew."

I knew she was setting me up by saying *Thomas.* The name of someone that I should have known and didn't. Instead of taking her bait, I searched her finger for a wedding ring. Nothing there.

"Look, I have to get to work," my sister said. "So if you could get to what you need, I'd like to speed this little visit up. And if you're looking for money—"

"I'm not," I said. "I just need a few days to hide out."

"Forget it," she laughed. She actually laughed.

"Rain . . ." I said. That's right, let's pause to register that my sister's name was Rain. Sunshine and Rain. My father was a musician (and perhaps high at the time of our births) and he'd made a deal with God that if he named us in that way, his art would be protected. It's too bad he hadn't been interested in a deal protecting us.

"I want to be perfectly clear with you about this," my sister said. "I don't have any desire to help you."

"I have nowhere else to go."

"You have nowhere else to go? Why don't you try Georgia? Isn't that where you're from?"

I looked away, not wanting to enrage her further. She blamed me for leaving her here with our father. She blamed me for leaving Montauk at all. It didn't seem like a good moment to remind her that she was the one who had chosen to stay. It didn't seem there was ever a good moment for that.

"Or, here's an idea. Hang out in your gorgeous Manhattan loft. Order takeout until things calm down."

"I can't."

"Why not?"

"Danny sold the apartment right after everything happened . . ."

"So . . . when he found out you were sleeping with someone else?" She shook her head, laughing a little. "He sold the place out from under you? Well, not the nicest thing to do. Can't say you didn't deserve it."

She picked up her phone and started texting. I was hoping it wasn't the police. I couldn't handle another five-hundred-dollar no-visitor fee.

"I don't particularly care that you're guilty of plagiarism on a major scale. Or that you deceived thousands of true fans who believed in you. And I've always liked Danny, but that's really your business too. Just to be clear, I'm not helping because you're a lousy fucking sister. And you were long before you did anything wrong to any of those people."

She stopped texting, returned to pulling the peanut butter from her hair.

"I don't hear from you until you need something."

"That's not true, Rain."

"A card on my kid's birthday isn't hearing from you."

"It's not like my phone has been ringing off the hook either."

"And if it had been?" she said. "What would've you done? Swooped in and helped out with the house?"

I looked around her shitty guesthouse and tried not to think about what it must have been like when she and Sammy ended up here.

"I don't even know why I'm getting into all this. I don't have the time. Sammy! We're leaving."

"She goes with you to work?"

"Tonight she does."

I touched her arm. "Why didn't you tell me you had to sell the house?"

She moved her arm away, as though my touch actually stung her. "In our many lengthy conversations?"

"Wasn't there another option? I would've helped. Or, if you didn't want my help, you could have rented it out, made a fortune doing that."

"Thank you for the brilliant financial advice! That didn't occur to me."

"I'm not saying . . ."

"I had to sell the house, okay? The maintenance was too much. And I needed the money for Sammy's education."

I looked at her, confused. Great public school was one of the few advantages of being in the Hamptons year-round.

"What do you mean?" I said, concerned. "Does she have learning issues?"

She shook her head, more offended that I might actually have the nerve to care than about anything else I'd done. "Why are we even discussing this? You want your share of the house?"

I did, as a matter of fact. "I told you, I just need a place to stay until everything quiets down."

She pulled at her hair, free of gum and peanut butter, soaking wet. "No."

"Can I just stay here until you get back?" I said. "Please? Use the computer. Get organized. If I go back out there, I'll probably get arrested."

I held up the ticket as proof.

"Who do you think called the cops?"

"Seriously?"

"I'm sorry, are you outraged? Did I, like, offend your moral compass?"

I shook my head, exhausted by her narrative—her same narrative that cast me in the role of evil villain. And she must have registered it on my face—my anger at her. Which only made her more angry. And, like that, there we were again, right where we'd left off, convinced that the other person was wrong and impossible.

"Hello."

We both turned to see that Sammy was standing in the loft (her bedroom apparently), wearing wire-rim glasses and overalls, her hair in two braids, Pippi Longstocking–style. The glasses took up most of her face—which, combined with the braids, made her look older than she was. Or maybe it was neither of those things. Maybe it was the way she was tilting her head, studying me. Like, at six years old, she had the ability to study anything.

"Sammy, where's your jacket?" Rain said.

"I checked the temperature. I'm fine."

That stopped me—the way she spoke. Grown-up, pitched. Her eyes still laser-focused on my face: piercing blue eyes, stunning and mildly absurd behind those glasses. And then there was how much she looked like my sister. Rain was two years older than me, and I had spent my childhood looking at her and trying to decide how I should be. It was bizarre to look at this small version of her, trying to figure out who I was.

Sammy climbed down the loft's ladder and stood right in front of me, studying me more intently. She might have been six, but I wanted to look away.

"Are we related?" she said.

"What makes you ask that?" I said.

"Well, we look alike, for starters.

Rain hoisted up her daughter. "Sammy. We're leaving."

They headed for the door, Sammy hanging over her shoulder.

"Just be gone before we're home," Rain said.

"Thank you, Rain."

Then she did look at me. "Don't thank me," she said. "Just don't come back."

She opened the door, a bag over her shoulder, Sammy still dangling, a balancing act she had mastered. And, yet, her face gave her away. My sister had always been the classically beautiful Stephens sister: five foot eight (to my five foot three), with shiny blond hair and strong features, a smile that lit up her face. But she wasn't smiling now, her eyes creased, her hair short and uninspired. Now she just looked tired.

As they headed out the front door, I heard Sammy say, "Who is that, Mommy?"

"That," she said, "is nobody."

15

I intended to find a place to stay for the night and leave as promised. I had no money and no good options—though staying with my sister was proving to be impossible. It would be one thing if we had a five-thousand-square-foot house to avoid each other in. There was no avoiding each other in six hundred square feet. Except I fell asleep with the laptop right on top of my stomach. And I hadn't been searching last-minute, reasonable hotel deals, like I should have been. I was trying to write an email to Danny, something that would make him understand—maybe something that would make us both understand. I hadn't gotten too far.|
This was what I had written before I fell asleep.

Dear Danny, so you're probably
Clearly, that would fix everything.

I woke up when I heard the key in the lock. My sister. I reached for my laptop and grabbed the rest of my stuff—not even zipping closed my bag—and raced toward the door. Rain wasn't kidding. She would call the police if I wasn't out of there before she stepped inside. My plan was to run out, even if that meant running right past her. But I ran too fast, and instead of squeezing past Rain on my way out, there was a man there. Large, imposing.

"Whoa!" he said.

He grabbed my shoulders, trying to avoid a collision. This guy was dirty and smelly, in fisherman gear, a garbage bag in his hand.

I flinched on his impact—on the feel of his hands on me—and my things went flying all around him, my laptop hitting the floor with a crack.

I bent down and started picking everything up.

He looked down at me, like he was trying not to laugh. "Where are you going in such a hurry?"

I looked up at him. "Don't you knock?" I said.

"Is that protocol where you're from?" he said. "If I'm the one with a key?"

He got down on the ground and started helping me corral my things—his hands on my folded underwear, his hands on my lipstick.

"Hope you didn't have anything too valuable in here," he said.

"You know, just everything I own," I said.

He picked up my computer, a crack running down the front. "*Owned* may be more accurate," he said.

I looked at him, his water bib undone, his suspenders by his waist. He was so dirty that you could almost miss that he was also pretty good-looking, in a burly kind of way. All muscles, with these clear blue eyes, smile glowing.

"So you did show up," he said. "I thought you would."

"Congratulations."

"Thanks," he said. "I believe someone owes me a hundred bucks."

"You would have to be Thomas?"

"I don't know that I would have to be," he said.

I wasn't in the mood for this guy, who was so obviously charmed by himself. I didn't want to pretend I was interested in having anything like a relationship with my sister's boyfriend, let alone with my sister herself.

He stood up, and I followed suit, my clothes stuffed back in my bag. He pointed toward the bedroom. "I'm just here grabbing a few things," he said.

"Well, Rain is at work—"

"I know where Rain is."

"So does she know that you're here grabbing a few things?"

I couldn't read his look. "You're asking a lot of questions, considering I'm the one with the key," he said.

"It was one question, actually. And you know what? I don't care, I'm leaving."

"Are you going through Sag on your way out of here?" he said.

"No, why?"

He smiled, dirty and mean. "No reason. There's just a little billboard. For all the new Food Network shows."

I closed my eyes, taking a breath in. "Great, so everyone is going to recognize me."

"Well, you're more like the corner of the billboard," he said. "And, no offense, you look a lot better in the billboard version of yourself than you do in person, so . . ."

"Thank you."

"I'm just saying, I'd relax about that. Not sure how many people around here care about someone stealing a few recipes."

"So why'd you tell me about it?"

Thomas shrugged. "Thought you'd like to drive by it on the way out of town."

I drilled him with a look, but then I heard a key in the lock.

My sister opened the door. Sammy was sound asleep in her arms. She looked back and forth between us.

"I don't fucking believe this," she said, straining to keep her voice low.

Thomas raised his hands in surrender. "It was my fault," he said. "I was asking a ton of questions."

"And whose fault are you?" she said.

She stormed past us and put Sammy in her bedroom, on her bed.

He laughed. "She is pissed!"

"I wouldn't laugh, some of that anger seemed directed at you."

"Nah. Just caught in the crossfire."

Rain walked back into the living room. She crossed her arms over her chest, turning first to Thomas.

"I had to keep Sammy at the hotel my entire shift."

"I'm sorry about that," he said.

"Where's Thomas?" she asked Thomas.

I looked at him, confused. "I thought you were Thomas."

My sister pointed at him. "No, this is Ethan."

"You told me you were Thomas."

He shook his head. "I think if someone rewound the conversation, it was you who told me I was Thomas."

"So who are you?" I said.

He held out his hand. "Ethan Nash. And you're Rain's sister. YouTube sensation." He paused. "Kind of."

I stared at his hand, not taking it. "You could have corrected me."

"I could have." He smiled. "Just one question. Why Macon, Georgia? It's not a particularly lush farming community. Why not go to Texas? That still has a Southern feel."

"We clearly needed your help."

"Clearly."

135

My sister rolled her eyes. "Look, where is Thomas?" she said, completely uninterested in this. "He was supposed to grab Sammy at the hotel and take her home. She's going to be exhausted!"

Ethan turned toward Rain. "There was a small car accident."

The anger washed off her face and in its place was terror. "What?"

"He's fine. He's totally fine."

She pushed Ethan. "For fuck's sake, Ethan! Would you open with that next time?" she said.

"He was on his bike heading to East Hampton to get Sammy."

I looked at them, confused. "He was going to put Sammy on the bike?"

Rain put her hand up to stop me. "Really? Can you refrain from offering your opinions on my parenting skills?"

Ethan shrugged. "Anyway, some teenagers were going too fast on Ocean and they threw him off. He may have a couple of cracked ribs. And his knee is toast."

"Where is he?"

"Southampton Hospital. In surgery."

"What? How is that completely fine?"

"Thomas didn't want me to tell you tonight. He wanted me to just get some of his things."

She started running around frantically. "I

don't fucking believe him. That fucking bike."

"I can't imagine why he didn't want me to tell you," Ethan said.

She headed toward the bedroom. "I'm going to wake up Sammy. And we'll head to the hospital . . ."

"I can watch her," I said.

She stopped and turned around. "You'll say anything to stay here," she said.

"Yes, that's true. But I'm still happy to do it."

She looked back and forth between us, as if Ethan was going to weigh in.

"But she doesn't know you."

"It's a good thing she's sleeping, then," I said.

Rain looked down at her watch, out of any good options. "If she wakes up, which is never going to happen, but if she wakes up, I want you to call me. No, I want you to have her call me."

Ethan stepped past us into the bedroom, started filling his garbage bag with Thomas's things.

"She usually gets up around seven, seven thirty, if you're lucky. Our friend Gena is watching her tomorrow. She will be here at six thirty A.M., will you not burn the house down until then?"

"I'm pretty sure I can handle it."

"I'm pretty sure you can't, but I don't really have a choice right now," she said.

"You can probably be there when Thomas comes to, but you're going to have to stop insulting me to do it."

Ethan walked back into the living room. "Yeah," he said. "We've got to go now."

"Fine." She was flustered, grabbing her purse, her keys. "What does Thomas need for the hospital, Ethan?"

Ethan touched her shoulder. "I've got it," he said.

Rain stayed frozen in place, not sure she was willing to leave. "I don't have a good feeling about this."

Ethan heaved his sloppily packed garbage bag over his shoulder. "What's the worst thing that could happen? I mean, it's more ideal than waking the poor kid up and dragging her to the hospital."

She pointed at him. "You! Don't talk to me."

"What did I do?"

"You got Thomas the bike!"

Ethan opened the front door.

"We've got to go," he said.

Rain nodded and started to walk out. Then she turned back. She met my eyes, and I was thrown by it. What I saw there. It was a little bit of concern and a little bit of anger. But beyond that, there was something else. Something that looked like how Danny looked. Like she didn't know me at all. And maybe she never was going to want to.

"This doesn't change anything," she said.

And with that, she was gone.

16

When I woke up in the morning, it took a minute to figure out where I was. I sighed loudly, thinking of Amber, feeling a crick in my neck from sleeping on Rain's couch. The terrible last few days came screeching back. And I vowed that this was the only night I'd wake up in last night's clothes, sleeping in my sister's house.

"Gena isn't coming," she said.

Sammy. The sound of her voice surprised me. I looked down to find her sitting on the floor by the head of the sofa. She was fully dressed, in jeans and a button-down shirt, reading a book, patiently waiting for me to wake up.

I rubbed my eyes, confused and still exhausted. "You sure?"

She held up her wrist, where she wore a little watch with SAMMY on the band in glitter. "It's eight A.M. and she isn't here."

"Doesn't mean she won't be."

"Actually, statistically, ninety percent of the time someone shows up within a half an hour of a scheduled obligation, or they don't show up at all. Her half hour was up over an hour ago."

"How do you know that?"

"Thomas told me."

"How does he know that?"

She shrugged. "You're going to have to ask him."

I tried to will myself the rest of the way awake—to figure out what I was going to do with Sammy now.

"So I guess we should call your mother."

She shook her head. "My mother called a little while ago and told me that Thomas had a boo-boo and you were going to watch me until Gena arrived. So I told her she already did."

"You lied to her?"

She shrugged. "She'll just worry, and there's no sense in her worrying."

I tilted my head, took her in. "How old are you?"

"Six." She paused. "How old are *you?*"

"Older than that."

She looked down at her book. "Obviously. Way older."

Rain and I hadn't discussed what I should tell her about who I was—or who I was to her. Gena was supposed to be on duty.

"Has your mom mentioned anything about your family?"

"Not a lot, really. Just that I'm named after my grandpa."

I cringed, not wanting to react in front of her, irritated to think of anyone being named after my father. "Has she told you anything else?"

"Mom told me on the phone that you're her sister. The one that sends the checks."

She seemed to have no discernable reaction to this, not needing or wanting any further information.

"Thank you," she said.

"For what?"

"The checks."

She looked confused by my slowness. Which gave me the opportunity to look away, my heart breaking a little at her gratitude.

I threw off my makeshift cover (a throw blanket with the ABCs on it). "You must be hungry," I said. "What do you want for breakfast?"

"Cinnamon toast."

Toast. Great. My mind went to Amber and her terrible toasts. She'd recently done a special episode on sweet treats—and made her own version, which had cinnamon and nutmeg on seeded wheat, smothered in olive oil and butter. I had watched that episode, for some reason or other, and remembered her pride at the addition of the nutmeg. Like she had single-handedly reinvented the cinnamon-toast wheel.

I got up, ready to cobble it together for Sammy. But then she stopped me.

"I only get it at John's. Eight thirty sharp."

I turned and looked at her. "Would you like to go there with me now?"

"Isn't that what I just said?"

"No, you said you only go there."

"Samesies."

She looked back down at her book, and I bit my lip trying not to laugh at this confusing child, who apparently acted forty-eighty and eight in the same conversation.

"Considering summer traffic, we will have to leave now if we want to arrive on time," she said.

"I'm ready when you are."

She looked up, taking in my wrinkled clothes, snug against my body. "Are you sure about that?"

17

The ride to John's Pancake House, which took five minutes in the winter, was so far taking us five times as long.

And we were less than halfway there.

Sammy sat in the back, reading a book, unbothered. I was very bothered—not only by the traffic, but by what the traffic represented. Over the last few decades, Montauk had stopped being the one place in the Hamptons that was still undeveloped and became the place that prided itself on a different kind of development. It wasn't quite as showy. It was more quietly fancy, drawing in the kind of wealthy people who thought they were better than their counterparts because instead of spending money on fancy cars, they spent it on their Priuses and perfectly done cottages filled with shabby chic furnishings. They purchased fluffy couches that cost twelve thousand dollars (the Montauk Sofa, that's actually what they were called) and cast-iron pots that were never used. It was its own cult of obnoxiousness: the show that didn't look like one, which was a show all in itself.

The village reflected that. On the surface, it was less a glamorous beach town and more a town of yesteryear: surf shops and restaurants, all desperately needing a face-lift. And sprinkled throughout these Montauk evergreens were the fancier new additions: a yoga studio, an overpriced bar, a designer clothing boutique— all hiding their glamour with the same rustic chic exterior, the occasional six-figure sports car giving the whole enterprise away.

And getting in my way.

A Range Rover took a sharp right turn, forcing us to miss another light.

By the time we actually pulled into John's Pancake House's parking lot, I was in a pretty surly mood, irritated by Montauk, irritated by all these people who were pretending to be something they weren't. How was that any different from what I had done?

Then I was reminded about what I had done. On the way inside the restaurant, we passed the newspaper kiosk, full of the morning papers. And there was the *New York Post*, front and center. And on the upper half of the cover, there was a headline. CELEBRITY CHEF REVEALED AS PHILANDERING FRAUD p. 10.

I pulled a paper out, turning quickly to page 10. AIN'T NO SUNSHINE. *No Stars for This Farm-Fresh Phony*, the header read, right above a small (unflattering) photograph of me sitting in a vegetable garden.

Sammy pointed at the photograph. "Why are

you in the newspaper?" she said. "And why did they use *that* picture?"

I heard a knock on the window and looked up to see Karen McCarthy, a girl from high school—twenty pounds lighter, and twenty years older—but it was undeniably her. She kept waving through the windowpane.

"Get your ass in here!" she mouthed.

I quickly tossed the paper as Sammy froze.

"Oh, no," she said.

I held the door open, but Sammy shook her head. "I don't like to sit in Karen's section," she said.

"I have a feeling you're not going to be alone in that," I said.

Sammy looked upset. "I'm serious. She lets the toast get cold."

But it was too late. Karen ran over. "As I live and breathe!" she said. "Sunny Stephens!"

She squeezed me toward her. Then she patted Sammy on the head. "And Sammy Stephens too."

Sammy patted her hair back in its place. "Please don't touch me."

Karen laughed. "Right. Sorry, Sammy," she said.

Then Karen folded her arms and turned back toward me.

"How long has it been?" she said.

"A long time," I said. "You look fantastic!"

"I know, right?" She looked me up and down

as if figuring out a way to return the compliment. "What's going on with you? Returning home in infamy?"

I flinched. "So you heard?"

She tilted her head, confused. "What are you talking about?"

And for a great moment, I actually thought Karen had no idea. It was one of my favorite things about Montauk. It was suffocating when you lived here—everyone in everyone else's business. But if you had the gall to leave town, you stopped existing. It was entirely possible Karen had not picked up the *Post* that morning and had no idea about what had happened with *A Little Sunshine*—or maybe she didn't know about *A Little Sunshine* in the first place.

Karen leaned in. "If you believe that, I have pancakes from yesterday that I'm happy to serve you!"

Then she started laughing, beyond amused at her sense of humor. I made myself a deal that she had thirty seconds to stop laughing or I would swipe Sammy's book and hit Karen across the head with it.

She caught her breath and smiled. "Of course I know. We are in the same biz!"

"Not exactly," I said.

"Well, not anymore!" she said. "But you had a good run before the hack. I mean, thanks to our loyalty."

I looked at her, confused.

"Everyone." She motioned around herself—I assumed to encapsulate all of Montauk. "We all assumed you pretended to be from somewhere else to protect your father's legacy. So we weren't going to out you. I mean . . . he was famous. He couldn't exactly have a daughter doing what you were doing."

Was she seriously saying that having hundreds of thousands of *A Little Sunshine* viewers would embarrass him? Or was it selling 150,000 cookbooks? Perhaps it was having so many loyal followers that the Food Network had decided to feature me prominently in prime time? But then I realized the part that would embarrass him. The part where I couldn't cook. The part where I was only pretending to be who I told everyone I was.

"I'm hungry," Sammy said. "I want to sit and I want to eat."

Karen looked down at Sammy. "Sit! By all means, sweetie," she said. "Can I get you your toast?"

Sammy looked back toward her book, turning the page. "I don't know. Can you?"

Karen laughed again. "You're a hoot, Sammy!" she said. Then she turned to me. "We'll catch up, okay? And, man, I should have reached out when it happened. I'm sorry about your father. He was truly a great man."

I felt a tightening in my chest. I didn't know what to say, never knew what to say when someone talked about my father. Especially someone like Karen, who seemed committed to talking about him as long as I would let her. Karen, who probably knew as much about him as I knew. He came to John's every morning to read his paper, to enjoy a short stack of buttermilk pancakes. Not the usual three they brought. Bad luck.

"We still miss him around here," she said.

"Oh, well, that makes one of us."

I was unnecessarily harsh, but I was pissed off about her takedown, and I didn't have the energy to pretend my father wasn't who he was.

Karen stepped back. The insult of my father was apparently something she took personally.

"I'll tell the hostess to get you guys menus," she said.

Then she walked away.

On the upside, Sammy smiled. "Wow, you really told her," she said.

She apparently liked rudeness directed toward her chilly-toast nemesis.

"Was she talking about Grandpa?"

I nodded. She had never met him, and yet there was a familiarity to how she said the word. What had Rain told her?

"Can we sit by the other windows now? Alisa is a way better waitress."

"Great idea," I said.

18

The story about my father was one I hated telling. He wasn't an alcoholic. He didn't hit us. He didn't do much of anything, which I guess was the best way to describe what was wrong with him.

Steve Stephens. His parents had actually named him that, which he liked to say explained something about how he had grown up. I thought it was more telling that he was raised in Charleston, South Carolina, above his parents' restaurant. They had planned for it to only be a lunch spot, but no one seemed to like their food. So, to make ends meet, they started dinner service as well. No one liked the food then, either, but they served alcohol, which everyone liked. They would play old ballads on the stereo, and people would stay late drinking, the music drifting upstairs into my father's childhood bedroom until two A.M. If this sounds romantic, he didn't consider it to be. My father would always say that it made him long for quiet.

Wouldn't you consider it ironic, then, that he went on to become a famous composer? He was most notable for his film scores, composing the scores for eighty films. And he won all sorts of awards, his little gold statues and magazine covers lining his music studio.

His music graced the screen and the theater worlds for decades. Then his success stopped. He kept taking jobs and striking out. The awards stopped. The phone calls stopped. The A-list jobs disappeared.

It would be nice to line it up with the moment my mother left. I was five years old, and she walked out the door. But that exit didn't hold him back. He actually found even greater success. It was the woman after her (the trophy wife) who held him back. Louisa Lorraine, my erstwhile stepmother. When Louisa walked out the door (shortly after walking in it), his career started to suffer. That's when he created the rules. The rules that he had to follow so his music would come together again. So his composition would be successful. So he could give it meaning. Example: He could only eat white foods on mornings he worked in the studio. He had to wear one specific pair of jeans on days he was meeting with potential clients (and when those jeans fell apart, he had to go to the same store to get a new pair to replace them). Rain and I were only allowed to drink certain things (apple juice okay; soda terrible). We could only leave the house (or return) at certain times during the day. This rule became particularly difficult to navigate when my father deemed two to five in the afternoon unlucky. The two of us would stroll around the village, trying to look like we had somewhere to be. This was Montauk. There were limited places to pretend to go.

And if you think I turned into a liar, I had an excellent role model. You should have seen the type of lies my father told. In order to keep his rules intact, he lied to everyone in his life—the people he worked for (he would make up reasons he had to turn new music in on certain days), the people working for him (he would provide a variety of tasks so they would walk in and out of his studio door the right number of times), our school (he'd make excuses to avoid a student-teacher conference because he decided it could jinx his work). What he actually had to work on was honoring his intricate system of rituals. He betrayed anyone and everyone in order to maintain it—to give himself the room to adhere to new rules whenever they came up for him.

My sister and I had different reactions to the rules. She was the typical caretaking firstborn. She tried to help him keep everything intact. She would put on the coffee in the morning so he wouldn't have to walk into the kitchen before working. (If she did it for him and delivered it to him in the studio, he was allowed to drink it.) She would make dinner at night on the safe plates (so she could easily cajole him into having something to eat).

On the other hand, I was the second born. And

I tried to do everything I could to mess with his rules, to show him they didn't add up to anything useful. I would serve him breakfast on the bad plates and only tell him afterward. I thought it would prove to him the rule had no merit— he hadn't been unable to work after eating, he hadn't passed out with the first bite. He never saw my lessons as loving, though. He saw them as acts of hostility.

When I tried to point out that if the rules were actually working he would have already started composing scores he was proud of again, he would shut down entirely. He didn't see it that way. He saw the rules as the only way back to artistic success. My inability to accept that seemed like proof to him of my defiance. It was proof to him that I lacked imagination in my own life.

So, since Rain would oblige, he dealt with her. And he slowly—and completely—retreated from me.

I think my sister never forgave me for that. She forgave him for having the rules. Maybe she figured he couldn't do anything to get rid of them. But she felt that I should have helped to maintain them—helped *her* not have to maintain them all on her own.

She was furious at me for leaving Montauk and going away to college. She, after all, had made the opposite decision upon graduating from high school. But as angry as she was that I left, she was even angrier that I hadn't done what I needed to do while I had been there to pretend my father was functioning, to make our lives work under his regime of crazy.

Which led us to our current relationship, or lack thereof. It explained why we had seen each other a grand total of five times since our father's funeral nine years before. The first time was to go over the will. There was no money to divide, only the house to consider. The second time was for my wedding to Danny. Rain was a fan of his, probably because our father had been. The third time was for her wedding to the man that would become Sammy's father. He was a professor at Southampton College—*Rain's* continuing-education professor at Southampton College—and it was our best reunion, Rain too happy to focus on hating me. The fourth time was when Sammy was born. Sammy's father, who had left a pregnant Rain for a different student, was gone by then. And the fifth time was when Sammy was two months old. Danny was working on a house in East Hampton. I made the mistake of telling her that was why I'd come to visit. She made the mistake of not seeing it as a gesture, nonetheless, and telling me to leave, Sammy a delicious little baby, held tightly in her arms as she closed the door.

All these years later, my sister still didn't know

how to forgive me for leaving her alone to handle our father. She still wanted to close the door and walk away.

I still hadn't forgiven her, either, but for the opposite thing. I hadn't forgiven her for spending so much time taking care of our father and his rules, even though she was the only mother figure I had, that she had stopped taking care of me.

My sister thought I left her. But, if she was paying attention, she'd see that she had stopped being around for anyone to leave.

19

Sammy read her novel during breakfast, not engaging with me at all.

When we got back to the house, she went up to her loft, and I walked into the bedroom to find Rain fresh from the shower, putting on her clothes for work.

Rain was a senior manager at the Maidstone, a sweet little hotel in East Hampton. She had worked there since she was twenty-one, starting off at the front desk. She now practically ran the place. And there was nothing wrong with her job, except how wrong it was for my sister. For one thing, she hated people—and she had to deal with them all day. For another, she had graduated number one in her class at East Hampton High and was nothing short of a math genius. Harvard had wanted her, and Princeton. She could have gone anywhere and done anything. She could have taken a job in some think tank where she never needed to be nice to a single person ever again. She should have gone somewhere other than down the street.

She crossed her arms over her chest, not trying to hide her disdain for me.

"Where's Gena?" she said.

"She never showed up," I said. "You really

might want to rethink your childcare choices."

She shook her head, walking toward her closet. "Sammy has got to stop lying to me."

"How is Thomas?"

"He'll be okay." She sighed, clearly upset about him, and clearly uninterested in discussing it. "Did she make you take her to John's?"

"Yep," I said. "Karen McCarthy was there. She's pleasant."

She laughed. "She called you out? That must have been fun."

"Your daughter doesn't seem to be a fan."

"She's a smart girl."

"Right? She read through her whole breakfast. I mean, I don't know what most six-year-olds do, but . . ."

"How would you?" she said, clearly not interested in my interest. Nor in the familiarity of my question. Then she dinged me for it.

"There was a *USA Today* at the hospital," she said.

I looked away, trying not to engage her further.

"I think the headline read: 'THE PRINCESS OF COOKBOOKS REVEALED TO BE A PAUPER.' "

I shrugged, pretending it didn't upset me. "They've done better."

"I could do better right now."

She reached into her closet, pulled down a scarf. "They focused mostly on the affair, actually, which I think sucks. Who you're sleeping with shouldn't be the issue. The issue is that you can't cook worth a nickel."

I didn't correct her, though she was missing the point. There were definitely people who cared that I couldn't really cook. Everyone else cared about something more primal—that they'd decided they knew me, and then decided they were deceived. That was the transaction we had traded in. I was supposed to have let them in to my lovely marriage, my gorgeous home, the recipes I warmed it with. And, in their minds, that was what I'd robbed them of.

"It actually made me feel badly for you," she said.

Was my sister taking my side a little? "Well, that isn't the same as saying I didn't deserve it, but I'll take it."

"I wouldn't."

So much for a nice sisterly moment.

She looked at herself in the mirror, doing a once-over of her tired face, giving up. "So there's a wedding at the Maidstone tonight. And usually when I have a wedding, Thomas is the one watching Sammy."

"Are you inviting me to stay?"

"Not exactly." She swayed from foot to foot uncomfortably. "I'm saying that the world has conspired in your favor and injured my boyfriend."

I thought of the awful story in the *New York Post*, Danny's face when a punk at work showed it to him. Would he throw it away, feeling a small pang and moving past it? Was that what I was to him now? Someone he needed to figure out how to move past? I thought of Danny and then I thought of my gutted career: my cancelled contracts, my lack of liquidity, the fact that there was no one in the world who wanted anything to do with me at the moment. Karen McCarthy was tweeting out to her hundred gossipy followers about our run-in. Amber Rucci was relishing in her victory. "I'm pretty sure that's not the case, but again, I'll take it," I said.

"Well," she said, "Thomas has been hospitalized five times since he started riding that thing, so probably not."

"Someone should take that bike away from him."

"Nobody's perfect," she said, her voice defensive, the way she used to get about our father.

She looked down, as if considering how she'd gotten herself into this bind, then deciding there was no time for such contemplation.

"Sammy has a science experiment she needs to do for camp on Monday. Would you be able to help her with it?"

"What kind of camp is that?"

"A camp where they like to learn," she said.

"Sammy is a special kid, isn't she?"

"How many ways are you going to ask that?"

I didn't have a good answer, and Rain wasn't looking for one anyway. She didn't want to talk about Sammy with me—which was fine. I didn't want to talk to her, either.

She paused. "Here's the thing," she said. "I don't want her getting attached to you today."

"There's not much risk of that if I have to make her do a science experiment."

"Forget it. I'm going to take her with me."

"No, no! Rain, it's fine."

"Just leave out any stories about our childhood. Anything about how her mommy used to be. I'm serious."

I nodded, and it occurred to me that we were both hiding who we used to be from the people that mattered the most.

"Look, Sammy's in camp Monday to Friday. She's been going since school let out, thank goodness, because last year she refused." She shook her head. "But Independence Day at the inn is very busy, and I have no weekend plan for her. Thomas *was* my weekend plan for her. So I guess, for right now, we're both out of great options."

"It's nice to have something in common."

20

In case you're worried that this was going to turn into a story about a woman realizing her childhood home was where she always belonged, please keep in mind that I hated being back in Montauk. I hated dealing with my sister and her unfair judgment. I hated looking at our childhood house and knowing she got ripped off, selling it for a quarter of what it was worth.

The address alone should have scored her a hefty sum. It was entirely about what was just outside those windows: the most gorgeous view of Montauk's pristine beaches.

You walked out the back door and down a pair of rickety stairs, and there you were. The Atlantic Ocean was stretched out before you, its quiet white beaches as far as the eye could see.

My favorite part of growing up in Montauk was taking those stairs down to the ocean, feeling the cold air hit my face, starting to feel a little bit free.

At this moment, though, even that turned into something else. Sammy had a game in which she tried to beat her previous time to the ocean. She was down to twenty-five seconds.

Chasing Sammy down those stairs, hoping she didn't trip and fall, took most of the pleasure out of it.

By the time I arrived at the ocean's edge, I was winded. And Sammy was bending down, putting water in a mason jar.

"We are making rain today," she said. "I just need to close these lids tight. And we can head back upstairs."

Down the beach, a group of kids about Sammy's age were playing catch with a large volleyball. No mason jars in sight.

"Sammy, we can stay on the beach for a little while. Hang out."

"Why would we do that?" she said.

"There are a bunch of other kids down there," I said. "Why don't we see what they're up to?"

She shook her head, not even looking in their direction. "No, thank you."

"Why not?"

"I don't really want to."

"Do you ever hang out with anyone except your mom?"

"Thomas," she said. "And sometimes Ethan."

"I mean anyone your own age?"

She sighed. "Not recently, no."

She didn't even look upset about it, which was sadder than if she did. It was like she had resigned herself to friendlessness.

She was done chatting about it, though, and ran back up the stairs toward the house, me lagging as I tried to keep up with her.

As I climbed the stairs, I looked up toward the

main house. The entire back of it was lined with bay windows—making the most of those views. I tried to see if anyone was inside. I could barely see inside at all, the house dark.

But there was a red sports car in the driveway, a Porsche, shiny and bright. It looked out of place on the gravel, too showy, which reminded me of when my father threw parties while we were growing up. Fancy cars would fill the driveway, squeeze in on every side of my father's beat-up Volkswagen Bug. My father kept that car during his rise to fame, and my entire childhood. He never traded up—even though he could have, financially. It wasn't about rules, he said. It was about loyalty.

When I got back to the guesthouse, I found Ethan sitting on the porch steps, smoking a cigarette. He was in his fisherman gear.

He motioned in my direction. "And she's still here," he said.

"Do you live here or something?"

He shook his head. "Nope. I live near the docks."

"So what do you want?"

"I'm friendly with the people who live next door." He paused. "The wife, really."

"The celebrity no one will dare name?" I said.

He nodded. "Exactly," he said. "The wife."

He smiled, and then I understood what he meant. He was *friends* with the celebrity wife.

"Seriously?" I said. "And who smokes anymore?"

He motioned toward the Porsche. "Her husband came home unexpectedly. So I'm hiding out. The cigarette is just my cover."

"I'm sure!"

He put the cigarette out on the heel of his shoe, as though proving the point. "And besides, people have all kinds of arrangements. If anyone should know that . . ."

"You don't know anything about me."

He looked up thoughtfully. "I'm sure that's true," he said.

I sat on the bottom step, too exhausted to figure out if he meant that, or if he was still making fun. "Sammy went inside?"

"Safe and sound."

I must have made a face, the stench of the fish coming off of him strongly.

"Sorry, I didn't have a chance to shower yet."

"There are worse things," I said.

He smiled. "I think that's the nicest thing you've said to me since we met," he said. "Thank you."

"So what do you fish, anyway?"

"Today? Swordfish. But it depends. I'm part of a seafarers' collective out here with Thomas. We fish sustainably, so that kind of dictates how it goes."

He leaned in.

"Sustainably means fresh caught, local fish. Not a lot of food miles, softened carbon footprint."

"I know what it means."

He shrugged. "I wasn't sure how deep the fraud went. If they taught you anything."

I ignored him. "How's Thomas doing? Rain didn't want to talk about it."

"He'll be fine. But he's not going on the water anytime soon. So my summer just got a little more complicated."

"I'm sure you can rally up the fish on your own."

"I'm guessing that's true." He tilted his head and considered. "Are you looking for some work? While you're here?"

"I can't smell like you."

He smirked. "I wasn't offering you a job. I just happen to know that the first bait shop on the harbor is looking for extra help. I could probably get you some work at the cash register."

I laughed loudly.

"I know it's not sexy, but . . ."

"You think?"

He put up his hands in surrender. "I was saying that I would put in a good word. That's all."

We heard a door slam and both looked up to see his girlfriend's husband walk out the front door and head to his red sports car. He was tall and handsome, in a pretty-boy kind of way. Tall and a little too thin. City slick.

He looked over at us on the steps. "Ethan! I thought that was you," he said.

Ethan waved. "Hey there, Henry. Did you just get into town?"

"I 'coptered in a couple of hours ago," he said. Then he turned toward me. "You look familiar."

My heartbeat sped up, and I tried to act casual. "I don't think so," I said.

Ethan pointed. "Sunshine Mackenzie née Stephens, the TV chef who was just hacked."

I forced a smile, elbowing Ethan in his side.

"Oh, sorry, the *internet* chef who was just hacked. Never quite made it to TV. Though there is a great billboard over in Sag."

Henry smiled back. "That's right! I think my wife is a fan of yours. And I *know* we have your cookbook."

"She's not," Ethan whispered, and continued waving. "And they don't."

"Are we going to see you later, buddy?" Henry called out. "Maybe get a little surf in?"

"Definitely," Ethan said.

Henry gave him the thumbs-up sign.

Then he disappeared into his car and peeled out.

After he was gone, I looked at Ethan, who shrugged. "I've provided them with fish for some dinner parties, so he knows we're friendly," he said. "He just doesn't know *how* friendly."

"That's lovely," I said. "Did you really have to embarrass me like that?"

"Please, in front of the guy who used 'helicopter' as a verb?"

"I'm trying to keep a low profile. Until I can pretend this never happened."

He considered. "No offense, but isn't pretending how you got into this mess? If you ask me . . ."

"I didn't."

"Seems to me that you probably should stop pretending."

He got up and headed toward the house, the one where I grew up, which now belonged to his celebrity girlfriend.

"Let me know if you change your mind about the job at the fish shop," he called out as he walked away. "I'll put in a good word."

"And why would you do that?"

He turned. "I don't know. 'Cause I can."

"Yeah, where I come from, people don't just do nice things for each other."

He smiled, motioned around himself. "This is where you come from."

21

The truth was that I did need a job.

I needed a specific job—and it was why I had acquiesced to coming to Montauk. I needed a job that would start me on the road to redemption: a new show, a new crack at the whole thing. I was already formulating a plan in my mind. A new story, if you will. Sunshine returns to her childhood home to embrace who she really is, and in the process learns to cook, and for real this time. But not just from anyone. From a master chef. From *the* master chef of the Hamptons.

It would be the first step in getting it all back. The cookbooks, the show.

I already had the feel of the new show worked out. It would be elegant, real, beachy, earthy, and wish-fulfilling. We'd shoot it in a kitchen that looked out onto the Atlantic Ocean, with fresh fish on the counter, a centerpiece of lemons and white seashells.

I would emerge as a pared-down version of myself, tanned and happy and more effortlessly graceful than before. All that would be needed was a quick mea culpa that when you surround yourself with the wrong people, you can become wrong yourself.

But now I had surrounded myself with

everyone right—my family, my old friends, and an extraordinary chef, my new friend, who anointed me as his protégé. And I couldn't wait to share new, homespun and delicious recipes from the sea.

I would be legitimate again. Amber Rucci would be put back in her place.

But first, he had to anoint me—which was going to be no easy task, considering who *he* was. In a world where every chef wanted the cookbooks and the shows and the attention, he wanted none of the above. He wanted to be left alone—which was one of the main reasons he'd opened his restaurant in the Hamptons.

The restaurant, which he named 28, was a few tree-lined streets off Montauk Highway, on the way to Amagansett. It was called 28 because of its intimate twenty-eight-seat dining room and chef's counter. The five seats at the chef's counter were the most coveted, but getting a table anywhere in the small dining room was a serious coup. If you knew about food (or even if you didn't), you knew about this restaurant. It was a destination restaurant, a place-you-get-engaged restaurant, a place-you-get-married restaurant, a place-you-can't-even-get-a-reservation restaurant.

And, with any luck, it was also going to be the start-of-my-redemption-tour restaurant.

I got Sammy an ice-cream cone at Craig's (two scoops, chocolate and vanilla) and left her to it in the foyer, so I could walk inside 28 alone. The dining room was perfectly understated: wooden rafters, dark stone tabletops, Windsor chairs. There were two paintings on the wall— one of Montauk, circa 1938, *Hurricane* written at the bottom; the other of a wooden spoon and fork, crisscrossed over a white canvas. I couldn't explain why that painting was as compelling as it was, so simple and decent. And yet, kind of like the restaurant itself, you wanted to be a part of it.

A woman was standing at the hostess stand, placing the evening's menus in their holders. She was in her early sixties and perfectly coiffed, in a white sweater and dress pants. Formal. And so slight that you could have missed her, if it weren't for her perfume—a pungent mix of lavender and dandelions—as though someone had told her that if she bought a natural perfume, she could put as much on as she desired. And, apparently, she desired to wear a lot.

She looked up and noticed me in the doorway. "We're closed until dinner service," she said.

"I'm actually looking for the manager . . . Lottie Reese?"

She offered a forced smile, probably thinking that I was there to beg for a reservation. "I am she."

I nodded like I didn't already know that. I had known it. I'd done my homework and had picked this exact time to walk in, knowing she would be the one in the main dining room. Lottie Reese: Chef Z's right-hand woman, the first employee he'd hired when he opened 28. Chef Z avoided the dining room whenever possible—didn't like mingling with his guests—and Lottie handled everything front of house for him every evening. By day, she handled everything else.

I offered her a large smile, taking in the restaurant, listening to the noises already coming from the kitchen. And taking in the smells—a mix of citrus and freshly cut herbs—reminding me that I hadn't eaten all day.

"What can I do for you?" she said.

"Peter Gerbertson told me to ask for you directly. I used to work for him at Per Se."

Her eyes went wide, and I saw her trying not to react. Peter had been the general manager there and was famous in the world of high-end dining. Considering that I was lying to her—I didn't even know Peter, let alone had ever worked for him—it was a risky move to use his name. But it added legitimacy. I knew she cared about Per Se. Even if Chef Z deplored the business of the restaurant business, Lottie liked to think the Per Ses and Blue Hills of the world knew of 28, that they were talking about her the way she talked about them.

Her smile went from forced to real, and I could see her take in my attire, which I had carefully chosen: a white peasant shirt, classic jeans. My hair was curly and loose. And I wore tortoiseshell eyeglasses: thick and oval, covering my eyes, obscuring my face. I didn't look so much like myself with the glasses on—and without makeup. It was my Clark Kent disguise, in case I needed one. Though, of course, I'd never been Superman.

"How is Peter?" she said.

"He's good," I said. "He sends his regards. And he told me you're the person to talk to about the possibility of working at 28."

"Well, it was kind of him to send you my way . . . uh . . ."

She was searching for my name, which I took as a good sign. "Sammy. Stephens."

I probably should have thought harder before using the kid's name. But it was the first that came to my mind.

"It's nice to meet you," she said. "Though honestly, we're already overstaffed for the season. But if you want to leave a resume, I can let you know if something opens up."

I pretended to reach into my bag for a resume I had no intention of handing her. I'd win or lose this battle in this moment.

"That would be great," I said. "I imagine it must be hard, training people and then retraining them every summer season."

"It's fine," she said.

Which was when there was yelling from the

kitchen. A British accent. Strong and intrepid. Chef Z.

Lottie blew right through it, and took me in. For a second, she looked at me as though his loud screaming would give me permission to call her out on the obvious: how many people Chef Z fired. How hard it was for her to keep any staff at all here, no one good enough for Z, no one meeting his standards, the task all the harder in the Hamptons.

"It's largely a summer community, so that's the case with most establishments," Lottie said.

I nodded. "Absolutely, but I'm from here. Born and raised. Not going anywhere. My sister had a kid, and I want to be around for that. So, if this worked out, you could count on an employee even in the quieter seasons."

She tilted her head, considering. "And how long were you at Per Se?"

I killed her with a smile. "A long time. And I was at Gramercy Tavern before that. I'm very familiar with how a kitchen like this runs."

She smiled. "Until you've worked here, no one is quite familiar with how a kitchen like this runs."

"A fair point. But I would love to find out."

Her smile disappeared. I wondered if I'd overplayed my hand, too eager. "I'm sorry, I'm just trying to figure out . . . why do you look familiar?"

"I've probably waited on you."

"All right, if Peter sent you, I'll give you a shot, but you'll have to make it through training, like everyone else."

"Understood."

"We do two dinner services a night. Six thirty and nine. Be here at five. I'll have you shadow Douglas. And depending on how you do, we'll start you on the floor."

"Great," I said, and started to leave.

She called out after me. "Wait a second," she said. "I know why you look familiar."

I braced myself and turned around.

"Anyone ever told you that you look like that girl? The cooking star . . . the one who can't cook. What's her name?"

I pushed the glasses higher up on my nose. "I think . . . it was Sunshine."

"Right, you look a lot like her."

My heart started racing, but I shrugged, not showing it. "People have said that to me before. I don't really think so."

Lottie nodded. "Well, she is thinner."

"I'm not really familiar with her . . ."

"A *lot* thinner," she said.

22

When we got back to the house, Rain was sitting on the porch, drinking a glass of wine. She looked exhausted, but tried to hide it, giving Sammy a huge smile.

"How did the science experiment go?" she said.

"Relatively uneventful. How was the wedding?"

"If I ever hear the word *orchid* again . . ."

Sammy tilted her head, taking her mother in. "I think you could use some pizza," she said.

Rain looked at her daughter, amused. And I could see the joy she took in her child, surpassing any other disappointments.

"I think that's a fantastic idea," she said.

Rain ushered Sammy into the house, apparently to order. No invitation. Not even a *hello*. I was nothing more than a babysitter whom she was never planning to hire again.

Rain turned around in the doorway, forced a smile. "Maybe you want to head into town?" Rain said. "Get something to eat?"

And I heard the implication. Make yourself scarce. It was the last thing I wanted to do. I wanted to sit in front of the computer and see what was going on with Amber and Ryan. I wanted to break into Danny's email and see if

174

he had calmed down yet, and was ready to talk more reasonably about our small relationship hurdle. I wanted to strategize for the first night of work with Chef Z.

"That's a good idea," I said.

She sighed loudly, as if she were unhappy with my response. "What are you going to do there?" she said.

I couldn't answer that. If Rain thought I was doing anything to stay, she would make me leave. "Do you really care?"

"I only care that you don't wake us when you're back," she said.

Then she shut the door.

23

You name a favorite world-class chef, and I could probably tell you about an experience I had at his or her restaurant. Thanks to Ryan (and his various attempts at cross-promotion) I had been in some of the most spectacular kitchens in the world. I'd spent an afternoon learning from Thomas Keller how to make his signature oysters and pearls, a creamy tapioca pudding infused with caviar and oysters. On the next episode of *A Little Sunshine*, I gave it a farm-girl twist—substituting juicy mushrooms for the oysters, caviar making way for sustainably cured salmon. I'd spent an evening at Blue Hill at Stone Barns learning how to cull the most perfect piece of lettuce.

So you might think it's surprising that I'd never met Chef Z before. There were a couple of reasons why I never met him. The main one was that in the modern cooking world, where TV shows and Instagram feeds were king, Z was as reclusive as he was talented. He didn't play the food-as-porn game. He didn't fight for Zagat reviews or a guest blog at Epicurious. No one even knew what Z was short for—it was a name he chose not to share with anybody— which told you a lot about Z: a Le Cordon Bleu trained chef who spent years as the executive chef at Michelin-starred kitchens in France and Spain before relocating to New York, where several investors got in line to open his flagship restaurant. It was located in a former Midtown West bank, which had been done and redone to Z's exact demands.

The reviews during the soft open were stellar. Z was set to rival Daniel and Jean Georges. But a week after opening—that's right, one week—Z had an enormous fight with his investors and fled. The investors sued, and he countersued, and the whole thing went on for years. All the investors wanted was for Z to return to the restaurant, and all Z wanted was to never again have anything to do with a restaurant of that size, which he thought made it impossible to focus on the food the way he wanted. Eventually they settled, and everyone thought that was the end of Z. Until Z moved to the Hamptons, where he opened 28 to worldwide acclaim and the elusive three-star *New York Times* review.

After which, rumor had it, Louis (my former publisher and friend) offered him a $600,000 advance for a cookbook entitled *Z*. And Z wrote back: *Not for six times as much.*

Z refused to do any press about 28 at all, except one interview he did for a small magazine about botany that his friend edited. In the interview, he spoke mostly about his garden and how the vegetables and fruits he grows dictates 28's menu. He did take a swipe, though, at his former business partners, and grand fare dining in general. "It is a step away from a wedding," he said. "Unless you're personally controlling every plate that hits your tables, you're a caterer."

So even when Ryan had made some headway at having *A Little Sunshine* do a special lunch at 28 (Z's silent investor hired a PR consultant who apparently liked Ryan), I declined to pursue it further. Z wouldn't have attended, but it didn't matter. I had no interest in returning to the Hamptons or discussing the Hamptons. And I certainly had no interest in honoring a nasty chef who would hate any press we got him anyway.

Which made it somewhat ironic that I was now walking into his kitchen, willingly, convinced that he was the only person who could get me out of my current jam.

The kitchen was pristine and mirrored the dining room in its simplicity. Everything was sterling silver and chrome. Everything was spotless. Workstations glistened, every chef and waiter already at work, moving through their early evening prep. The waiters were all dressed in their simple uniforms. Button-down blue shirt, dark pants. Loafers.

I knew enough not to disturb anybody, so I kept my eyes out for Lottie and watched the kitchen move. Sous-chefs were chopping and sautéing, waiters folding napkins. Everything was eerily silent and Chef Z was nowhere to be seen.

Lottie walked briskly past, not noticing me and heading to the other side of the kitchen. She put her hand on a cook's shoulder, whispering something into his ear.

When she looked up, I caught her eye, and she waved. Then she pointed at a heavyset guy, sweating profusely as he walked up and down the cooking line.

"Douglas," she mouthed.

It was as if he heard her, because he looked up. And she pointed at me. "Her," she said.

Douglas walked over quickly. "I'm Douglas," he said. "I guess you're following me tonight," he said.

Nothing. Not even a smile.

"There's a uniform for you in the break room. Get dressed and come back in here. I move pretty quick so try and keep up."

He said it with a straight face, but something about his girth made me wonder if he was kidding.

"Get your instructions from me. Talk to no one but me. And no matter what you do, never look at Chef Z. If you make eye contact, you'll be fired."

"Is he here tonight?"

Douglas shook his head. "Those kind of questions, and you'll be fired. And don't think I don't know, okay?"

He added it in so quickly, so smoothly, I thought I'd misheard him. "Excuse me?"

"Don't pretend," he said. *"Sammy."*

I looked around the kitchen. There was no one going out of his way to stare at me.

"Who knows?"

He shrugged. "I haven't taken a poll yet. Would you like me to? I can imagine the dishwashers don't care."

"Please, I really need this job."

"And I really need a good server. Lottie just fired someone else. And tonight's menu is particularly demanding. So if you can keep up and do your job, your secret is safe with me."

"Thank you."

"Probably shouldn't thank me until you hear my definition of *good job.*"

Before Douglas could say anything else vaguely resembling a threat, the kitchen door swung open, and there he was. Z. He was in his chef's jacket and pants, wire-rim glasses covering his eyes. He was in his fifties and surprisingly good-looking, considering his red hair, his never-even-seen-the-sun skin. It wasn't entirely a surprise. He was, for a time, as well known for the women he dated as for his food. There was something about him. Call it confidence, call it not giving a shit. He was hard not to notice.

"All right, people, let's do it," he said.

Lottie stood to his right, and everyone else

gathered around him in a semicircle. There were several dishes lined up on the counter behind him—piping hot pastas and a lamb shank, an elegant arctic char.

Chef Z picked up a plate of what looked to be some kind of flatbread pizza.

"That's Z's strawberry *sofrito* pizza," Douglas whispered. "Garden-grown strawberries, heirloom tomatoes, homemade ricotta cheese, balsamic vinegar, fresh basil . . ."

I swear, my stomach started to rumble. I was scared that Douglas had heard. But his eyes were firmly on Z. Everyone's were.

Z broke off a piece of the sweet, ooey-gooey goodness, which looked like a work of art—the ratio of tomatoes to strawberries to the dense thick cheese—perfectly decadent.

Z seemed less than pleased, though. "Kristin, where's the basil?" he said.

One of the sous-chefs stepped forward, not answering at first.

"Kristin?" he said.

She pointed to the other five pieces in the pie, which were strewn with gorgeous julienned pieces of the herb, so fresh and abundant, I could smell it from several feet away.

"Chef, it's right there," she said.

"Are you planning on going to each table tonight to make sure our guests happen to pick up a piece that you decided deserved fresh basil?"

"No, Chef."

He pointed at his piece. "It should be right here," he said.

Then he whispered something to Lottie and dropped the pizza on the countertop, disappearing out the same door he came in.

Lottie sighed. "An hour to service, folks," she said.

Then she motioned for Kristin to follow her out of the kitchen.

I looked up at Douglas. "She's not seriously getting fired over that?"

Douglas shook his head. "What did I tell you about those kind of questions?"

Douglas could move. In the first half hour of dinner service, I think I ran a mile just keeping up with him. I started to sweat, and not the cute kind of sweat—beads of perspiration dripping down my back, staining my new shirt. I was desperate for a glass of water, but too smart to dare ask. I was trying to keep mental notes, Douglas racing through responsibilities he assumed I understood from my imaginary years working at restaurants as fancy as—and far busier than—this was.

I tried to sneak peeks at Chef Z, who stood opposite his cooks line, monitoring the orders and doing quality control on every single plate before it went out into the dining room. He didn't talk to anyone except his cooks, and he spoke to them constantly, giving them orders. *I need a* sofrito. *Where is my salt? Steak, five times.* It was like he was a different man from earlier in the evening. Calm, evenhanded, in his element. I started to think: *Why was everyone making such a big deal about this kitchen being a nightmare?* Then I heard his voice.

"Taylor!" Chef Z screamed. Loudly.

I swung around toward the cooking line, expecting to see Chef Z. But he was standing at an empty workstation, in the back of the kitchen.

"TAYLOR!" Chef Z screamed again.

A thin and scrawny guy came running from the bathroom, back to the workstation. He had tattoos up and down his arms—one in notable block letters. I tried to read it without being too obvious about it. *You're the reason I'll be traveling on . . . Don't think twice, it's all right.* Why did it sound familiar? They were lyrics to a Bob Dylan song. I loved that song, though a little less on someone's arm.

He wiped his hands on his apron. "Yes, Chef."

Chef Z held up a dirty dish in his hand, a few tomatoes scattered across it.

"What is on this plate?" Z said.

"Those would be tomatoes, Chef. I believe from the strawberry pizza."

"So you do recognize the fruit, then?"

The kitchen got quieter than before. Everyone was pretending they weren't doing exactly what everyone was doing: looking back and forth between them, no one saying a word.

"Before you took off on your little break, or wherever you've been, did you or did you not mark that a plethora of tomatoes were left behind?"

"I did not."

"And why not? Isn't it your one job to note which foods return from the dining room uneaten?"

"I didn't consider the amount to be a plethora."

"Is that sarcasm?"

"Absolutely not, Chef. We're early in the evening, and before I disturbed you with it, I wanted to see—"

"A diner leaves a dozen tomatoes on his plate, I want to know. A diner leaves a single tomato on his plate, I want to know that too. Who leaves a tomato behind? I sat in the garden. I planted it myself. That is heaven. They left a bit of heaven on their plate."

"And in a few weeks, it won't even be around to waste," I said.

He looked around the kitchen, meeting my eyes. "Who are you?"

Everyone turned and looked in my direction. I cleared my throat, knowing I'd just taken a risk, but knowing I had to, if I wanted to get anywhere with Z.

"I'm your new server. In training to be, at least."

"So you're not particularly useful."

Douglas moved slowly away, as though the inevitable firing was something he could catch.

"What do you think about waste?"

"I'm against it."

There was a chuckle in the group, but I knew that my answer was the right one: succinct, sure of itself.

Z tilted his head, taking me in. His attention was on me; the room's attention was on me as well.

"Come here, please," he said.

I hesitated, and Z started flapping his arm.

"Let's go," he said. "Let's go."

I walked over, and he motioned for me to step behind the workstation, next to Taylor. I looked at Taylor, who turned away.

"Here's the deal. Watch everything that Taylor writes down. If he misses anything, if he misses one tomato, you tell the captain and you take his job."

"And what if he gets everything right, Chef?"

"Then there's no use for you here."

Z turned and walked back over to the line, started checking on the next course's dishes.

Taylor leaned in toward me, tidying his station. "Why did you get us into that?" he said.

"I didn't mean to cause trouble," I said.

He shook his head. "Well, you meant to do something," he said.

He dropped the tomatoes into the trash.

"He does this every few nights. Threatens his regular staff with someone new, makes them work a little harder for their job. But there is no way he's actually giving you my job."

His station was spotless, ready for the next rush of dinner returns.

"I was just promoted to trash too," he said.

"That's something you get promoted to?"

"It's not my strength. But if you want to cook for him eventually . . ."

"Trash is the path?"

He nodded. "Trash is the path."

"So, the idea is that you're writing down what people don't eat?"

"Has anyone ever told you that you ask way too many questions?"

"Yes, they have. And I totally understand if you don't want to answer them, considering that I'm now the competition."

He smiled, my honesty having warmed him. Imagine that!

"Noting for Chef what is left behind helps him ascertain whether it's presentation that isn't working or the item itself, so he can adjust accordingly. It's pretty important. At least as far as he is concerned."

"Weird. They haven't done this at the other places I've worked."

"They don't do most of what Z does anywhere else," Taylor said. "He's fastidious."

Taylor nodded, proud to work there. And I started to feel conflicted that he was trying to help me out, even though I was trying to take his job.

I suddenly wanted to do something else.

"So maybe we can figure out a way to convince him he needs two people to do it," I said.

He laughed. "No, it's you or me."

"I was suggesting an alternative."

"No offense," he said. "But the alternative is that you're ending your little regime at 28 right when it's getting started."

The thing about working in a restaurant kitchen, even under intense pressure, is that it gets really quiet, really quickly. The only sound is the noises of the kitchen, its own life-form, stainless-steel pots and fire and bubbling water, finding their rhythm together. Especially a restaurant like 28. The waiters and line cooks move like a machine. I didn't know how I'd do on trash, but I realized it was a good thing my career as a waiter here had been short-lived, or I would have been fired before the night was out. The rapid movements, the heavy plates lining arms. Getting hit by Z on one side and the snooty guests on the other.

Staying in my small trash workstation, surrounded by garbage pails, was certainly preferable. Yes, even considering the garbage pails. And I found myself watching intently, trying to keep up, trying to learn. I watched the plates come back from service, making mental notes as to what people were eating well. And what they weren't touching.

Some of it wasn't surprising. There wasn't a stray noodle from Z's homemade *cacio e pepe*—rich and peppery, covered in cheese. And Taylor had been right: The leftover tomatoes were an anomaly. Besides those stray tomatoes Z had sulked about, every plate of strawberry pizza returned to us clean.

In fact, over the course of the evening, the only unpopular dish was the vegetarian tagine.

It was midnight before Chef Z came over.

"What's the word, Taylor?" Z asked.

"The tagine's sauce," he said.

"What in the sauce, specifically?"

I looked down into the thick sauce, uncertain how he expected Taylor to answer that, when I realized what the answer was.

"I would say the preserved lemon, Chef," Taylor said.

"Would you?"

"Often, there were several chunks left in the bottom of the dish."

Chef opened up the trash bag and peered inside. Then he looked at me. "Is that right?"

I paused. I needed this job. I needed the proximity to Z for my plan to go as needed. Then I looked at Taylor. It seemed like if I gave a different answer than he had, he'd be out of a job. Or would he? Was that too easy for the game Chef Z was playing here?

"Preserved lemons, Chef."

It wasn't that I'd developed a conscience. It was that it suddenly occurred to me that there was a smarter way to go.

Z looked surprised that I backed up Taylor. As for Taylor, he looked downright shocked.

"Okay," Z said.

"But I don't think the lemon is the problem," I said.

"And what is the problem?"

"The dried cherries. They're close to the lemons in consistency. And once people have the sweet, they're probably less interested in the savory."

Chef Z moved incredibly close to me, whispered in my ear. "Did I ask you to evaluate my dish?" he said.

"No, Chef."

"So do not offer it then, especially when you have no idea what you're talking about," he said. Though I could see it. He was just a little bit insulted. Which, for a narcissist, was a step away from impressed.

Z looked between us. "So which of you is staying?"

It wasn't a question. "I'd say we both should," I said.

"Not possible."

"Except the issue with the food that is thrown out is twofold, Chef. Taylor accurately noted everything that didn't leave the plate, but there is another important aspect—the other elements in the dish that were preferred. That has to be taken into account in considering what they chose to consume and what they chose not to consume. That's really a two-person job."

He looked down at his watch. "That was almost ninety seconds that I'm never getting back."

I nodded, a subtle apology.

Chef kept his eyes on me. "Taylor, walk away."

"What?" Taylor said.

"Walk away."

"Chef, Sammy will tell you . . ."

"Who is Sammy?"

I raised my hand.

"Stupid name." He shook his head. "Is that what your parents named you, or did you shorten it all by yourself?"

I looked around the kitchen, wondering who would react to the lie, who knew my real name. Everyone continued working, cleaning up their stations, closing down for the night. If anyone was interested in outing me, they were going to do it when they hadn't been on their feet for fourteen hours already and were dreaming of getting into their beds, confrontation free.

Z turned away from me, looked Taylor up and down.

"Taylor, why are you still standing here?"

Taylor walked out of the kitchen, leaving me alone with Z.

"So, *Sammy.* This is your entire job, trash. You look at what people left on their plate. And write it down. Then you throw it out. Is that understood?"

I nodded, trying to contain my joy. "I won't let you down, Chef," I said.

"Of course you will," he said.

Then he walked away.

24

On the way home from the restaurant, I stopped at a pay phone off of Montauk Highway to call Danny. I knew he wouldn't pick up if I called from my phone, so I had to try a different way. It felt wrong to have a night like I'd just had and not tell him about it—not hear him laugh about how scary Chef Z was—and how scary Douglas was. He would probably say Douglas was scarier. And it felt wrong not to tell him that I had scored a first victory on the way to getting a life back.

We'd had a tradition when one of us had a big day—something at school or work, something worth reporting—of bringing home some super-unhealthy takeout, dealer's choice. It had started in the first apartment, the garden apartment, when we were so broke that any takeout was a treat. And we had stayed with it.

The night that *A Little Sunshine* was picked up to series, we hadn't gone to some fancy restaurant. And of course, I didn't cook. I had ordered spicy chicken and extra egg rolls, and we ate on the couch while imagining what we were going to do with the (small) influx of money. It was enough to put a dent in the down payment on the town house. But I hesitated.

Ryan had already signed a lease on the studio in Chelsea. He wanted Danny and me to get a place not so far from there.

As hip as Red Hook was, Ryan decided that my living in Manhattan was more relatable—especially to people unfamiliar with New York. That was the dream people aspired to, as opposed to our dream of living off the beaten path. It wouldn't appeal to viewers in the same way to engage with someone who was living miles from the nearest subway station.

They wanted what they'd seen on television—what they thought New York was supposed to be—lively streets crowded with sexy people and late-night bars. Fancy restaurants. And a dream apartment in spitting distance of the action—where they could dream they would have a chance to live too.

Danny was holding his ground on staying in Red Hook—not ready to give up our dream just yet. But, as I enjoyed my greasy takeout, I was already happily envisioning the East Village apartment that Ryan thought could be perfect. It was right by Astor Place, shiny and new, with a shower that was larger than our current bathroom. I told Danny that we would figure it out together, but I think I already decided that was the way I wanted to go. Takeout and dreams be damned. I was already willing to sell us out.

As I dialed Danny's number, I remembered the

night of the surprise party. Danny had offered me the takeout option. Sushi and a terrible movie. Why hadn't I taken it? Maybe if we had been home when those tweets came through, I would have handled it better. I would have convinced him it didn't define us. Which, of course, it didn't.

Right now, there was no chance of takeout. The most I could hope for was just to hear his voice. And, at 1:45 A.M., that was unlikely too.

Still, my heart dropped when he didn't pick up. The phone went right to voice mail, and all I heard was the machine-operated version of him, saying he'd give a ring back.

I knew he wouldn't.

So instead of leaving a message, I held the phone out so he could hear what I was hearing. The late night breeze, the ocean kicking up, and somewhere on the beach in the distance, someone laughing at something I couldn't see.

25

I tiptoed into the guesthouse a little after 2 A.M., and turned on the kitchen light.

"I thought you disappeared on me!"

My sister was sitting on the living room couch, arms folded across her chest.

I jumped back. "Holy shit! You scared me."

She was pissed. "I scared you? I thought you just took off."

"And left all my things?"

"It's what you did last time."

I looked at her, not saying anything. I had to catch my breath from finding her sitting there. It was like I was suddenly fifteen again, and walking into the house late. My father didn't give us a curfew. But if I arrived home even a second after ten, Rain would have a million questions about where I'd been. It wasn't that she was actually worried about me. She was worried about my father. She didn't want him to be woken up or to manage what that would mean for him the next day. And for her.

She stood up. "Where were you?" she said. "I wanted to go to the hospital and see Thomas. Isn't that why you're here? You get a place to stay and you help me with Sammy? What the hell were you doing?"

I sat on the edge of the couch, my feet throbbing. "See? Why do you have to ask like that?"

"Because I know how you work," she said. "And I know when you're up to something."

"I got a job at a restaurant."

She laughed. "Where?"

"28."

"28 hired you for two weeks?"

"I didn't tell them it was just for two weeks."

She shook her head. "Of course not."

I motioned for her to go away. "As fun as this girl talk is, I'm exhausted, so if you'd please . . ."

She ignored me. "Did anyone there recognize you?"

"A couple of people, but it doesn't seem like they're going to say anything." I paused. "Until it benefits them to do so."

"So how did it happen? The job? Ethan pull some strings?"

"What kind of strings? He's a fisherman."

"No, he's *the* fisherman. Look him up. Ethan Nash. He's very impressive."

I put my legs out in front of me, ready to fall asleep in that position—lights on, clothes on—as soon as she stopped her lecture.

"He takes the ferry to New Haven every week to teach a class at Yale on climate change and oceanography. Generating a safe food supply."

She paused, as if waiting for me to jump out of my seat, impressed.

"There is a thirty-restaurant wait list to even get his fish. Le Bernardin uses them, Per Se . . . Chef Z won't serve fish from anyone else. A national restaurant group offered him a million-dollar contract if he would ensure that his fishermen worked with them exclusively this season."

"And he didn't take it?"

"That's not why he's doing this. Not that you'd understand that . . ." She headed toward her bedroom. "Well, congrats on the job. I can't believe that you made it through a shift. Bet you're gone by the end of the week."

"Thanks for the faith," I said.

"So I guess this means I'm on my own with Sammy again."

"No, I'm only working nights. I'll still take her for the day tomorrow."

She looked surprised. "Thank you."

I didn't add that the restaurant was actually closed for the Fourth—it seemed better to just take the credit. Especially when I knew I was about to press my luck.

"If you want, I can get her ready for camp in the mornings this week, so you can go and see Thomas before work. And I can drop her at the Maidstone on my way to the restaurant at night."

She tilted her head and considered. "I guess that'll work. For this week, at least."

I nodded, pretending to look pleased. Had it really come to negotiating with Rain in order to stake a claim to her lousy couch?

Rain paused, tapping on the bedroom doorframe. "So why did you take the job?" she said. "What's your play?"

"Nothing."

"Nothing? Bullshit."

I looked away, irritated that she was calling me out, even if she was right.

"Not everyone is gaming everyone, you know," I said.

She smiled. "No, not everyone. But you definitely are."

"You know . . . you looked kind of sad that I might have been gone," I said.

She stopped smiling. "I can promise you it wasn't for the reason you think," she said.

Then she disappeared into her bedroom.

26

You can easily get complacent.

When I was younger, I never did. I was vigilant. Consider it a side effect of growing up in my father's home. His shifting rules made anything close to complacency an impossibility. We never knew what would be required of us, based on what he thought was required of him. There were some rules that we could count on lasting, like his pancakes, and others that shifted entirely on a dime, like forbidden hours. It taught me a good lesson, though. Complacency was dangerous.

So why was it that I kept forgetting such a basic tenet?

I woke up on the uncomfortable couch, rain pouring down outside, and I actually had the thought: *Amber's hack was in the past.* I was onto the redemption plan. Step one: getting my career back on track. Chef Z knew me. Chef Z would soon love me. Step two: starting to deal with my personal life. I sat down to send Danny an email. A long email explaining a little better how I thought we'd gotten here. It would be useful, I decided, not to let him completely off the hook. I would strike the perfect tone between sensitive and strong. I wouldn't overly apologize.

He, after all, had things to apologize for now too. His haste in the aftermath, selling our apartment. I wouldn't castigate him, but I'd allude to it.

I would also fit in that I was driving my niece to camp every day. If he thought I was trying to heal my family, he'd be impressed. And he would remember that was the woman he loved. One night in fourteen years hadn't changed that.

Except, when I opened my computer, I saw the new hack.

An email from Aintnosunshine.

Checking in. Happy being yesterday's news?

And there was a link to my YouTube channel, *A Little Sunshine.* I clicked on the link, and instead of a new video from me, there was *Toast of the Town* written in large letters and a link to Amber Rucci's YouTube channel. I stared at the screen in disbelief. Was Amber actually that shameless? Sending people from my channel to hers?

Reluctantly, I clicked on the link and saw Amber sitting in her Upper West Side apartment, curled into her couch in a comfy sweater and jeans (and full makeup), announcing her cookbook release and saying she had exciting news to share.

"I'm hitting the small screen!" Amber said. Then she clicked on her TV, which was tuned to the Food Network. "Stay tuned! Literally."

My Food Network hosting gig. It was now her Food Network hosting gig. She was the ideal replacement. A marketing executive was ordering new billboards. A producer was happily convincing the higher-ups that Amber was better for the job anyway.

I hit pause, trying to control my anger.

On Amber's checklist to steal my career, she had checked another box. An important one.

Publishing contract. TV show.

I looked at Amber's smug face, so pleased with herself for stealing my life. So pleased with herself that she was getting everything she thought she deserved.

I couldn't help it. I hit play again.

"A perfect toast to enjoy the premiere episode with?" Amber said, springing into cheery action. "I vote for . . . grilled pineapple and hazelnut chocolate on dark pumpernickel bread. For the win!"

She held the toast up, the chocolate dripping off the rich pumpernickel bread, the pineapple bright and luscious.

She took a large, crunchy bite and smirked right at me.

I felt faint. I actually felt faint.

So I turned off my laptop, complete with its crack.

And then I threw it against the wall.

"Wow, that's loud!"

I turned to Sammy, standing there, watching. "Sorry, Sammy."

She shrugged. "It wasn't my laptop," she said.

I almost laughed.

Sammy walked over to the window, looked at the rain. "I'd like to watch movies today," she said. "Considering the weather."

I bent down to pick up my laptop, still thinking about Amber. "Good decision," I said, only half listening.

She plopped down on the couch, wrapping my blanket around her. "You'll watch with me?" she said, more of a command than a request.

"As long as it's not a horror film," I said.

"Not allowed," she said.

I thought of Amber and her pineapple, my fury bubbling up again. "Or about food."

"Not interested," she said.

I sat back down on the couch, the laptop in my hands.

She motioned toward it. "Why did you throw that, anyway?" she said.

"It was stupid. I was mad at this woman, who did a mean thing."

Sammy looked confused. "Is it her computer?"

"No."

Sammy reached for the television remote. "Then that was pretty stupid," she said.

27

A weird thing happens when someone tries to blatantly take you down: You let cruelty win or you let it fuel you.

I chose fuel.

I knew that the first step was to win Chef Z over quickly, and that meant taking big swings.

For my swing that Monday morning, I would head to 28's local farm in Amagansett. In Z's one and only botany interview, he'd said he tended to his vegetables at 10 A.M. daily in order to prep the menu for that night. I sussed out that the sous-chefs arrived a little before he did. I was going to befriend one of them, and convince them to walk me through the gardens (show me the springing mushrooms and tomatoes and herbs). I would "happen" to be there when Chef Z arrived. So he would see my eagerness to understand another aspect of how he did what he did. How many members of his kitchen staff did that? How many people in charge of the trash?

My plan was to take Sammy to camp and then head to the farm. Except, just as we arrived, Sammy hesitated before getting out of the car.

"I won an award at camp," she said.

I was reviewing my knowledge about summer

fruit, thinking of something interesting to say to Z. So I didn't respond at first—and then Sammy continued.

"I made a contraption that waters the plants at night," she said. "While we sleep. It's pretty great."

My eyes ticked to the clock on the dashboard. "That's great, Sammy. Good for you."

"They're having assembly today to show the inventions."

"Did you tell your mom? She definitely would want to be there."

"I know she has to be at work, so . . ."

I knew what she was asking. I knew what I was supposed to say. What she wanted.

Sammy shrugged. "It's no big deal."

I closed my eyes, doing the math. If the ceremony took less than an hour, I'd probably be okay.

"So how about if I come?"

She turned and looked at me, and I guiltily hoped she'd argue. "All right," she said.

She didn't look out the window. She looked right at me, as if calling my bluff.

My heart dropped, and I almost rescinded the offer. Six or not, she was getting in my way. Amber's irritating vlog was playing on repeat in my head, and I knew the only way to get rid of her *was* to get rid of her. To beat her at her own game. In order to do that, I needed to get to the farm and intercept Z. And I desperately wanted to stop for a coffee before I did. The thermos I'd brought from the house was making me incredibly nauseated. Normally I could drink any drudge, which seemed like further proof that I was allergic to Montauk.

And now there was a little girl, making a little girl face—which was hard to resist. If I were stronger, I would have resisted it. Or maybe that would have been proof that I wasn't strong enough.

I put my hands back on the wheel. "Show me where to park."

28

The assembly lasted for five hours.

At least, it felt that long.

All these little kids did their demonstrations—sometimes in groups of twos and threes. And it seemed like Sammy was never going to be up. Sammy hadn't mentioned that she was getting her award last—the finale to the entire assembly. Sammy was given her award last because, as Sammy hadn't made clear, it was the most important award.

She headed to the front of the auditorium to do her demonstration, and the head counselor, a woman named Kathleen, stood proudly behind her. Kathleen was pretty in a librarian kind of way. She had porcelain skin, and long red hair, which she wore in a low ponytail. Her adoration for Sammy was obvious. After each part of Sammy's demonstration, she cued up the audience to applaud, which we did.

When Sammy was done, the counselor put her hand on Sammy's shoulder. "Was that fantastic or what?" she said.

From my seat in the second row, I tried not to laugh as Sammy did everything in her power not to physically remove that hand.

"Sammy Stephens has proven herself to be

quite a star," Kathleen said. "The fact that she is already designing a self-sustaining irrigation system, when we are only touching on water during geology . . . well, I just want to say, H2U. Here's to you!"

Everyone started laughing. Water humor, really? I had clearly stumbled into the nerdiest camp in America.

Kathleen handed Sammy a ribbon—they still gave out ribbons?—and I saw a smile break out on Sammy's face. It stopped me. What was I feeling? There was no denying it. Pride.

As everyone started to exit, Sammy ran up to me, holding up her ribbon.

"Did you watch?" she said.

"I sure did. Congratulations!" I said.

"Thanks," she said.

"I've really got to run, but let's get ice cream when I pick you up later."

Her face fell. "There's cake, though. For the parents. *Now.*"

Seriously? Were there no points earned? "I'm sorry, Sammy. Next time, okay?"

"It's really good cake," she said under her breath.

How many times was I going to make her ask me? Was I that freaking selfish? "Next time," I said.

I patted her awkwardly on the shoulder, already searching for the nearest exit.

Then I heard someone call my name. "Sunshine?"

I turned and saw Kathleen walking toward us, her long hair now loose. She waved excitedly.

I forced a smile. I was never leaving this place.

"Hi, there," she said, picking up speed as she neared. "Kathleen Teague."

"Hi, Kathleen," I said.

She held out her hand. "Great to meet you. Sammy mentioned that her cool aunt was going to be joining us today."

I looked down at Sammy, wondering if *cool* had been her word. Whatever she'd said, it was probably nice, or Kathleen wouldn't be so friendly now. Which made one person in the world who didn't loathe me. Even if she was only six.

Kathleen leaned in and whispered in my ear. "And, FYI, I don't believe what I read in the papers."

I pulled away. "I've really got to run."

"Before you do, would you let Rain know that I've left her a few messages?"

"Sure," I said.

But then she reached for my arm. "I need her to give me a call back," she said.

I looked at Sammy, who was focused on her ribbon. "Is everything okay?"

"Oh, yes! Sammy is wonderful. It's more than okay. She is having a great time at camp. And I'm so happy with how the summer is going for her."

She put her hand on Sammy's shoulder again, Sammy squirming away. Was this woman oblivious?

"I understand why Rain's avoiding my phone call," she said. "Sometimes it can be just as scary to hear that something is right with your kid as something is wrong with her."

"I'm guessing she's just slammed at work."

"Perhaps," she said. "Do remind her though. And please feel free to come anytime. Our doors are always open to Sammy's family."

She gave Sammy a smile and headed away.

Sammy looked up at me. "She's the head of the camp," she said. "I kind of like her."

"She seems nice," I said.

"She talks a lot, though."

I nodded. "That's all right."

"But you're late," Sammy said. "I'm sorry. I shouldn't have asked you to come."

Sammy played with her ribbon, eyes down. And I regretted my previous tone immediately— I regretted everything I'd done that made her feel badly that she'd wanted somebody to be there for her.

I bent down so we were eye to eye. "No," I said. "I'm happy you did."

"No, you're not."

"I am." I took a deep breath in, almost in disbelief at what I was about to do. "And I can't

209

believe I was going to let an errand get in the way of cake. That was really crazy talk."

She smiled. "Really?"

She looked up at me like she was trying to figure out if I was truly happy I'd come. Apparently, she decided it didn't matter.

We started walking toward the cake reception, and Sammy took my hand. Intertwining our fingers. Little fingers circling big ones. Like it was the most natural thing in the world.

I looked down at our hands, trying not to make a big deal, holding on to hers a little tighter.

Maybe I had been lying earlier when I said I was happy to be there. But it felt like the truth now.

29

After I left Sammy at the Maidstone, I barely made it to work on time. I ran to my station and put on my glasses when I heard a voice behind me.

"Of all the gin joints."

I turned to see Ethan, dressed in a hoodie and jeans, holding a cooler. His hair was freshly washed, his scruff gone. He looked nice, for him at least, though the smell of fish, maybe from the cooler, still seeped out of his edges.

He smiled. "What are you doing?"

"Setting up my station."

He laughed, literally out loud. "Z did not give you a job cooking here," he said.

"No, I'm more in a quality control role."

He tilted his head, and considered. "So you're the new Taylor?"

"You know Taylor?"

"I know trash overhaul is a long way from quality control," he said. "That's what I know."

I looked at him, my face turning red. "It's part of a larger plan."

"I don't doubt it," he said. "Those glasses mean business."

"And I tried to save his job."

"There's no saving anyone from Chef Z," he said. "But it was nice of you to try."

I thought of my day with Sammy and I started to say that it was possible I was turning over a new leaf, but it occurred to me that turning over a new leaf probably involved saying it less and doing it more.

"What?" he said.

"Don't take this the wrong way, but the smell of you truly makes me sick."

Ethan smiled. "How could I take that the wrong way?" he said.

I motioned to his outfit. "You're almost dressed up," I said. "What's the occasion?"

"I have a dinner later tonight," he said.

"With the nameless celebrity?"

He smirked. "You'll have to peek in the dining room and see," he said. "Z is going to fit me into the second seating."

"That's incredible," I said. "I now have the answer as to who can get into 28 without a reservation without any advance notice."

"What can I say?" He shrugged. "The man loves me."

"Many people do."

"What's that mean?"

"My sister was bragging about your accomplishments the other night. You didn't mention that you founded the whole fishing community."

"The whole fishing *community?*"

"You know what I'm saying, *Yalie*."

"I don't think you're called that when you teach there."

He heaved the cooler up higher.

"So you guys were talking about me the other night?"

"A little. In between her lectures on what a terrible person I am."

He grinned. "I've got to run, so you'll have to tell me another time." He paused. "And by the way, try not to feel too badly about Taylor. Z fires people from Cordon Bleu. I'd give you until the end of this shift."

"Would you put in a good word? I kind of need to hold on to this job at least for a little while."

"Chef Z is the most influential chef on the East End. He's eighty percent of my high-end business in the Hamptons."

"So you will?"

Ethan nodded, started walking away. "Absolutely not."

30

E than did come in for dinner, but he was with an older man I didn't recognize. There was no celebrity in sight.

I peeked at him through the small kitchen window.

"What are you doing?" Chef Z said.

He was still standing on the line, facing away, so for a second, I didn't think it was me he was talking to.

He motioned to one of the line cooks. "Is she hard of hearing?" he asked.

I froze. Was it me?

Chef Z was putting the finishing touches on the grilled sardines with pickled onions. Light on the citrus, heavy on the capers. Vinegar and sugar and salt. A pickled feast.

"Why are you looking through my window, Samantha?"

I pointed toward the door. "Sorry, Chef," I said. "I'm friends with Ethan Nash."

Name-dropping—trying to save myself. I wasn't proud.

"Do you spy on all your friends while they eat?"

"No, Chef."

He inspected another plate, still not turning around. "So stop spying on this one," he said.

I didn't have an opportunity to talk to Chef Z again until the end of my shift. Twelve thirty A.M., the restaurant nearly empty.

He came over to my station, already in a huff, and asked for a report. I was ready to make up for the earlier mishap. I'd procured from the garbage a small plate of the least popular item, which was still fairly popular, but which had been left fairly regularly on people's plates. Braised fennel. Z had served it alongside a ginger-infused cod. People didn't leave even a piece of the flaky fish on their plates—its gentle yellow sauce admirable—though their fennel was apparently less enticing.

Chef Z called out to Douglas. "Get me a fresh dish of it," he said.

Douglas ran over with a small bowl of the fennel, piping hot, the butter seeping out of its skin.

Z started to lift a forkful to his mouth. Then he turned to me instead. "You taste it," he said.

It felt like an opportunity to redeem myself. I took a bite eagerly, already thinking of something smart to say so Z would know he could trust my palate. I would tell him that the fennel was the ideal texture—hardy and light—and how

215

the aromatics were lovely, the anise highlighted by the garlic.

These were words of praise I was familiar with. I had offered a similar review on my show, regaling in a fresh fennel dish (my fennel sausage and eggs were a particular hit) hot out of my own phony oven. Now I would recycle them for Z.

But something was off. The fennel was sour and wrong in my mouth.

I tried to hide the reaction, but he saw it. Disgust. I thought I was going to be fired right there. Fennel sticking to my tongue as I tried desperately not to throw up.

But Z walked away, not saying anything.

I caught Douglas's eyes, trying to decipher if I was fired.

"That's the closest thing to praise you're ever going to get," he said.

31

The fennel episode led to several nights in a row where Z sought out my opinion—where it felt, for a moment, like I was falling into the rhythm of the restaurant. But how many times did I need to relearn the same lesson?

At this moment in time, there was no rhythm for me to find.

On Friday morning, I woke up to Rain moving fast around the kitchen, pulling Sammy by the arms. Sammy was laughing.

"Mom! I can't go that quick."

I looked up at them from the couch, rubbed my eyes. "What's going on?" I said.

"We're playing hooky from camp," Sammy said.

"But you love it there," I said.

"Sorry, did I ask your permission?" Rain asked, annoyed.

Sammy looked back and forth between us, and I saw it. She was going to defend me. Rain must have seen it too, because she pulled back.

"I'm not going into work today or to see Thomas," Rain said. "I need a day. We're going to the park."

That was great news. There would be no driving Sammy to and from camp. Maybe I'd get to work early and get some points during pre-service.

"Come with us!" Sammy said.

I saw Rain flinch, not sure whether to jump in and rescind the invitation. I decided to throw her a lifeline.

"That's okay," I said. "I'm just waking up."

She paused, as if considering whether to say it. "Do you want to come?"

I was so surprised to hear her actually offer. I did. "Really?"

"Don't make me ask twice."

When my sister said they were going to the park, she meant they were going to Montauk Point Park. It was a state park on the easternmost tip of the Hamptons. There were places to fish and trails for hiking. Picnic tables and a great playground. And, of course, it was adjacent to the fabled Montauk Point Lighthouse, which was something of a tourist destination, and also Rain's favorite place in the Hamptons. Most people liked that it was pretty—an imposing force on top of its hill—but Rain loved its history. I always wished she had volunteered at the museum there while we were growing up so she could bother other people with all the details, not just me.

Every Sunday, Rain and I bagged sandwiches for lunch and went to the lighthouse. While we were there, we agreed that there would be no fighting. Not about Dad, not about his money troubles (quickly becoming ours), not about anything. One Sunday, Rain told my father we were heading there at precisely the wrong moment. He was having trouble with a movie score he was working on, and he decided that the lighthouse had become bad luck. He went so far as to ask Rain not to go—in the way he asked for things, which was to tell her.

It was the first time I'd ever heard her refuse him. She reminded him that we had been going to the lighthouse long before the rules were in place—that he used to take us. That maybe the unlucky part didn't come from us going, but from his *not* going.

He seemed wooed by that argument. When we left for the lighthouse, my father even came along. Or, rather, my father dropped us there. Because, on the way, he had an idea for his score and went immediately back home. Also, he had a rule about being off the property for too many hours on Sunday, and he probably didn't want to risk losing track.

Rain chalked it up to a victory. It made it harder to convince her that validating his insanity was just the opposite—and the very way that his insanity could trap her too. When I told her she should have just told him the way it was, she put up her hands and said, *It netted the same result. I kept my lighthouse safe.* She wasn't going to be forced to justify the means by which she did it—not in her favorite place, not in the one place we promised we wouldn't fight.

So it made it a little weird to be there with her now—her daughter with us, so many years later—when we weren't even close enough to fight, and we didn't particularly want to make up.

We sat on the rocks, Sammy between us, and had peanut butter pie that Rain had made.

If peanut butter pie sounds elegant—if you're thinking of a professional mix of whipped peanut butter and homemade crust—that's not the kind I speak of. Rain's pie was peanut butter stuffed into cupcake liners with smushed bananas and Hershey's chocolate chunks. Old-school. And, really, not even pie. She would freeze the whole enterprise, and it would come out tasting like the sweetest, creamiest brownie you'd ever tasted.

Her peanut butter pie had been my favorite treat growing up, and it felt like a gesture when she took it out of the bag.

I didn't have the heart to tell her that it tasted wrong. The chocolate chunks were bitter. The bananas were too ripe, or not ripe enough. And the peanut butter tasted sour. Could peanut butter go sour? Apparently Rain's had.

Sammy finished her second piece. "This is great, Mom," she said.

Rain licked her wrapper clean. "It's pretty good, right?" she said.

I didn't want to seem ungrateful, so I nodded enthusiastically. And asked for another.

"Mom, can I go down to the water?" Sammy asked.

"Go ahead," Rain said. "Just stay close."

Sammy ran down the hill, and it seemed like she was heading toward a group of kids who were eating pizza. Instead she turned away from them, and started picking flowers alone.

I looked at Rain.

She put her hands up to stop me. "Don't say it."

"I'm just sitting here, eating pie."

"I know she doesn't have a lot of friends," she said. "She's different."

"That's a good thing," I said.

"I think so." She looked over and caught me playing with the wrapper. "What are you doing?"

"Savoring it."

She shot me a look, trying to decide whether she believed that. "Anyway, I never had a lot of friends growing up. And I'm fine."

Was this a good moment to say, *That's debatable?* "I think Sammy is fantastic," I said. "So no argument from me."

She looked at me with something I almost didn't recognize coming from her. Gratitude.

"Well, her counselor, this woman who runs the camp, I should say, she doesn't think so."

"Kathleen?" I said.

She nodded. "Kathleen," she said. "I mean,

she thinks Sammy is great, but she is concerned . . ."

"About what?"

She shook her head. "I don't know . . ."

I held my breath, not wanting to interrupt her, not wanting her to stop when she realized it was me she was confiding in.

"Kathleen thinks Sammy needs certain challenges in order to excel. To reach her potential. And I've heard that from her teachers, too, which is why I'm putting her at a private school next year in East Hampton."

Private school. The good ones had fifty-thousand-dollar price tags out here. *That's* why she sold the house.

"So what's the problem?"

"She thinks the private school here isn't the answer. She wants me to send Sammy to this gifted program in the fall. She never nominates anyone and she nominated Sammy, and she got in."

"That's great."

"There's nothing great about it. It's in New York. I'll never be able to make that work."

There were apartments in New York. And there were jobs at other hotels. Didn't she owe it to Sammy to get her the best education she could—to help her find a place where she would find friends?

But Rain wasn't going to leave Montauk. And

222

I wasn't going to convince her that she should. It was a fight I'd had with her when I meant a lot more to her—and I'd lost it then.

"And Thomas is no help," she said. "He's so impressed by the program. Loves talking about how families move from California in order for their kids to go."

"Sounds like he's trying to be supportive."

She turned toward me. "There is a way to be supportive. Quietly."

I nodded, knowing that was the only tack I could take here. If she was mad at Thomas, whom she loved, she would be furious with me for saying a word.

"I just don't need him telling me that he and I could make it work," she said. "As though the issue is about the two of us. The issue is that we live here. Right here."

She motioned around herself, as though that were the end of it. As though people didn't move all the time. She didn't want to hear it, though.

So I looked out at the shoreline, the water hitting the rocks, letting Rain have the last word.

Then I saw her. Meredith. I did a double take.

She walked along the water's edge, one kid in her arms, two by her feet. She was wearing the black pants she never seemed to take off. And she was on the phone—with Ryan?—laughing loudly.

I tried to catch my breath. There was something

about seeing her there. It brought it all back. Ryan and New York. The night of the party. That look—that horrible look she had given me—as she raced out the door.

The pie did a hurdle in my stomach.

I tried to ignore it. And to ignore what I was feeling. Something I hadn't felt, at least in terms of her. Guilt. I felt awful about Danny. And I was sorry I ever touched Ryan. But looking at Meredith with her kids now—even as she rudely talked two decibels too loudly—I was overcome with guilt. It was all I could do not to walk over and apologize to her.

I threw up instead.

"Seriously?" Rain said, jumping back. "That is so gross!"

It was too late. My sticky throw-up landed right on the edge of her dress. A little extra goo dripped down her legs.

"That's disgusting," she said.

"Sorry."

She started patting herself down with paper napkins. "You're not forgiven."

I pointed down to the water. "Meredith is here."

She kept patting, following my eyes to Meredith. "Is that the wife? Or the scorned girlfriend?"

"The wife."

She put down the napkins and moved farther

away from the small puddle of vomit. "Serious overreaction."

Then I looked closer. It wasn't Meredith. The hair was more red than blond. The legs were thicker than Meredith's had ever been. And whereas Ryan had two boys and a girl, this woman had only girls, towheaded beauties following the fake Meredith around.

"Never mind. It's not her."

"So definitely an overreaction!" Rain said. Then she looked at me, handed over a paper napkin. "What's going on with you?"

"I just don't feel very well. I ate fennel at the restaurant the other night, which didn't agree with me. I haven't felt great since."

"That would be your fault, not the fennel's." She paused. "Maybe you're allergic to Montauk."

I laughed.

"What's so funny?" she said.

I started to tell her I'd had that exact thought when my thermos of coffee hadn't agreed with me.

Then I threw up again.

32

There is something that people don't tell you about trying (and failing) to get pregnant. That every time you take a pregnancy test you get the same result. The NO shining at you, a condemnation that you dared to hope for a different result. So you stop trying. Stop counting days. Not interested in even knowing when you should have taken the test. Not interested in more of that hateful condemnation.

So when my sister suggested that maybe the reason I had thrown up three times in an hour was that I was pregnant, I thought she was wrong.

I argued with her on the car ride home when she insisted I take a test, *just to be on the safe side,* spelling the implicating words for Sammy's benefit.

Then gave in when Sammy spelled back, *A cousin!*

Of course, when I got back to the guesthouse and was sitting on my sister's bathroom floor and I actually got a YES, it was surreal. It was like there was a mistake of nature or something.

I looked at the box, unsurprised to see that it was expired.

Rain went to the store and got another test, not expired, and it also said YES. It said it without equivocation. It said there was going to be a baby.

"Now what's the excuse?" she asked.

"It's just . . . we had been trying for a while. Like, really trying."

"And nothing good?"

I shook my head. Pregnant.

The nausea these last several weeks, the dizzy feeling that I'd attributed to the upheaval in my life. It hadn't been that—or hadn't been entirely that—it had been a little baby, trying to make herself known.

How had I missed it? My strong reaction to the fennel, to Ethan's smell. I had missed it because it hadn't even occurred to me as a possibility. Danny and I hadn't been particularly active recently. We'd put the trying on hold until we got to Italy. We'd put a lot of alone time on hold—and for once that had been his choice more than mine. He'd been so busy prepping the Upper West Side job, he was almost never home.

Though, apparently, he had been there at least one time.

I could figure out when. It was either the night he came home and found me in an old University of Oregon sweatshirt in my egg chair watching *When Harry Met Sally*. Or the night when he came home and found me in his sweats on the bed, half-asleep. Despite all of my stylish work dinners over the last few months—meeting the players at the Food Network, prepping for the new cookbook—the times he was actually up for having sex were probably the times I looked the worst. A weird guy, my husband.

My sister stood up. "This is Danny's, right?"

I drilled her with a look. "Yes," I said.

She raised her hands in surrender. "Okay, just checking as to what level of tragedy we are looking at here."

33

Pregnant. I couldn't believe it. I carried the news around for nearly a week—trying to get used to it. But I knew it wouldn't feel real until I told the one person who would make it real. Except how was I going to tell him? I was tempted to drive to New York and tell him in person, but I didn't even know where he was staying. And the thought of ambushing him at work again—even with happy news—seemed like the wrong tack to take.

Danny had wanted a kid so badly, even more than I did. Regardless of what was going on between us, he'd be thrilled to know he was going to be a father. So why was it that I was so scared to pick up the phone? Why did it feel like if I picked the right time—or the right way— to tell him we were going to be parents, he'd forgive me? That he'd do more than forgive me?

Finally, I gave up on finding the right time, or even a reasonable time. I called Danny from the restaurant, a little before midnight. It wasn't smart for several reasons—not the least of which was that the dining room was still full, the second seating finishing up dessert. I had most of my trash report ready from the previous courses, but I never knew when Chef Z would come over, wanting a rundown.

The losers of the night were the heirloom peaches. They had been diced up and served with a roasted lamb and mint chutney.

The lamb was a hit—as was the chutney—though some of the small peaches were left behind. I had the plates lined up and prepared to show Chef Z, before I snuck off to talk with Danny. Still, if I heard him shout my name, I'd have to hang up on my erstwhile husband, even if I was in the middle of telling him he was going to be a father.

There was also the issue that at nearly midnight, there was a very good chance Danny would be sleeping.

But as soon as his cell phone rang, my heart started racing, and I couldn't wait to get the words out of my mouth. Even if I was greeted by his sleepy voice. Even if I was greeted by his voice mail.

Pregnant.

Except it wasn't his voice on the other end of the line. It was a female's voice—one that I recognized—though it took a second to place who had answered.

"Hello?" she said.

Maggie. Our friend Maggie, who had designed our apartment. Really, she was Danny's friend Maggie. They had gone to high school together in Iowa, and worked together all the time, recommending each other for jobs, their designs often shown in tandem. She had recommended Danny for the job on the Upper West Side. She had helped land our apartment in *Architectural Digest*. His work, and her work, were displayed prominently on the same pages.

A formidable team, the writer had called them. We had toasted to it, all together.

As silly as it sounds, I assumed they were out drinking with our other friends. She had probably seen it was me on his caller ID and picked up to say hello. Except she didn't know it was me, since I was calling from the restaurant's phone. And the familiarity of her *hello* sounded like the question wasn't why she was picking up my husband's phone at midnight; the question was who had the audacity to call so late.

"Who is this?" she asked, her voice high-pitched.

"It's me."

And she went silent. "Sunny. I uh . . . I thought you were my sister. She's out in the Hamptons with the kids for vacation, and I saw the area code. I thought you were her. Sorry."

"Why would she call you on Danny's number, Maggie?" I said.

She got quiet. "I'm going to get him for you, okay?"

I had no idea where she was "getting him"

from. I didn't know where I'd reached him. Or her.

"One sec," she said.

She started moving, the pitter-patter of her feet. And I could hear it in the background, the distinct sound of the shower.

Maggie knocked on the door and called out his name. "Danny!" she said.

The clock said 12:02 A.M.

Another woman was getting my husband out of the shower.

I hung up the phone.

I started pacing the kitchen, trying not to shake. Taking deep breaths. Thinking of the baby. Stay calm for the baby. Which was when I saw her through the window, eating the flourless cake and laughing. It was Z's thick pudding of a cake, all sugar and vibrant sea salt—one of the only smells in the kitchen I could handle. And now she had ruined that as well.

Amber.

She was wearing a sexy black dress, a thick gold necklace. Her boyfriend was with her and three other people, at the one table Z reserved for big parties.

Amber was performing, talking loudly as she took another bite, probably analyzing the cake for the group. The textures of the sweet custard, the genius of the sea salt finish. As if she were an expert on such things. She *was* the expert as far as everyone she was dining with was concerned. Soon she'd be the expert as far as America was concerned too.

I didn't know what I was doing until I was doing it. I moved all of the rejected peaches onto one plate.

Then I swung through the kitchen door, peaches in hand, and walked into the dining room.

A few of the guests at the chef's counter looked up, taking in my apron, my sweaty bun.

I nodded in their direction.

Confused, they nodded back.

I walked right past them, right to table 5. Amber's boyfriend now had his arm around her, and he was gently nuzzling into her neck. She was seductively eating the last bite of the flourless treat—licking the plate clean.

Amber looked up, eyes wide, as she recognized me there in my kitchen garb, in serious need of a shower.

"Oh, my God!" she said as she looked me up and down. "What are you doing here?"

"Saying hello," I said.

Then I smiled and dropped the peaches in her lap.

34

I woke up the next morning to Sammy standing over the couch, which was a good thing, probably, as the last thing I wanted was to review the night before. Maggie's voice on Danny's phone. The irritating sight of Amber Rucci. The end of my illustrious career at 28. I had stormed out following my plate-dumping, not waiting to officially be fired. I turned off my phone, knowing Danny wouldn't call back. I didn't understand how things were still going so awry. How had that happened? I was supposed to be on my way to redemption by now, and I was nowhere. Jobless. Husbandless. With the lovely and charming Amber Rucci poised to take over the world.

Sammy shuffled from foot to foot, a little nervous. She had a new novel in her sweet little hands.

"I don't want to go to camp," she said.

"Why?" I said.

"I don't want to discuss it," she said.

"What do you want to do instead?"

"Reading day?" she asked.

"You know what? Why not?"

She smiled, large. "Great!" she said.

Then she proceeded to move my feet out of

the way, plop down on the couch, and crack open her book.

I watched her turn the pages, a nausea in my throat kicking up. It was a combination of what I assumed was morning sickness and the realization that a small person—not unlike Sammy—would belong to me soon.

"Why are you staring at me?" she said, eyes still on her book.

"I need you to tell me why you don't want to go to camp," I said. "Was someone mean to you?"

"No."

"Sammy, if someone was mean to you, I'll go with you to the camp and make sure that the counselor knows. You don't have to give up camp."

She closed her book. "It's nothing to do with that," she said.

"So what happened?"

She met my eyes, as if trying to decide whether to say. "Kathleen's daughter is coming to camp. She wants us to sit together at lunch."

"And you don't want to?"

Sammy looked exasperated. "Her daughter goes to the school, the one in New York."

I nodded. Now she was getting somewhere.

"I know she's going to try to make us be friends and stuff. So I'll want to go."

It was a strange reaction—as though Sammy

was skipping a couple of steps. The one where she decided if she liked Kathleen's kid, and the one where she decided if the school seemed interesting to her.

"Why do you feel badly about that?"

She shrugged. "I don't know. I mean, Kathleen says it's a great place, so . . ."

Then I knew what was upsetting her. "Your mom."

She nodded. "She thinks the school is a bad place, I guess."

"What do *you* think?"

"I don't know. I think it could be fun."

I felt my heart break a little. What was wrong with Rain that she was making Sammy feel like it was the school versus her? And what was wrong with the counselor that she was sending in undercover recruiters? Would she get some kind of bonus if Sammy showed up there? Suddenly I was mad at everyone, except for the kid sitting on the edge of the couch.

"All right," I said. "You don't have to go to camp. But no reading day, okay?"

She sighed, exhausted. "Why not?"

"You're not going to sit around. If you don't want to go to camp, that's fine. You're going to do something, though."

"I am doing something. I'm *reading*."

I looked out the window at our old house, the red car in the driveway, the nameless celebrity inside. And I thought of her boyfriend. "Let's go fishing," I said.

A real Montauk fishing boat—not the kind rented out for bachelor parties and beer, but a fishing vessel—was not exactly meant for a comfortable cruise around the harbor. Ethan and Thomas's offshore boat—forty-eight feet long, two-sleeper cabin—was no exception. It wasn't exactly uncomfortable, but it wasn't luxurious, either. The deck was wiped down from the morning haul, but it still felt slimy and sticky. And there was a distinct odor in the air that, in comparison, made Ethan smell like fresh chocolate cookies.

Still, as soon as we left shore, I felt better, the ocean breeze helping my nausea, helping to empty my head. Ethan and I sat at the helm, Sammy at our feet, lifejacket tightly on, watching the ocean swirl, mesmerized.

Just kidding. She was reading in the sleeper cabin. She could have still been at the house.

Ethan folded his hands over his mouth, tried to warm them.

"I ended up having a lengthy conversation with my friend's husband earlier," he said. "He was trying to relate to me, I guess, and said all these people who say there are two Montauks, one for the summer people, one for winter people, they don't get it. He said it's about the people who fish here and the people who don't."

"So what's wrong with that?"

"Henry doesn't fish here. He takes a fancy charter out with his corporate buddies and pays someone to take a photo of him with a marlin. That's not fishing. That's a photo op. With a marlin."

"Okay."

"Do you not see the irony? Sammy, by herself, could reach into the ocean and catch a marlin." He shook his head. "This guy pisses me off."

"The man whose wife you're sleeping with pisses *you* off? That's who you're talking about, right?"

"He thinks he fishes here. He thinks he can say something that stupid. If he really fished here, he would never say something that stupid." He paused. "He might just think it."

I took a deep breath in, the shoreline moving farther away. "Why are you still talking?"

"Hey! You wanted to come out on the water today. Hell, I don't know why I agreed to it," he said.

"Because you have a soft spot for Sammy," I said.

He smiled. "I guess so," he said.

He looked out at the water, navigated us farther north.

"So how's the job going? I'm impressed you've lasted this long."

"I haven't."

"What happened?"

"Spilled a plate of peaches on someone." I paused. "Dropped. I should say that I dropped the peaches on purpose."

He laughed, a little impressed. "Did she deserve it?"

"Don't think that's the question Chef Z is going to be interested in. I ran out of there too fast to find out."

Ethan killed the engine. "Well, I'm interested."

"It was Amber Rucci, the woman who hacked me. She took my cookbook deals and my Food Network show. She can't even cook."

"Either."

I looked at him, confused.

"I'm just saying, you should probably say, *She can't cook either*."

"She makes toast, Ethan."

"I like toast." He shrugged. "But I'm not much of a recipe guy. I like to wing it. Put the toast in the toaster oven. Turn it on high. See what happens."

I laughed. "I don't know what I was thinking. She was just sitting in the restaurant, and I snapped."

He pulled a joint from his pocket. "Sounds like she deserved it."

It should have made me feel better, Ethan justifying my feelings about Amber. But it didn't. I thought of Amber destroying my life to better her own. I'd been angry before, but thinking of the kid I was carrying, I was more than angry. I was heartbroken.

Ethan lit up the joint, and I gave him a look. "What? It's legal."

"I'm not sure it is while operating a boat."

"So, it's a good thing we are sitting still."

Then he handed me the joint.

I shook my head.

"Not interested?"

"Pregnant."

"Wow." He pulled the joint back, the smoke blowing away from us. "That's a buzzkill. Literally."

He stared down at the joint, and I watched him taking the pregnancy in.

"Does the husband know yet?"

I flinched. *The husband.* The ex-husband. How was I going to tell him now? How was I going to tell him anything ever again? I shook my head.

"Why not?"

I shrugged. "He's too busy showering with his new girlfriend."

He took another drag. "Wow."

Then he focused on the joint, neither of us talking.

"Have I told you I have three kids?"

I looked at him, shocked. "What?"

He nodded. "All different mothers."

"That's some sperm."

He smiled. "The first one, I don't know. I couldn't handle it. I was eighteen, I behaved terribly. I spend most of my time making it up to the other two," he said. "It's not the same thing. My daughter, she's my first, deserves to have a better father than I've been."

"If you're trying to make me feel better, it isn't exactly working."

"Make you feel better? I'm trying to make *me* feel better."

"You were eighteen when you screwed up."

"True," he said. "And it's not like I lied about everything in my life."

"All right, enough."

"Sent my husband into the arms of another woman. Threw away my job on a plate of peaches."

"Please stop talking."

"Pretty honest move, tossing the peaches like that," he said. "No regard for the consequences."

I looked at him, trying to read if he was still making fun.

He put the joint out. "I'm serious. When was the last time you did anything like that?"

"Crazy?"

"Honest. Without thinking about how it would appear to your many fans," he said. "Just allowing yourself to have a moment that wasn't curated."

That stopped me. *Curated.* It was a perfect

word for what was required of me in order to present *A Little Sunshine* to the world, in order to present myself to the world. Everything I'd done—for so long—had required it: sifting through photographs, sifting through perfect phrases, to capture the moment I was supposed to be having. Sleeker, more interesting, more photo-ready.

Danny had been the first casualty of that removal from reality. Every night out—even a night at home—there was the untaken shot of what was actually happening (bad pizza while I worked late), and then there was the "impromptu" Instagram photo of the night, which actually meant taking dozens of selfies until the camera had me at the right angle, "enjoying" the scrumptious pizza, and binge-watching the hottest show. #homemadepies #squeezingintohubby #Waltforpresident

What was the consequence of that? Of suggesting to both of us that the way it actually was hadn't been enough?

Ethan turned the ignition on. "Maybe the point is that you're done lying now."

"I have nothing left to lie about," I said.

He turned the wheel, his boat kicking forward. "I'd take a compliment where you can get it."

35

When we arrived back at the house, Rain was pacing on the porch. Furious. It took me a second to notice it, which it shouldn't have. Furious was pretty much the usual way she greeted me.

I walked around to let Sammy out of the car.

"Hi, Mom!" she called out.

Rain crossed her arms over her chest. "Where the hell have you guys been?" she said.

"We went fishing," I said as we walked up the steps. "Relax."

"*Relax?* The camp called because Sammy didn't show up. You didn't think you should maybe call me before hitting the high seas?"

"I did call you," I said. "And left a message."

"I did too," Sammy chimed in.

"Sammy, get inside."

"Mom . . ."

"Inside!"

Sammy paused at the doorway. I smiled at her, and she waved back, this sad little wave, like she didn't want to be pulled away.

Rain apparently saw her with the eyes in the back of her head, which only made her angrier.

"Inside now!"

Sammy disappeared, Rain drilling me with a look. "How could you do that?"

"Rain, I swear to you, I didn't think you'd be upset."

"I picked up the camp's call before I heard your message. Do you know what that was like for me? I thought that maybe you guys had an accident. I thought you flaked. I didn't know what had happened."

"So you had a really rough five seconds?"

"Do you think this is funny?"

"No, I'm sorry, Rain. I thought it would be fun to do a field trip today as opposed to just sitting around the house."

"Why on earth do you think you get to decide where to take my kid?"

"You let her skip camp."

"*I* let her! Not you," she said. "You don't get to make those decisions."

"Rain, she didn't want to go. And, I'm telling you, she had a great day. She read and got some air, ate some nachos. There's nothing to be upset about. She had a blast."

She turned and stormed into the house, slamming the door behind her. "So now you're the expert on my kid?"

I swung the door open, followed her inside. "I'm helping you with her. How about saying thank you?"

"Please, I could have gotten a college kid to

drive Sammy to camp the day after Thomas's accident," she said. "Everyone knows who's helping who here."

She looked away, which was when I realized why she was so angry. She didn't want Sammy having a great day. Not with me. It didn't matter—the day we spent together, the pregnancy. Rain didn't want Sammy having anything to do with me.

"This was just a mistake, okay?" she said. "I want you to pack your bags and leave."

"No."

She shook her head. "No?"

That was right. I wasn't going anywhere. Maybe it was the pregnancy, maybe it was the trauma. Maybe it was what Ethan had said about me and the peaches and getting honest. But I wanted to stay where I was. At least until I knew where I needed to go.

Rain laughed, bitterly. "What are you even doing here? I mean, really. It's certainly not to reconnect with us."

"Maybe it is."

"Bullshit."

I looked up toward Sammy's loft. "Would you keep your voice down?"

Rain ignored me, kept talking loudly. "So what is the play? Getting Chef Z's approval and using it to reinvent yourself in one way or another, right?"

"And what if it is? You think I should just take this all lying down? Amber stole everything I worked hard for. And, I know, you don't think it was legitimate work, but I worked hard for it," I said. "Not that that's something you'd understand."

"I don't work hard?"

I kept my voice low, even if she refused to. "I just think running a hotel isn't exactly a dream come true for you."

She looked at me, surprised. Maybe even hurt for a second. Then she laughed, deflecting. "Well, since we're talking about dreams, which dream did you make come true again?" she said.

"I'm not talking about me, Rain."

"Are you kidding me? It's all about you." She shook her head. "Just because you think the picture would be prettier if I had an impressive career doesn't mean I'm not happy. Did it ever occur to you that if you weren't living in fear of other people's opinions of you, no one would have the power to take anything away?"

"Is that right?"

"It is, as a matter of fact."

I looked up toward the loft, moved toward my sister. "So why are you so scared to hear other people's opinion about your kid?" I whispered.

She reached for my arm, pulling me back out to the porch. "Excuse me?"

"That's why you took her out of camp, right?"

I said. "Because the counselor had the gall to tell you that Sammy is special? That she needs special things?"

"So in all of your experience with Sammy, you've already reached the conclusion a woman you don't know is correct, and her mother is wrong? That I haven't considered what my kid needs?"

"Rain, don't hold her back."

"Right. 'Cause staying here is holding her back. Staying with her mother is holding her back."

"So go with her. There are hotels you could run in New York."

"It's not that simple. I like it here. I've built a home here. I have a relationship here. It may not be sexy, or get us a television show, but some of us value building a home somewhere."

"You don't think it's weird that yours is five feet away from where you grew up?"

That stopped her. She got quiet. "What's that supposed to mean?"

I paused, knowing I shouldn't say it, that there were some lines you shouldn't cross. But she was so mean, and I was so tired. I couldn't seem to stop myself.

"I don't know. I recall certain rules about never being away from this property for more than a few hours at a time. Never, ever sleeping off the property for any reason."

"That is so out of line."

"Taking the steps down to the ocean every other day. Getting the mail at five P.M. at the edge of the driveway. Eating dinner on Sundays facing the ocean. Feel free to interrupt me if I'm forgetting any. Maybe you have some rules now about never venturing far from the life Dad set up? Or maybe you're a little more like him than you want to admit?"

She looked right at me—so angry, so hurt—like she couldn't believe it. She couldn't believe that I still had the power to affect her.

"Ten minutes to get your things and get out of my house," she said.

Then she turned and walked away.

36

I sped down the driveway, my belongings hastily thrown into the passenger seat, and drove to 28, fighting back tears. Sometimes you're glad you got something off your chest. This wasn't one of those times. I was sorry I'd said any of it. I hadn't meant it, really. Rain was just coming at me so hard, and even when I thought I was doing something right—giving Sammy a fun day, not taking the easy way out—she still would hit me for it.

How do you win with someone like that? Especially when I was so confused as to how I'd ended up here—again. Stuck in Montauk. Stuck in a house with the one person who was a mirror of all of the things I was trying to escape. It wasn't that I'd been trying to hurt her. It wasn't that I wanted to make her feel as lost and isolated as I did.

It was really that I didn't know how to ask her to stop, for just a second, doing everything in her power to remind me that she thought I deserved to feel terrible. That I deserved to have my career taken overnight, and to lose my husband, who had apparently already moved on.

I pulled into the restaurant parking lot, took a

peek at myself in the rearview mirror, and wiped at my tears.

And now there was Sammy, her weird and wonderful kid. Thing was (chalk it up to the pregnancy hormones), I was getting used to her. I hated the idea that I didn't even have a chance to say good-bye to her, that she wouldn't even get to hear that I hadn't wanted to leave. At least, I hadn't wanted to leave her.

I walked into the kitchen and headed right to my station. Douglas was standing there with a young guy, showing him the ropes.

"What are you doing here?" Douglas said.

"Douglas," I said. "You have two seconds to get away from my station . . ."

"My station now," the young guy said.

I drilled him with a dirty look. "Who are you?"

"I'm in charge of trash," he said.

"I have five hundred dollars in my pocket. It's yours if you just go to the bathroom for the next five minutes."

"Deal!" he said.

"No deal," Douglas said.

"What's going on?"

We turned to see Chef Z standing behind us. He had his chef jacket on, his arms folded over his chest.

"Douglas, move away," he said. "And take Lance with you."

"I'm not Lance," the young guy said.

Chef Z raised his hands. "Nobody cares," he said.

As Douglas disappeared and the young guy headed toward the bathroom (did he really think I would pay him now?), Chef Z leaned in.

He whispered in my ear. "What are you doing in my kitchen?"

I cleared my throat. "I apologize, Chef. I just thought if you knew the details of why I did what I did, you'd let me stay with you at work."

"Details of why you threw a plate of food onto one of my guests?"

I had a whole plan of what to say to him—an entire story. I was going to tell him that Amber had ordered the last lamb entrée of the evening and left the entire plate. And it had just seemed wrong that she would take advantage of everyone's hard work. Of Chef Z's hard work. Especially when she was served the last lamb dish of the night. Other people would have loved and respected the food. But thanks to Amber, they hadn't.

How could that not work? I'd be speaking to every single narcissistic impulse the man had. To deny it would be to deny himself.

Except I was too tired to lie to him. And, I suspected, too out of practice to sell the story. That was the thing about lying. You got used to it, and it was what you did. The truth became a low groan that you could hear, but didn't really

251

need to address. When you were out of practice lying, though, the effort it took to lie well—the energy to turn a story—became obvious. It was almost as hard as telling the truth.

So instead, that's what I did. I told him the truth. "She's not good enough to eat your food, Chef."

He paused, considering. "No one is."

Then he stepped away, motioning for me to take my usual spot.

"Consider yourself on probation," he said.

I nodded, swallowed my tears.

He shook his head, disgusted. "There are no tears in my kitchen," he said.

"You don't have to tell me that, Chef," I said.

"Apparently, I do," he said.

37

I showed up at Ethan's at midnight, completely spent.

He had told me he lived near the docks, and a quick search of his website told me exactly where.

He answered the door in his boxer shorts, nothing else. "Haven't you had enough of me for one day?" he said.

"I need a place to stay," I said.

He rubbed his eyes. "Come on in."

From the outside, his place looked pretty run-down. It was a yellow Craftsman in desperate need of a paint job and some different shutters on the windows. Inside, his place was pretty rugged too, though it had a certain charm. Almost in spite of itself, the house had a way about it. There were these thick wooden floors (definitely the originals, which he must have sanded down) and fresh green walls, great photographs of gas stations scattered throughout. The furnishings consisted of decent rugs and a great leather chair. And there was a gorgeous bay window that looked out on the docks and let in the moonlight, putting a soft sheen over everything.

Ethan led me into the bedroom, where he pointed at a mattress on the floor, Frette sheets on top of it. Like the Frette sheets I had at home. And in a million years, I wouldn't have imagined this man would have purchased Frette sheets, and I realized he hadn't. They had been a gift from someone who hadn't wanted to sleep on whatever sheets he had purchased. The celebrity.

He shrugged, not exactly apologizing. "It's what I've got to offer," he said.

I was too tired to care. We both lay down, back to back, heels touching.

"Don't try anything funny," he said.

And, like that, we fell asleep.

38

When I woke up, it was still dark out.

I looked at the clock. 5 A.M. Thankfully, Ethan was gone. It took a minute to acclimate to where I was. Strange bed, familiar sheets. For a second I let them take me to the last time I had been in these sheets, "Moonlight Mile" on the radio, Danny still sleeping in bed, the sheets up to his shoulders, the sheets up to my chin. Where was I now?

I assumed Ethan had gone to the docks and went into his kitchen to make myself a cup of coffee. There was no going back to sleep. I sat on a wooden chair, waiting for the coffee to brew, and pulled up Danny's number on my phone. I needed to tell him about the baby, whatever his situation was. I still couldn't wrap my head around it. Maggie. And Danny.

How was it possible? That wasn't how Danny worked. He wouldn't want to be unfair to Maggie. She was a good friend. He wouldn't want to start something with her until he was ready. Was there a world in which he was ready so soon? Maybe I was a complete fool, but I didn't buy it. I still thought there had to be another explanation.

I poured myself a large cup of coffee and was about to call Danny, when Ethan walked back in the door, a bag from John's Pancake House in one hand, a tray of coffee cups in the other.

He motioned toward the mug I was holding. "I definitely wouldn't drink that," he said.

I put my phone away. "If you're judging me for drinking coffee while I'm pregnant . . ."

"I'm judging you for drinking that coffee," he said. "I haven't used that coffeemaker since the early eighties."

He handed over his tray of drinks.

"Sugared. Decaf. Caf," he said. "Wasn't sure which way you'd want to go."

"Thanks. What's in the bag?"

"Egg sandwich. That's for me, though. I need the sustenance."

"And why's that?"

"I'm driving to New York today to meet with some investors."

He pulled the sandwich out of his bag, unwrapped it, the steam pouring out.

"We're thinking of expanding to a few restaurants in Southern California. Los Angeles, primarily. That was the dinner I took at 28," he said.

I looked longingly as he held up the greasy sandwich, piled high with cheese and tomatoes.

"What? I'm not running a bed-and-breakfast here."

I must have looked terribly disappointed, because he rolled his eyes and handed over half.

"Apparently, I am."

I took a large bite, stuffing most of my half into my mouth. He waited for me to swallow and then smiled.

"Sexy," he said.

In response, I shoved the rest of my half right in behind it.

"So I didn't want to tell you last night," he said.

"Though five A.M. feels like a good time?"

He took a bite of his eggs. "Amber is having a fancy cookbook release party over on Tyson Lane tonight. That's why she's in town."

I immediately regretted the sandwich. "How do you know that, exactly?"

"Her publicity person was trying to get a discount. And she used Amber's name, talked about the party and all the people who would be eating our fish." He kept talking, mouth full. "I guess she's having stations set up. Each station is going to serve one of the recipes in the book. The station she wants us to supply fish for is a ceviche station."

"What is she supplying? The toast?"

"I asked the publicist the same thing."

I laughed. "Did you really?'

"Yep. Apparently she doesn't share our sense of humor."

I thought about what that party would entail. Everyone would be there. Louis, food journalists, folks from the Food Network. Everyone who had turned their backs on me, and who were now thrilled to be honoring her.

Ethan took another large bite, apparently scared I would try to steal it.

"Anyway, I'll give her a dirty look."

"Can you get me in?" I said.

He looked surprised. "Of course. Why?"

I shrugged, not having a good answer. I knew that I shouldn't care—that Amber and her party were beside the point. In that moment, though, it somehow felt like the entire point, all over again.

"Will you do it, even if I don't have a good answer for you?"

"Consider it done," he said.

He handed over his last bite.

"I'll even bring extra fish," he said. "In case you want to drop something else on her."

39

People love to talk about the most prestigious roads in the Hamptons. Dune Road. Flying Point. Ocean. Meadow. Tyson Lane was often too small to make the list. And yet, there it was, right off Further Lane—steps to the ocean—and home to several of the most stunning addresses in East Hampton, including a gorgeous abode owned by Helmut Lang.

Amber's party was at the house next door—also oceanfront, also exquisite—owned by a venture capitalist and his cooking-enthused wife.

Lanterns lined the driveway and led up to a stunning cottage (not that *cottage* was really the appropriate name), its wraparound porch crowded with people. And candles. And flowers—solely white, solely orchids. Enormous trays of caviar and shrimp sushi were being passed. A jazz band was playing standards on the party's edge. It could have been the nicest wedding I'd ever been to.

I took a breath as I stepped out of my car and headed toward the porch, wearing the only dress I had grabbed from my sister's house after our fight: a purple halter-top that swung wide and, thankfully, covered my slowly growing belly.

"I don't believe it," she said.

I turned to see Violet, wearing a set of headphones and a black pencil skirt, looking beautiful and put-together.

"What are you doing here?" she said, a large smile on her face.

I wasn't sure how to read her. "Just coming by to say hello to everyone," I said.

"Not the party," she said. "Here! The Hamptons. I thought you were hiding out where you were from. Nashville, or wherever."

"I'm from here, actually," I said.

She looked confused. "I didn't know anyone was from here," she said.

I smiled. "How are you, Violet?"

"I think that's like the first question you've ever asked me. I mean, about *me*."

I motioned toward her headset. "Where are you working now?"

"Well, I was helping out on Meredith and Ryan's new show. But I quit. It's going nowhere fast. I promise, it's going to get cancelled before it even hits the air." She shook her head. "Meredith is terrible. Just awful in front of the camera. And she's actually like a pretty terrible person, too, if it makes you feel any better."

"About sleeping with her husband? Not really."

"Well, it would make me feel better." She shrugged. "Anyway, I started working for Julie Diaz, who is fantastic."

Julie was the agent I liked. And she was a

260

perfect boss for Violet. She would grant her access to everybody.

"She's getting into production, and we've talked about my running development for her," Violet said, beaming.

"That's great, but I thought you wanted to do your own show?"

"Not so much anymore. Too many skeletons in this closet." She pointed at herself. "I don't want my nudes hitting the internet."

I smiled, trying not to let it gnaw at me—the feeling I had whenever I thought of my own photograph somewhere on the internet. Even after it had been scrubbed, it wasn't completely scrubbed. Enterprising people would be able to get at it.

"I really love working for her, and it was my experience with you that got me the job, so . . ."

She smiled, grateful. It was all water under the bridge as far as she was concerned. Why wouldn't it be? She had gone on to do better things—things she should have been doing anyway. Maybe a bigger person would have been glad to see it. And part of me was. The other part of me was sneaking into Amber's party with the hope that I would ever again have good career news to tell anyone.

Violet's headset went off. She pulled the microphone to her ear. "I've got to jet! Duty calls."

"Is Julie representing Amber now?"

"No, she's representing a certain celebrity who's a friend of Amber's. I think Amber catered a bridal shower for her. She didn't end up getting married. Though it did end up on the cover of *Martha Stewart Weddings*, so . . . everybody won. Anyway, the former fiancé is also stopping by. So I'm on duty in case he brings the new girlfriend, and our girl needs to make a quick exit."

She started walking away.

"Let me know when you're moving back though, all right? We should get coffee or something."

I nodded. "Definitely, sounds great."

She looked at me like she was trying to decide whether she believed me. "I mean, you're not going to just hide out here forever? It gets creepy in the Hamptons after Labor Day. Like, I'm talking *The Shining* creepy."

I laughed. "That it does."

"Besides, your scandal is so over. There have been like fifteen better ones since. There was a better one this morning. A certain sexy-if-sexually-ambivalent hunk of a movie star's male assistant just got hacked, and I have two words for you. Camping trips."

"I'll keep it in mind."

The porch had cleared out.

When I walked inside, everyone was turned

toward the front of the vaulted living room. I actually thought they were turned toward me.

After all, it could have been a party for me. I had eerie flashbacks, looking around the exquisitely designed room—rustic beams and a fireplace. All the usual suspects were milling around. Julie and Christopher. The food writers and journalists. It reminded me of my party at Locanda Verde. It could have been my party at Locanda Verde. Except instead of me being feted by Louis and a variety of Food Network and publishing brass, it was Amber. She was standing a little to my left, behind a rustic farm table covered with farm-fresh ingredients and cookware, wearing a Dolce & Gabbana dress.

I quickly stepped down into the room, before she saw me, before any of them did.

"Ladies and gentlemen!" Louis said, putting his hands together for quiet. "If I could please get your attention. Thank you for joining us tonight to celebrate the release of *Tender Toast*."

There were whoops and cheers from the crowd—which Amber pretended to be embarrassed by. It was all I could do to not vomit.

"We couldn't be more excited to be releasing Amber's cookbook. Her recipes are not only inventive, but they reflect her rustic approach to cooking. And of course, they are pulled together by her signature ingredient. Toast. Made tenderly." He paused while a couple of people let out cheers. "We are thrilled to welcome her into our family, and for you to welcome her into your home."

Amber put her hand on her chest, as though touched by this. And the crowd smiled at one another—at her humility, at her talent. It was funny being on the outside of it all. How bullshitty it seemed. After all, Louis was saying all the same things he would have been saying about me.

"Amber is going to make us a little something, aren't you?"

She nodded. "That's right. I wanted to pick something both sexy and homey. Something that really exemplifies my cookbook. My ricotta and raw honey toast, if that sounds good to everybody?"

"It sure does!" someone called out.

Amber threw her head back, laughing.

Then she went to work, whipping together a fresh, homemade sheep ricotta, drizzling it with raw honey.

As she prepped, she explained what she was doing, and I could already see it. She was going to be great on television.

"I made the buckwheat toast from scratch, of course," she said. "As can you, if you go to page fifty-five in *Tender Toast*."

The crowd laughed.

"I feel the buckwheat is a great platform for

appreciating the salty and sweet synthesis of the toppings, but if you don't have five hours to spare, you can also head to your local bakery and pick out any dark bread."

She was stunning up there. She was talking bullshit, but she was stunning all the same. And it wasn't new to me that the look was all that mattered. I knew that better than anyone.

"Who wants a taste?" she said.

Everyone started to applaud as waiters in matching TENDER TOAST aprons started handing out the ricotta and honey toasts.

"I whipped these up for you. Enjoy!"

The crowd broke into more applause, grabbing for the waiters, eagerly having a taste.

My curiosity got the better of me, and I reached for a triangle of toast off a tray. I took a small taste. It was delicious—creamy and light, with just the right amount of sweetness coming from the honey. It occurred to me mid-chew that I probably shouldn't have been eating it. Raw cheese was a pregnancy no-no. But I had no idea if it was actually homemade—and, if it was, if it was homemade by Amber. For all I knew, what she made up there wasn't what was being passed around. The ricotta was from Murray's Cheese. The honey was from a great farm in North Carolina.

Even if it was the case, who was going to tell on her? No one. Or maybe someone, one day. There would have to be someone she treated so badly that they were compelled to undo the mirage she had created.

As Amber stepped toward the crowd, greeting people, I tracked Louis, heading toward the bar.

I dropped the toast and made a beeline toward him. But I felt a hand on my arm, stopping me right before I reached him. Ryan. He looked pretty great in jeans and a relaxed button-down shirt.

"I thought that was you," he said. He focused in on my thickening waist. "I wasn't sure."

I forced a smile, watching Louis order his drink, knowing I was about to miss my chance.

"What are you doing here?" Ryan said.

I turned to him reluctantly. "Night out. You?"

"Well, these are still my people."

I smiled. It was such a ridiculous thing to say—such a Ryan thing to say—that I couldn't even take him seriously. "That's right! Violet was just saying that you're gearing up to air. How's it going?"

"Great. Really great. The focus groups are just in love with Meredith. Not that Violet would ever tell you that." He leaned in. "We had to let her go."

It was all I could do not to call him out. What did I expect from him, though? Honesty? What did I expect from any of these people, from a world that was built on perception? Their whole business was to make people long for a perfect meal—a perfect night, a perfect life. And then they held it, just outside of reach.

Ryan was still talking. "We just shot the pilot up in Scarsdale. And we're really doing stuff that no one is doing. It's like this Korean fusion, but in the French tradition . . ."

He prattled on, and I nodded, as though I cared. How had this man ever been intriguing to me? And why did he think that, after what he did, I'd want anything to do with him? Then I remembered. He wasn't thinking about me. He hadn't thought about me for one minute since I hadn't done exactly what he wanted. And yet, for him—and his silly games—I had compromised my relationship.

My cheeks turned red, and Ryan clocked it. "Are you going to cry?" he said. "Really. C'mon!"

I was close to slapping him, right across the face, but I felt a tap on my shoulder. I turned to see Louis, a bourbon in his hands.

"Hello, Ryan."

"Louis!" he said. "How are things with you?"

Ryan put out his hand for Louis to shake, but Louis smiled instead. "Forgive me, but I'm going to steal her."

And without waiting for an answer, he moved us to the other end of the bar.

"Is it fair to tell you now?" he whispered. "I hate that jackass."

"Thank you for the assist," I said.

"It seemed like you could use it."

He tipped his bourbon in my direction.

"I'd offer this to you, but I'm not waiting in that drink line again."

"Actually, I'm not drinking tonight anyway."

Louis looked at me, considering. "I've never known you to turn down a drink. Five in the morning, five at night. Anything you want to tell me?"

I shook my head, not answering. Louis was friends with Danny, and it occurred to me that I might not be the only one with interesting information I was withholding. How could I ask Louis, though? *Have you seen my estranged husband and how does he feel about his new girlfriend? How do you think he's going to feel about this baby?*

Louis nodded, deciding not to press. "How you holding up, kid?"

I wanted to scream: *You abandoned me, how do you think I'm doing?* But I smiled. "Pretty good. You?"

He sipped the bourbon. "About to be a lot better. Despite the hundred people here I have to say hello to."

I motioned toward the deck, which was steps from the beach, the Atlantic Ocean. "We could sneak outside, and you could have your drink in peace."

Louis smiled, a little sadly. "Afraid I can't do that."

I nodded, knowing that would be his answer. Louis had forgiven me as much as he was going to forgive me. That didn't mean he wanted anything to do with me.

"Be well, though," he said.

"Wait!" I said. "I just need to tell you something . . ."

He shook his head. "Sunny, I was trying to lend you a hand, but I really don't want to do this."

"I know, but this is not about us. I mean, it's not about me trying to get you to forgive me or anything."

He narrowed his eyes. "I think in order for that to even be on the table, there would have to be an *I'm sorry*. Haven't heard that yet."

"There's something you need to know about Amber."

"I'm not interested," he said.

"Well, I am!"

We turned to see Julie, a mostly empty champagne glass in hand, a pantsuit highlighting her figure.

"Julie," Louis said.

She kissed Louis on each cheek. "Hello, sir! Congratulations."

Then she smiled at me.

"This is a surprise! Well, not really, Violet texted me the second she saw you walk in." She took a sip of her drink. "What's the Amber gossip?"

"There is no gossip," Louis said.

I shook my head, staying quiet.

Julie looked back and forth between us, intrigued. "Let her tell you, Louis. Let her tell us."

Louis paused, and I knew this was the moment. I leaned in, ready to jump into my story. My initial plan had been to tell Louis what Amber had done—to turn him against her—to remind him that I wasn't the enemy; to tell him that I was working for Chef Z, and I was trying to rectify it, trying to become what I had only before pretended to be.

Except, with Louis waiting to listen, it seemed wrong to talk about Chef Z, wrong to say I was fixing anything, even wrong to talk about Amber. It was just a different form of pretend.

I shrugged. "You know what? I forgot."

He looked over at Julie and then back at me. "I don't follow."

My heart started to race, the room closing in. "I need to go," I said.

Which was when Amber intervened.

"That's certainly true!" she said loudly.

Several people at the bar turned toward us, a few groups of people turning to look as well.

"I want you out of my party!"

Julie put her hand on Amber's arm. "Darling, you should probably calm down."

"Get out, or I'm calling the fucking police!"

Julie pulled back. "Or not."

Amber lowered her voice. "Do you know how much that skirt cost that you ruined? A lot."

"Do I want to know what you're talking about?" Louis asked.

"Sunny publicly attacked me with a plate of peaches."

Julie laughed. "I'm . . . uh . . ." She cleared her throat. "Sorry."

Amber shot her a look. Then she turned back to me. "What are you even doing here? No one invited you. And believe me, no one wants you here."

I turned toward Louis, my desire to take the high road disappearing with Amber's entitled display. Now I just wanted Amber knocked down a few pegs.

"Amber is the person who hacked me."

She laughed a little too loudly. "That's ridiculous."

I put my hands up in surrender, no need to raise my voice or make a big deal. Telling the truth was funny that way.

"And how do you know that?" Louis said.

"She told me."

"She told you?" Julie said. "She confessed?"

271

"More like gloated."

"I did not."

"So you just happened to show up at my apartment the next night?"

She tried to pull off confused, as though trying to remember. "I think I had dinner reservations near there."

"Please."

"And even if I did go a *little* out of my way to revel in what happened, I still didn't do it. I swear to you." She turned to Louis. "I swear to you."

Louis looked back and forth between us, he and Julie both, like they didn't know whom to believe.

I met Louis's eyes. "I don't expect you to give me another chance. Please, though. Don't reward her for what she did."

Amber shook her head. "This is *insane.* I'm done defending myself. No one would do this for professional reasons."

"How about what you think happened with your boyfriend?" I said.

Julie leaned in. "What happened with her boyfriend?" she said.

"Nothing!" Amber said. "Louis, would you help me out here? I have a whole party of people I should be talking to."

I looked at Louis apologetically. He turned to Amber and I could see it. He thought if anyone was lying, she was.

Amber shook her head. "I don't believe this," she said. "I'm a feminist! I love women. Even the ones I don't particularly like."

She looked at all of us, exasperated.

"And how dumb would I have to be to show up at your apartment if I actually had done this?"

"So you admit that wasn't a random run-in?"

"Yes, you caught me! I admit it. I was happy someone had finally taken you down, and I wanted to gloat. I'm only human. I can't always be sweet Amber."

"When are you ever sweet, Amber?" Julie said.

Amber shot her a look. Then she turned back toward me. "I don't know what to tell you except that it wasn't me," she said.

And the weirdest thing happened. There was a look on her face that I couldn't deny. She didn't look guilty. She looked like she had nothing to hide. And suddenly it was too much. It was too much looking at her, because I started to think she wasn't lying. And if she wasn't—if she really wasn't behind this—then who was? Not Ryan. Not Violet. Not Amber. Not some random guy—I was sure of that too. So who?

"I'm going to enjoy what's left of my party," Amber said. "But I'll expect five thousand dollars from you. For a new skirt."

Julie blanched. "You paid five thousand dollars for a skirt? I guess you really want to hold on to that boyfriend."

Amber put up her hands in surrender. "Charlie's not my boyfriend anymore. Can everyone stop it with that?"

"Amber, he's here tonight," Louis said.

"I know. No one will seem to let me finish." Amber paused. "Charlie's not my boyfriend anymore," she said. "He's my fiancé."

Then she held out her ring finger like proof.

"We bought the ring together months ago. So there was really no need to punish you for anything. I won."

I held Amber's stare, Louis falling away, Julie falling away. Everything falling away except for Amber. "What did you just say?"

"We're getting married. I won."

Which was when it hit me. Who I was married to, and who had lost. Who had really lost as I had been rising. As I had been forgetting where I'd started. Forgetting what was important.

And all of a sudden, I knew who had hacked me. I knew who had done this.

Standing over our bed when the first tweet came in.

Selling our apartment out from under us.

Forcing me to end up in this exact moment. Having lost as much as he did.

40

I drove the two and a half hours to New York in under two hours. It would have taken even less time than that, except I had to stop twice to eat. Once for ice cream. And once for a cheeseburger. In that order. Those people who say they can't eat when they're upset? I ordered an extra scoop of chocolate for those people. And then in my anger I threw it against the wall.

And still, when I arrived at my old apartment in Tribeca, I was famished. Not so famished as to not be worried that when I knocked on the door Maggie would be there. Though if I had puzzled this together correctly, my husband certainly would.

So I didn't knock. I turned the key and walked inside.

And there was Danny, sitting at the dining room table, working on a blueprint.

"Jesus!"

Danny jumped up, shocked and confused.

"What are you doing here?" he said.

"I could ask you the same thing," I said. "Though I guess I don't have to."

I looked around the apartment. He had gotten rid of our furniture. Refurnished. Or, probably,

Maggie had. The fuzzy and frilly couch had her shabby chic name all over it.

"I love what you've done with the place."

"Sunny, this is not what it looks like."

"Really? 'Cause it looks like you set me up. It looks like you orchestrated the end of my career, and stole my home away, probably to move in with your girlfriend . . ."

He shook his head. "I knew I should've called you back that night," he said. "Maggie is not living here."

"You are, though, right? When did you start planning this, Danny? Technology certainly isn't your strong suit. Who showed you how to send tweets on a timed schedule? Who even showed you how to tweet?"

He was incredibly calm, the way he always was, which at the moment was infuriating.

"It wasn't tough to figure out," he said.

I felt hot tears start pouring down my face. "I guess you were pretty motivated."

He met my eyes. Fourteen years. "I guess I was."

"So you found out about Ryan? And you sought revenge?"

"It wasn't about revenge, Sunny."

"Then what? Maggie? Was this all so you guys could be together?"

"There is nothing going on with Maggie. She is helping me redecorate, but that's all.

You should know that I would never do that."

"How can you ask me to know anything about you anymore?"

"Maggie is dating a new guy. Simon Callahan. He owns a couple of restaurants in Brooklyn. I haven't been going out a lot, so that night, the night you called, she said that she wasn't leaving unless I went out with her to meet him. I had just gotten off work, so I jumped in the shower. She was being a friend. That's it."

I made a mental note to look him up. "That doesn't explain why she was answering your phone."

"She forgot her phone. She needed to reach her sister because she was supposed to head out to the Hamptons, but she stuck around to see Simon."

That sounded like Maggie. I wasn't sure, though. I wasn't sure what to think of that—what to think of any of this.

"Not that I have to explain anything to you, but I would hate for you to think a woman would be the reason why. This only has to do with us. You, actually."

I looked at him, willing myself to stop crying. And failing.

He didn't look away, but he didn't move any closer, either.

He shook his head. "You were so far gone for

so long. There was no way to make you understand . . ."

"So you just thought you'd publicly humiliate
me instead?"

He laughed. "Do you honestly think I wanted
the world to know you cheated on me? You think
that's not humiliating? It was the only way to
make you see what you'd become."

"Oh, wow. You were making a sacrifice. I
should be thanking you, right?"

"Sunny . . ."

"How about having a private conversation?"

"I tried a million times. And I was running out
of time."

"What's that supposed to mean?"

"The Food Network. If that show hit the
air, you'd have gone from a couple of million
followers to twenty million. It would've been
too late." He paused. "I'm sorry if you hate me.
It had to be done."

"Really? Who asked you to take on the role
of moral authority? Whatever I did to you, I
didn't mean to hurt you. What this is, is
something else. It was cruel."

"Was it cruel? How are you doing?"

I looked at him, confused. "What's that
supposed to mean?"

"How are things out in Montauk? 'Cause from
what I'm hearing, it's going pretty well."

"I'm smelling trash every night and living on

my sister's couch. No, correction, I *was* staying on Rain's couch. Now I'm living with a smelly fisherman. It's thrilling."

"At least it's honest."

I was seriously considering hitting him. "What did you just say?"

"You used to value telling the truth. Over pretty much everything. Tell me you're not a little relieved to be in that position again."

I didn't know how to answer him—or maybe I just didn't want to answer him. If I admitted that it wasn't all terrible, that I didn't just fall apart, he'd feel like he did the right thing. Which was the last way I wanted him to feel.

"I just needed . . ." He paused. "Do you remember our first date?"

Did he really think I was in the mood for a walk down memory lane? "You've got to be kidding, Danny," I said.

"No, I've really been trying to remember it. I know that I dragged you for an hour and a half to some fancy restaurant in downtown Portland 'cause I was trying to impress you. And I know you wanted to split the squab. I thought that was so exotic. Who orders squab? Not something you order in the Midwest."

"It was quail."

"See? Can't remember."

I could. Without even having to try, I could tell

him everything about that night. We did eat the quail—which was terrible. Or I should say, I ate it. Danny, who was wearing a tie over a T-shirt (no joke), ordered truffle fries and tried to push the truffle part off of them, drowning them in ketchup to mask the taste. And I wore a short dress, which I thought made me look sexy, but it probably made me look like I was trying too hard. I forgot to be embarrassed. I forgot to decline the last bite of almond cake when he offered it to me. And I didn't even pause in front of my door debating whether to let him come upstairs. It was as if from go, I had no ability to play games with him. I don't know why I was so confident in my terrible dress. I was, though. I was confident I had found my person. Who happened to be twenty-one and a freaking jackass.

Danny shook his head. "I know at some point it started going well. But I don't know, the details are a little slippery . . . maybe it's because, whenever I think of you, I'm stuck on the day we met."

I stared at him, not sure where he was going with this, not sure I wanted to know.

"We were at the football game, right? And you were sitting in the row in front of me."

"I was behind you, Danny."

He shook his head. "No, definitely not. You were sitting in the row in front of me, and I tapped on your friend's shoulder to ask if she had an extra beer. And she did, she had brought a six-pack, which was right beside her, and there were two beers left, and she started to give me one. But then you stopped her, literally pulled the beer back and said, no way."

He was right. That was what I'd said. And he was also right that I was sitting in front of him. I had turned around and looked at him. This guy who had that killer smile—those eyes—and I realized that probably no one had ever turned him down before. No one had ever said that they didn't have an extra beer for him. They probably ran out and grabbed one for him, if they needed to.

But I had wanted that beer—had been looking forward to it—and I knew that if she gave it to him, she would keep the other one for herself. So I pulled it back, told him he would have to head up to the concession stand. You know, like everybody else. *Sorry, was I asking you?* he'd said. But he was already flirting a little. He was already leaning forward to see what I would say next.

Danny shrugged. "And, the thing is, you weren't playing games or trying to impress me. You just genuinely wanted the beer."

He looked right at me.

"I tried a million times to get you to see what you were doing, to get you to understand what the cost was. Putting us to the side. The cost to you."

"So I wasn't supposed to change at all?"

He shook his head.

"That's not what I'm saying. I didn't expect you to stay like you were at twenty-one."

"Sounds like that's exactly what you wanted."

"You were the most honest person I'd ever met. That's why I chose you. And it's why I wasn't particularly weirded out about the fake cooking videos or you playing make-believe. I didn't think you could lose what defined you. But that's exactly what got lost," he said. "I couldn't reconcile the woman you turned into with the person I know you are. Or were . . ."

My heart started racing. "So you should have just left."

"But it's my fault too. You would ask me, all the time, *It's not a big deal, right, if I lie about this? Or if I fake it a little?*" He shrugged. "I gave you permission to give yourself away. And the worst part was when you stopped even asking. I became someone else you would try to spin."

I put my hands up to stop him. "I can't listen to this."

"Why? Because you don't want to hear it?"

"Exactly."

He nodded. "So ask me again why I did this."

I stared at him, feeling like I might explode. Was he seriously looking right at me and telling me that he did this to save me? That he did this for love? Even if I believed him, who wanted love if this was what it looked like?

I hadn't taken off my wedding ring, not the entire time we'd been apart, but I took it off now. I took it off and put it on the sofa between us, the soft sofa that looked so wrong in there.

Then I stormed out the door, trying to ignore a tugging on my insides as I headed down the stairs.

It wouldn't go away, no matter how fast I moved, this tugging, like a despair I didn't want to feel yet, that I still thought I could outrun if I just got as far enough away from him, as quickly as I could.

41

I don't remember the drive home. I vaguely remember stopping at a rest stop, trying to catch my breath, trying to make sure that I arrived in one piece.

I finally got back to Montauk at 6 A.M., the sun rising up over the ocean and the dunes, the roads still empty.

Rain opened the door. She was already dressed, ready to start her day.

I was still in my dress from the night before, tears and mascara running down my face.

She looked me up and down. Then she turned to the couch, to a tall guy with a baseball cap on, extra-long crutches by his side, a ragged scar on his knee.

Thomas. Her boyfriend. He was looking at me with a far more sympathetic expression than my sister was.

Rain met his eyes. And she turned back toward me.

"What makes you think you can just show up here?" she said.

Then she moved out of the doorway and let me inside.

August

42

Did you know that chanterelles are picked, at their peak, in late summer?

Chef Z loved chanterelles, and counted down until a specific date in July (which he refused to share), when he picked them from the garden. Then he made them a centerpiece of a course each night for as many nights as the mushrooms would allow. It had been eight nights since Danny had shattered my world and, on each of them, Chef Z's world was shattered by chanterelles.

He started on Sunday night with a pear and chanterelle salad, moved on to stuffed artichokes with crab and chanterelles, moved from there to a crostini, a fricassee, a pasta with chanterelle mushrooms.

Every night, Z gave the staff a lecture about the versatility of the vegetable, their meatiness and flexible quality. And, every night, he almost cried (the closest I ever saw him to crying, at least) when too many of the chanterelles returned uneaten.

I tried to stay out of his way most of those nights, even though he came over every few seconds to ask why more people were leaving them behind. I shook my head, trying to look equally disgusted. And I was—though about something else. I was disgusted at myself. At how exactly Danny had accomplished what he had. At how I had missed it.

I couldn't stop going over it, each new detail like salt in the wound. And I remembered the strangest details. The oak floors in Danny's Upper West Side apartment project. He had obviously been working on that project longer than a few days—had it afforded him a way to buy me out of the loft? The morning it had all started "Moonlight Mile" had come on the radio alarm clock. What was that doing on the radio? Had Danny managed to plan that part too? Was it not the alarm clock, but his iPhone connected to the charger, scheduled to go off and play that song? My favorite song playing, like a chance, to remind me of who I was. Whom I'd been.

He had given me other chances that night. He had asked me not to go to the party. I remembered clearly. He had brought Gerber daisies home with him and said he would call the whole thing off if I wanted. Was the whole thing, which I thought was the party, really the unraveling of our life together?

Why hadn't I taken him up on that offer? Where would I be now if I had?

Chef Z would come over to my station, and it would be like looking in the mirror. Utter and total despair. For him, it was his underappreciated vegetable. For me, it was the reminder—as if repeated on playback—that I was completely and utterly alone. Career-less, husband-less.

It was almost enough to make me confide in him. It seemed to be enough to make him confide in me.

"The chanterelle is a tricky beast," he said, on night eight, his eyes on a gorgeous plate of pasta. "They need to be picked at precisely the right time to reach their full potential."

Was it happening? A connection? "For what it's worth, Chef," I said, "I think they're delicious."

He banged the plate on the table. "Not much," he said.

Then he walked away.

I seriously considered hiding them for the rest of the night. Just to see a different look on his face. Just to do something proactive, as opposed to sitting here, stewing in it.

Adding insult to injury, Amber's cookbook was a raving success. One week in, and she had already gone into another printing. I was yesterday's news. Literally.

Perhaps this was what I got for lying so publicly. Now everything I had was private. My life was so private that I was about to have a baby with someone who didn't even know about it.

Another plate of the pasta with chanterelle mushrooms was returned to the kitchen. Chef Z's homemade and quite exquisite bucatini was absent from the plate. Several mushrooms remained.

I looked around the kitchen to see if anyone was watching. No one seemed to be, so I scooped up a mushroom and dropped it into my mouth.

It was delicious, rich and meaty, with a perfect amount of spice.

I reached for another when I heard a voice behind me.

"No, you didn't," he said.

I turned around to see Ethan standing there, a stainless-steel thermos in his hands.

He shook his head, disgusted. "That's a new low."

Then he reached down and took a bite himself.

"So you've been keeping a low profile," Ethan said. "One day you're staying over, the next you disappear."

We sat on the bench outside the restaurant, after hours, Ethan pouring us each hot cocoa from his thermos.

He handed me a cup. "Are you all right? Thomas told me you're sleeping on the couch."

"I'm surprised he even noticed. I stay in the car until late at night after they've all gone to sleep. And I sneak out before they get up. We've avoided saying more than two words to each other."

"That sounds comfortable. And sustainable."

"It's great."

"Why don't you just stay with me?"

"You have the celebrity friend. And I can't impose like that."

He put up his hand to stop me. "First of all, it's not an imposition. And second of all, she's in Paris for the week. Doing her fall shopping."

I looked at his outfit, the same hoodie he seemed to live in whenever he wasn't fishing.

"You guys have so much in common," I said.

"It is our hobbies that bring us together."

I laughed, took a sip of the cocoa.

"So the party didn't end up going so well?" he said.

I paused. "It was Danny," I said.

"What was?"

I looked at him, waiting for him to figure it out.

"Holy shit. The husband was the one who hacked you?"

I nodded, afraid to speak—afraid if I said another word, I'd burst into tears. Fourteen years. The tears hadn't seemed to stop. Danny had been my person. I'd trusted him so much it hadn't even occurred to me he would have done this, regardless of his reasoning. What did that say about me? What did that say about how little I'd been paying attention to him?

Ethan folded his arms over his chest. "Why would he . . . just . . . why?"

"He said he did it because he loves me," I said, my voice cracking.

"There are other ways to love someone."

I met Ethan's eyes, desperate for a lifeline. "You think so?"

"I know so," he said, trying to process. "How do you think the girlfriend plays in?"

I wrapped my hands around the cocoa, held it to me. "She doesn't. There is no girlfriend."

He looked confused. "What about the showering?"

"She was redesigning our apartment, Danny's apartment now. I guess the guilt I heard in her voice was about that, about her choosing him in the breakup or something . . ."

"You believe him?"

I did. Would I sound like a fool if I admitted it? I'd looked up Simon Callahan when I got back to Montauk, and he was who Danny said he was. But I hadn't found any photographs of him and Maggie. Not on Wireimage, not on her Facebook page. I didn't find any proof. Danny's word was my proof. And it was really the only proof I needed. What did that say about where I was now?

"So if we take him at his word, what exactly did he think he'd accomplish?"

I shrugged. "He was hoping that I'd remember who I used to be. You know, before the world was watching, and I lost it."

"It?"

"Me."

Ethan nodded, considered. "Well, he's not wrong about that part," he said. "The husband."

I turned and looked at him. "What did you just say, traitor?"

He smiled. "I'm not justifying what he did. I'm just saying, he's not wrong. We do lose ourselves that way. It's almost impossible not to," he said. "The other night, I was with my friend when she instagrammed a photograph of herself hanging out with a couple of other women drinking wine on the deck, the ocean in front of them. No, correction: She sent out a photograph of their very newly manicured feet. #girlsnight. #thebestnights."

He refilled his cocoa, took a long sip of it.

"Only problem was that the other women were her assistant and her assistant's new girlfriend. And they were over for approximately five minutes to go over her schedule in Paris and pick up her dry cleaning. And, obviously, take the photo."

"So you're saying everyone is a liar?"

"I'm saying it's the way of the world now to display yourself. And there is no putting that genie back in the bottle," he said. "And some people integrate it well, they find social media connective. But for the rest of us, it's a different story. Literally. And no one's talking about it. The cost of curating your life."

There was that word again. *Curate.*

"And there is a cost to the people looking at that photograph and thinking that's how their lives are supposed to be. And to my friend sending it out into the world. My friend, who savored the comments coming in about how she was a girl's girl. About how the best women had lifelong girlfriends. It was like the feedback made her forget it was a crock, that she didn't have a night with girlfriends. That what she was actually doing was having sex on that deck while her husband played golf in Pebble Beach."

"That's a lot of detail," I said.

He laughed. "Believe me, it's not," he said.

I shot him a look.

Ethan looked right at me. "I don't approve of the husband's methods," he said. "But I guess it's possible he had good intentions."

I sighed. "Whose side are you on?"

"His," he said. "Obviously."

I smiled. But, the truth was, Ethan had nailed it. I hadn't begun to forgive Danny for what he had done, but I was starting to think that maybe he was right. I'd spent so much time playing make-believe, I'd lost the thread between who I used to be and the person I'd been presenting to the world. How do you begin to trace it back to when everything you did wasn't a perfectly calibrated extension of who you thought you were supposed to be?

That was the cost of my curated life. I had no clue where I'd gotten so lost.

"So you're sure she's away? Your girlfriend?"

"A thousand photos on Instagram don't lie." He paused. "Well, not all the time."

"Would you help me with something, then? It's illegal."

He was already standing up. "That's my favorite kind of help," he said.

43

Ethan put the keys on the credenza in the foyer and left me there.

I took a deep breath and started to walk through the house. My childhood house. It vaguely resembled the house I'd grown up in, but it had been renovated from the ground up. There were dark wood floors now and silky chocolate walls, covered in modern art. Colorful canvases lined the entranceway, art deco fixtures hung lavishly from the ceilings.

It was difficult to remember the house as it had been. The bleached floors and white walls, my father's black-and-white photography the only "art" hanging anywhere. Some of the photographs had been personal, but most were of Montauk itself. This town had been my father's escape and, for a long time, his dream. And he had captured his love for it in his house. The docks and the beach. Ditch Plains and the Montauk Association. The Atlantic Ocean right beneath it.

I walked toward the back of the house, the hallway narrowing, the door to the kitchen now a sturdy red wood. My father had refused to replace the door we'd had there, which was yellowing and nicked in the corners, the paint splintering off. He had jammed his foot on it the day he was nominated for his first Oscar—jammed it moments before he heard the news, his toe breaking badly on impact, turning an ugly black and blue.

Yet, he decided that the door was instrumental in that early victory, that somehow the way he'd banged it had led to the victory. So the rule was that the door stayed as it was and could not get altered in any way. As splintered and messy as it got, he wouldn't even paint it. My sister didn't like it when I joked that, by that logic, he shouldn't have fixed his toe.

I ran my hand over the new door, pushed through past what had been my father's small studio. It was now a grand opening to the kitchen, which they had blown out and doubled in size to accommodate the top-of-the-line commercial Viking ranges (two of them), an island that went on forever, a wood-burning stove. I opened the Sub-Zero refrigerator and, even though the owners weren't in town, it was perfectly stocked. Eggs and shrimp and vegetables, farm-fresh strawberries and glass-bottled milk.

Our kitchen never seemed to have food, and there had been nowhere impressive to cook it. There had been a small stove, an island that had enough room for two bar stools. It had been simple and serene, as if a reminder of what the house was there for—what, even with all the remodeling, the house was still there for—the exquisite wraparound porch looking over the ocean.

I stepped outside, the sweet smell of the beach hitting my nose. How many days had I sat out there as a child, taking that smell for granted? Dreaming of going anywhere else?

My eyes ticked up to the second story. I walked back inside and headed upstairs to the room that Rain and I had shared. We'd had twin beds, a large desk with two chairs, and bright purple walls. My father had let us paint the room that color when we were little. And we had never changed it.

The room was now a meditation studio—complete with a Buddha and a small Zen garden, a large mat. But they had kept the purple walls. That was what they'd kept? The color was startling, taking me back in time, and, like that, it all came back to me. I was five and ten and fifteen at once, sitting in the window seat in the corner. Rain never far away.

I remembered her walking in, the day she graduated from high school. She was still in her gown, and I was sitting there imagining what I would do with the room when she left. Rain had graduated at the top of her class and received a full ride to Princeton. She would get to study in one of the most impressive math programs in the country and she would still be near enough to

Montauk that it would be easy for her to come home regularly, which I knew was important to her.

Maybe that was why I didn't believe her when she said that she wasn't leaving, that she was staying in the house—staying where she was—and taking some classes at the college in Southampton instead. *I wouldn't leave you,* she had said that day.

At the time, I was furious. How could she give up an opportunity like that? And how could she pretend it had anything to do with me? I screamed that she was pretending to say something kind, that she was pretending to be worried about me, when we both knew it was our father she was worried about. He was the reason why she was stupidly giving up a *free* Princeton education. I was certain she thought that without her there—to act as his buffer, to act as his protector—I would try to break him. I would try to break him of all his rules, of all his trauma. And she didn't know if he could handle it. Would he get better if he were stripped of his crutches? Or would he just be defeated?

She was so angry that she stormed out. I thought she hadn't liked getting called out for the truth—that she didn't want to defend herself again for bending herself in every possible position to protect our father. But what if I had been wrong? What if the truth was that she *had* been staying for me? Maybe she had thought that, if she left me with him, he would crush me instead?

I walked over to the window seat, and sat down on a strange bamboo pillow. I looked out the window, at the front yard, the guesthouse in the distance.

I had always felt so subsumed by our house, by the rules that governed it, rules I never understood. That didn't change, being here again.

I'd spent the last eight nights in my car on the side of my childhood driveway, waiting for the lights to go off, so I knew my sister was asleep. One night, I'd watched through the window as my sister and her daughter had a late dinner. My sister's boyfriend hobbled around in the background. They weren't eating anything fancy. A pot of pasta, bagged lettuce. But she was happy, my sister. Her daughter ate as Rain leaned in and listened to her speak of her day. My sister had built a family—she had built a life she enjoyed—and I had judged her before she even started.

You had to ask yourself: Where did that judgment get you?

There was a sonogram hanging over the rearview mirror in my car. A healthy little baby. Strong heartbeat. The start of limbs. I didn't know if it was of a boy or a girl. But it was on the way. There was a baby on the way that belonged in part to someone who didn't think he knew me anymore. Where would that picture be hanging in the alternate reality where I hadn't become a stranger to him? Where I had confessed before it was too late? Where he had confessed too?

For the last eight nights, I'd waited until the lights had gone off, until I knew my sister was asleep, so she wouldn't look at me with a mix of pity and aggravation that I was still sleeping on her couch. So I wouldn't have to look into her face and see her dismissal. So I wouldn't have to think about her and her daughter and my husband and my father and everyone who'd once loved me and whom I had somehow lost.

Tonight, I didn't have to wait for her lights to go out. I curled up on the floor in my childhood bedroom, on someone else's soft mat. And I realized I'd been wrong about something else. Maybe the most important thing. I'd been wrong about the ways we move past the versions of ourselves that no longer fit. I'd thought it involved running, as far and as fast as your feet could carry you, from your former selves. I didn't understand that was the surest way to wind up exactly where you started.

44

In the morning, I looked out the window, feeling foggy and damp, like I'd had a bottle of wine the night before. My shoulders were sore from sleeping cramped up, my head spinning from the heat.

I opened the window, letting in the chill, the soft breeze, and I saw her staring at me from her tiny loft window.

Sammy.

She looked confused, for just a second, about why I was in the main house. Except her happiness at seeing me there must have trumped her questioning.

Because she opened her window wider.

"Hi," I mouthed.

"Hi," she mouthed back.

Then she peeked behind herself as though she was going to get caught.

When she turned around again, I pointed toward the stairs, leading to the beach and the ocean.

She gave me the thumbs-up and closed the window, already on her way there.

"So you and Mom had a fight?" she said.

We sat on the rickety stairs, the beach right

beneath us, the ocean winds strong and thick.

"We'll work it out," I said.

She fought to keep her hair pinned behind her ears. "I don't know how, if you guys are avoiding each other."

"You noticed that?"

"Well, I do live here."

I smiled. "I don't want you worrying about it, okay?"

She nodded. "What were you doing in the other house?"

"Visiting," I said.

"Why?"

I sighed. "That question deserves a longer answer than I think you'll be able to sneak away for. Where did you tell them you were going?"

"Seashells."

I laughed.

"Mom is already at work, but Thomas said I could go for a little while. He's waiting on me, though. We're going to the Pancake House on the way to camp."

"That sounds delicious," I said. "Thanks for sneaking out to meet me first. I'm really happy to see you."

She shrugged. "I don't really get to see you anymore."

"I didn't want you to think it had anything to do with you."

She scrunched up her face. "Why would I think

303

that? My mother didn't really want us hanging around together. There was no choice."

I felt my heart burst at her empathy, her understanding. At six years old, she had already surpassed her aunt and her mother.

I leaned in and gave her a hug, like I hadn't missed the first six years of her life, like I had any right. Maybe that was the thing about regret. Once you felt it, you went out on a limb to try and feel anything else.

"I think you're pretty great," I said. "And I want you to know that in case your mother kicks me out again."

She blushed. Actually blushed. "Okay, next time you can just say it."

I reached down to the sand and picked up a white seashell, handing it to her. "For your cover story," I said.

She looked over my shell choice disapprovingly. Then she tossed it back onto the sand and began searching for a different shell.

"Let's at least make it believable," she said.

45

Not the next night, but the night after that, I arrived at the restaurant an hour before my shift, in time to eat the staff meal and relax before the dinner rush.

As I walked into the kitchen, Douglas met me at the door.

"Hey, you have a visitor out front," he said. "And she's looking for you. The real you."

"I don't understand."

"I don't really know, *Sunny.* Ask her."

Then he motioned toward the dining room, where Julie was sitting at the bar, nursing a glass of wine.

I wiped my hands on my jeans. "What does she want?" I said, more to myself than to Douglas. Apparently, though, he felt compelled to respond.

"So you're pressing the extent of my knowledge. And my interest."

He stalked off, and I headed into the dining room. I instinctively looked down at myself—taking in my sweater, pulling my hair behind my ear, trying to look presentable.

"Julie?"

She looked up as I arrived by the bar. "Sunny! I didn't think it was true, but here you are."

I forced a smile. "What are you doing here?"

"What am I doing here? What are *you* doing here? You're a tough woman to track down."

She moved her purse so I could sit down beside her.

"Do you want some wine?"

I reluctantly took a seat on the bar stool next to her. "I'm good, thanks."

She tilted her glass in my direction. "I'll drink for both of us, then," she said. "Cheers."

Then she gave me a large smile, looked around.

"So this is where people hide out when their world turns on them. Paradise."

Some people's paradise. Some people's old hell. Whatever, I didn't correct her.

"How are you doing?" she said. "That was some party, huh?"

"I shouldn't have shown up."

"Well, if Amber had done that to me, I would have shown up too."

I cringed. The old me would have let it go. But it seemed wrong now. Amber was terrible and a phony, but she wasn't guilty of this. She wasn't guilty of outing me. "I actually think I was wrong about that."

She looked surprised. "Really? Well, I can't stand Amber anyway," she said. "Most people can't. And seriously, *toast?*"

I smiled. "You aren't going to get an argument from me about that," I said.

She took a sip of her wine. "After you left, I sat

down and talked to Louis. About you, actually."

I looked up at her. "Is he any less angry?"

"Well, no." She shook her head. "But it got me thinking about why."

"I lied about pretty much everything."

She shrugged. "A lot of people do. That's what Facebook was made for, right?"

I wasn't ready to let myself off that easily. "It's different. I wasn't tweeting a few friends."

"So? That's pretty much par for the course when living a public life these days. There's no time to tell the truth. Everyone's the *New York Post*, posting the catchiest headline they can think of. A little imagination and you can make yourself the story of the day. Even when there's no real news."

I looked at her and considered. Was it the same? Was telling a white lie or two on Facebook or Twitter different from lying about everything in your life? Maybe that's how you lose yourself to it. One small fabricated post at a time. Until your Facebook feed, which looked quite a bit like you when it started, starts to looks like someone you kind of know. Maybe someone you'd rather be.

Julie took a sip of wine.

"Everyone lies. Louis isn't irritated because you did. He's irritated because he thought you weren't. He's irritated because you were so convincing. He's irritated because he thought you were authentic."

I thought about that. She had a point. The hard part was trying to convince Louis now that who he was to me—who we were to each other—hadn't been part of the fallacy. He had mattered to me. He mattered still.

"But here's the thing," she said, leaning in with a smile. "I actually think you are authentic."

"I'm not following."

"Look at you. No offense, but you're kind of a wreck. There's remorse written all over your face. To me that means that, whatever misguided choices you made, deep down, there's a real soul in there. No one without a soul can sell authenticity the way you did. That's what made you a star. Not Meredith's recipes or Ryan's cheesy promos. And I'm betting we can sell that again."

"You're talking about a new show?"

She nodded. "I think there's an opportunity to put you out there again. But to do it right. To do it honestly."

She pulled her iPad out of her bag, pulled up an image.

Cooking from Scratch, in pretty blue lettering, over a picture of me photoshopped into a shabby-chic kitchen. The ocean in the distance.

"It's rough, I just had Violet throw it together. It's a catchy name, though, right? Even Louis thought it was a catchy name. We'll shoot it on the beach. Do lots of clambakes and fun-in-the-sun-type pieces. Very down to earth. Include your actual childhood stories. Go to the local places you went to growing up. The fish shop, the general store. Local girl makes good."

She smiled, clearly a little proud of herself. "What do you think?"

I smiled, trying not to look too thrilled. This was what I had been hoping for—why I had been putting up with Chef Z's abuse. A new show, a new chance to do it right.

I felt like it wasn't really happening, which may be why I realized there were still several reasons that it might not.

"So, that's all pretty great," I said. "But there are things that make it complicated."

"Okay. Like what?"

"I'm having a baby."

Her eyes went wide, and she smiled. Totally sincere. "Congratulations!"

"Thank you."

She waved me off. "And that's not complicated. Everyone loves a baby," she said. "So you're reconciling with your husband?"

I shook my head. "No."

She nodded, not pressing it. "Still. It's going to be great. And I know it's scary to put yourself out there again, but people loved you. And they'll want to see you doing well again. I mean, you've learned to cook, right?"

"Not really."

"So we'll get someone to teach you. Don't

worry, they'll be the easiest recipes known to man. That's what people want these days." She paused, considering. "Maybe we even teach you how to cook on the show! I love that idea. It's a good thing you've learned nothing."

I laughed. I wasn't sure she was right about that, but I did like what she was saying. I liked the idea of not pretending, of doing something legitimately. With the child on the way, I liked the idea of having a real way to support her. Or him. But I was getting stuck on what she was saying. Why would people invest in me again? Why, if everything I'd said before was a lie, would they have faith in me now?

Julie shook her head. "People have a very short memory. Look at Paula Deen. She came back from a lot worse."

"I don't know."

"I do. And I promise, we can figure out all the details. Anyone can follow a recipe. But you have that thing."

That stopped me. It sounded like what Danny was talking about too. A thing. An idea. That's what makes us *us,* isn't it? But what if we give it away? Distort it? Hand it over to other people and let them tell us what to do with it.

Except Julie wasn't asking me to distort anything. She was asking me to figure out a way to let people in, but honestly this time. If that was even possible—it had to be, right?

She stood up. "Think about it," she said. "After all, what's the alternative? Working as a line cook here?"

"I'm not. I'm on trash."

"Gross," she said.

Then she winked, squeezed my shoulder, and walked away.

46

Sometimes, just when you least expect it, everything lines up right again.

I couldn't hide my smile as I went through the courses that night, trying to concentrate on the squash risotto, the conversation with Julie running through my head. Thankfully, every plate was a success, so there were no patterns in the trash to report to Chef Z.

Still, when Chef Z walked over after the first dinner service was completed, he seemed annoyed.

"What's with the joy?" he said.

I shrugged. "Everyone either loves everything tonight or they're very hungry."

"Well, which is it?"

I shook my head, forgetting for a minute he had no sense of humor. "I was just being silly. Everyone has loved everything this evening."

"Fine," he said, not a smile on his face. "No need to get so celebratory. That's the way it's supposed to go."

I still had a stupid grin on my face. Who cared? Let him fire me. Let him show me the door.

He pointed at his own turned-down lips. "This is what I mean when I say stop celebrating."

"Chef, I'm just happy to be here," I said.

"Be happy quieter," he said.

· · ·

"*Cooking from Scratch*, huh?" Ethan said. "That's not bad."

I'd been way too excited to go home—especially when that home happened to no longer be mine—so I drove over to Ethan's after work.

We went out to the docks, put our toes into the water. It was one of the perks of living in Montauk. That late-night peace. The moon crawling down over the horizon, everything a gorgeous shade of blue. The sailboats resting in the harbor, the docks quiet and serene.

Ethan reached into his cooler, pulled out another beer, handed it over. "Non-alcoholic," he said.

I clinked the bottle against his. "Thank you," I said, taking a long sip.

"So you're going to do it, right?" he said.

"I think so," I said. "It would be pretty crazy to turn it down."

Ethan paused, hearing something in my voice. "Are you asking me or telling me?"

"Telling," I said. "And maybe asking."

"Why? What does it matter what I think?"

I shrugged. "It's just a little hard to trust yourself when you've made such terrible decisions in the past."

He took a long sip, considered. "Does it make you happy? To think about doing it?" he said.

"Well, I'm at war with my husband, and my

sister hates me. And I've been squatting in your girlfriend's house for the last couple of nights. So you know, happiness is a bit of a lofty goal."

He laughed. "That's really the only goal."

"How do you figure that?"

Ethan moved closer. "The issue with what you did before isn't that you hurt anyone else. It's that you were so unhappy. I mean, that's no way to live, embarrassed by who you are," he said. "Though I guess we're all doing that a little."

I smiled. "I'm not sure why I'm asking you for permission to say yes," I said.

He took a sip of his beer. "Well, it's yours, if you need it. I think it could be a good thing."

I met Ethan's eyes. "You're a surprising guy, you know that?" I said.

"Why do you say that?"

"I don't know. Of all the places I thought I might find comfort during all this, I wouldn't have put you high up there."

He put his arm around me. "I'm very comfortable."

I laughed. "If you do say so yourself?"

He laughed too. Then he leaned in.

Ethan leaned in and tried to kiss me. I was alone and pregnant and surprisingly hornier than I'd ever been.

But I pushed him away. "I can't."

"Why? Your husband coming back?"

"I'm guessing no . . . probably never."

314

"Well, you're already pregnant, so, you can't be worried about my super sperm. And it can't be that you don't find me attractive."

I smiled. I wanted to tell him that I found him unbelievably attractive, but that felt like its own form of betrayal—a line I could cross but shouldn't. And I was sticking to it. The right side of shouldn't.

"So the lady doesn't find me attractive. All right, then," he said. "What does it say about me that my lukewarm attraction to you just grew by leaps and bounds knowing that?"

I laughed. "Everything."

I put out my hand. How easy would it be to slip into this new life? How nice in so many ways. A clean slate, a new me. But that was how I had ended up here, and I wasn't going to do that again.

"What's this?"

"You're still the only friend I've got. And I really don't want to lose you."

Ethan sat back, and I could see it flicker across his face. My honesty had touched him.

"Then I guess I won't let you," he said.

And he took my outstretched hand. But instead of shaking it, he just held on.

47

I took a risk doing it, but there was one other person I needed to discuss this with.

So, the next afternoon, I stopped by her camp.

I arrived in time for afternoon snack, Sammy generously offering to share her applesauce and pita chips. I sat cross-legged with her on the floor and took a few grateful nibbles, making sure she ate most of it herself.

"You're never going to guess what I was just doing," she said. "Guess."

"Let's see. Were you learning to tap-dance?"

She laughed. "That's a terrible guess. This is science camp."

I smiled. "So you better just tell me."

"Our group went down to the pond and we dissected frogs! Or, the counselor did, but we got to watch."

"For fun?"

She dug into the applesauce. "No, for science."

I put the spoon down, officially done eating. Maybe done with applesauce for the rest of the pregnancy, its creaminess now wrapped up for me with Sammy's frogs.

"It was awesome," she said. "I got to see the heart."

I interrupted her, fighting back the vomit.

"That's great, Sammy," I said. "I'm so glad you had a good time."

She motioned in the direction of her classroom. "Do you want to come see the frogs?"

"Definitely not," I said. "I did want to talk to you, though."

"About what?"

"That school you were telling me about."

She looked up, and I could see it wash over her face. Excitement. And then the opposite.

"Okay," she said.

"I've been wondering about something. If there was a way to make it work, would you like to go there?"

She shrugged. "I don't know. Maybe."

I met her eyes, waited.

"I would like to," she said. "Why?"

"There's a job I could take. It would make it possible to help pay for it. Get you and your mom a place to live nearby there."

"My mother won't want that."

"Probably not, but . . . I think it's a good thing to know what you want. If you do, you have a chance of getting it. If you don't, you have a chance of getting only what someone else wants you to have."

She wiped her hands. "I think I'd like for you to take me home."

48

It started raining on the way back to the house—a summer shower—though by the time we pulled down the driveway, the shower had turned into a downpour. And we had to make a run for it, to not get soaked on the way inside.

When we walked in, Thomas was standing by the stove and making dinner. Or, more accurately, Thomas was hobbling on crutches by the stove, attempting to make dinner. It looked like a lasagna, rich and meaty, with about a pound of cheese on top. And totally burnt. The smell rose off of it, gnarly and intense.

Sammy pinched her nose as Thomas turned and saw us in the doorway.

"I thought we were ordering pizza tonight," she said.

He looked back and forth between us. "We are now," he said.

Then he pushed the lasagna away, dramatically for effect.

Sammy laughed. "Great," she said. "Call up when it gets here."

She disappeared up into her loft, leaving us in the kitchen alone. I watched her go, trying to will her downstairs.

I looked back at Thomas. I tried not to stare at

this guy who had been my sister's partner for the last several years. He was tall, if a little gangly, with a mop of blond hair on top of his head that made him look younger than he was. This was the first time we were really meeting, except for the brief exchange the morning I'd stumbled home from seeing Danny.

Thomas wiped his hand on a dishtowel. "I'm normally a pretty great cook," he said. "Rain will tell you. But moving around is a little less than ideal at the moment."

He hobbled to the fridge and took out a beer.

"Do you want anything?" he asked.

I shook my head. "I'm good, thanks," I said.

He tossed over a bottle of water anyway—a small indicator that Rain had told him I was pregnant. She had probably told him as a way of explaining why she couldn't seem to kick me off her couch.

He motioned toward the kitchen table. "Normally I wouldn't have any problem standing around awkwardly, but would you mind if we sit awkwardly instead?"

I smiled. "No, that's fine."

He headed to the table, pulling out the seat closest to him. I walked over and took the seat across from him.

"It's a little weird to meet you," he said.

I wasn't sure how to read that. But then he smiled—a bright and warm smile, which lit up

319

his whole face and made him look more welcoming than I'm sure he felt.

"I mean, I hear such different things," he said.

For a second, I thought he meant he was hearing different things from Rain herself. And I took solace in thinking she was at least conflicted about me. That she was at least talking enough about me to suggest she was conflicted. But then I realized he was talking about the things he was hearing from Rain. And from Ethan.

"You've made quite an impression on Ethan," he said. "He says you've become pretty good friends."

I smiled. "He's a really great guy."

"Is that what he is?"

I could see his protectiveness. These were two people he cared deeply about.

"Look, Thomas, I understand that you probably don't want me here . . ."

He shook his head. "I didn't say that."

"Well, I've been trying to make other arrangements."

He motioned toward the front door. "Like sleeping next door?"

"I wouldn't say I was doing a great job."

He took another swig of beer. "Well. Who is?"

Then he elevated his leg, pulling it up on the chair next to him, rubbing his knee.

"It hurts a lot?" I said.

"Ah, I'll be all right." He shrugged. "I'm just

a little bummed. I had this whole thing planned for Rain and my anniversary next weekend and it's going to be tough."

"What were you planning to do?"

"I was going to take her out to the North Fork, spend the weekend going on a long ride. That's probably out."

"You guys could go anyway."

He considered. "We could. I got my friend Gena to commit to watching Sammy and everything."

The elusive Gena. "If she bails for any reason, I'll do it."

"Yeah? That would be awesome. Gena does bail sometimes."

"I'd love to, if Rain would allow it."

Thomas smiled. "That would be great," he said. " 'Cause, you know, I was going to propose."

"Really?"

He nodded. "Really," he said. "I mean, the getting down on one knee thing might be out."

Then he reached into his back pocket and pulled out the ring, like proof.

It was an emerald stone, surrounded by diamonds. It was elegant and simple, a classic design.

I looked up at him, trying not to show my confusion. Why was he showing me the ring? Why was he telling me about the proposal at all? He certainly didn't need my approval. But he wanted to need my approval. It was the kindest way I could think of for him to tell me that he was hoping we would work it out. My sister and me. He was hoping we'd be okay.

It reminded me of Danny. He had done the same thing before proposing. My father had died, not too long before, but he had driven out to Montauk to talk to Rain, to tell her he was going to ask. He told me later that they had gone to the lighthouse with coffees, and he'd told her he would take care of me. He wouldn't tell me what she had said, and I imagined at the time it was probably something snarky about how it wasn't her permission to give. But he had won her over that day all the same. In the gesture. In the fact that he'd acknowledged how much we mattered to each other, even if we couldn't.

"What do you think?" Thomas said.

"It's stunning," I said.

He smiled. "Thanks . . . happy you think so."

I handed him the ring, trying to fight back tears.

"Are you going to cry?"

I shook my head, the tears already starting to fall. "Definitely not."

"That's convincing."

"I think it's the pregnancy," I said. "I keep crying at everything."

"I won't tell," he said.

Which was when the front door swung open, and Rain ran in. She was completely drenched.

"Holy crap, it's terrible out!" she said.

Then she realized that I was there.

"Oh . . ." She looked back and forth between us. "What's going on here?"

Thomas quickly pushed the ring back into his pocket as I wiped the tears from my eyes. "Nothing," he said. "Is it raining?"

She reached for a small kitchen towel and tried to dry herself off. "You're funny," she said.

She walked over to the table and stood behind Thomas, putting her hand on his shoulder, and nuzzled into his neck.

"Ah, so wet!" he said.

She leaned down and kissed him. "Deal with it," she said.

And he did, holding her face to his, the water from her hair splattering across his chest. She smiled and, for a second, my sister looked like my sister.

She looked up, nodded. "Hi there," she said.

I waved at her. "Hi."

Thomas took Rain's hand, held it to his chest. "She dropped Sammy off. We were just having a little chat."

Rain forced a smile. "Is that right?" she said.

I pointed toward the door. "I can go."

Rain shook her head. "I didn't ask you to."

Then it got quiet, awkward.

Thomas looked back and forth between us. "I'd leave you guys alone, but you know . . . not gonna get up unnecessarily."

I looked at my sister. "Can we go somewhere and talk?" I said.

She kept her hand on Thomas, motioned around the small house. Sammy was in the loft above the living room, Thomas was taking up the kitchen, the bedroom was all bed.

"It's raining really hard out there," she said. "There's not many places to go."

I held up the key to our childhood home. "I have one."

49

S o this is super freaky," Rain said.

We walked into the foyer, Rain taking in the house. The walls, the art, the enormous portrait of the celebrity and her husband in the dip-down living room.

"We can't just be here," she said.

"Humor me," I said.

"I don't think that's a defense for the cops."

But she kept walking down the hallway and into the kitchen, taking in the enormous stoves, the bay windows leading out to the porch, and the gorgeous views of the beach and the ocean beyond it. The rain was still coming down hard, the wind whipping up, making it all feel slightly magical.

"Please tell me she's a good chef," Rain said.

"No idea, but . . ." I reached into the fridge and pulled out a loaf of our favorite bread. "You hungry?"

"Now we are just stealing."

"She's got a stocked fridge, and it's all going to go to waste."

"*That's* what we'll tell the police."

"Grilled cheese?"

She considered. "All right," she said. "But I'm taking the seat with the view."

· · ·

Here was how I made the grilled cheese:

First—and the ordering of the ingredients mattered—I took a loaf of country boule bread and sliced two pieces half an inch thick. Not from the ends, but from the middle of the loaf. This was the second-most important part of building a great grilled cheese—the bread itself, and then its ratio to everything else. Once I'd cut the bread, I buttered the inside of each slice and started to add the goodies. I added a generous layer of good quality Swiss cheese, then very thinly sliced cherry tomatoes. Of course, cherry tomatoes were small and difficult to slice thinly—and, it was summer, so I could have used any fresh tomato—but the rest of the year, only a cherry tomato was sweet enough. I put five tomatoes on each side, then another layer of Swiss, even more generous than the first. If Danny was there, I would have added a top layer of avocado, but avocado (a grilled-cheese purist might say) is a controversial ingredient. And not needed. What was needed was that I focused on the most important part: I put the sandwich together and coated the outside of each slice with mayonnaise. No thin layer, a solid coating. The salty goodness of the mayonnaise sealed the sandwich together, and made it grill on the grill pan more smoothly. Five minutes or to your

lesired level of toastiness. (But the right level
of toastiness is five minutes on each side.)

This might sound simple. And that is because it
s.

It is also, without a doubt, the most delicious
sandwich in the world.

found the house's sound system and attached
my phone, turning on "Moonlight Mile." I
listened to it all the time now—I wasn't sure
why. It wasn't just that I loved the song. It felt
like there was something else it was supposed to
be telling me.

Rain and I sat next to each other on two stools
facing the ocean, facing the rain, the song quietly
playing, eating silently.

We each had an entire sandwich, and then we
split another.

"That's pretty much the best sandwich ever,"
she said, finally.

"Right?" I said. "And they all say I can't cook!"

She laughed. "Too bad they won't let you do
a show on just that."

"They probably would," I said. "They'd call it
Say Cheese. And it would be all things cheese."

"And toast," Rain said.

"No. There's someone else who has that market
cornered."

"The toast market? I was kidding. That's a
thing?"

I nodded. "Amber's."

She shook her head. "Exhausting."

Then she took our plates and walked to the sink, turning on the faucet.

"I'm going to wash these by hand," she said.

I followed her and reached for the dishtowel. "I'll dry," I said.

"Aren't you going to ask me why I'm not using the fancy dishwasher?" she said.

I shrugged. "I figure you have your reasons," I said.

"I've read that now you can attach all your appliances to your phone so you know when any of them have been used," she said. "I don't want her getting a *ping* somewhere that people have broken into her house."

"To clean it?"

"I'm sure weirder things have happened."

She focused on the dishes, handing over the first plate.

"Danny called looking for you."

"When?" I said.

"Last night," she said. "I didn't talk to him."

I nodded, taking that in. I had no idea why he would call her as opposed to calling me directly.

"He's called before."

I looked up at her.

"He's called a few times to check in and make sure you were doing okay. But he shouldn't have," she said. "Not after what he did."

"Do you believe him? That he had good intentions?"

"Yes. But that makes me angrier."

"Why?"

" 'Cause I don't know whether to be furious at him for what he did or to be upset that I didn't think of it first."

I smiled at her and, almost in spite of herself, Rain smiled back.

"Anyway, don't call him. At least not yet."

It was the first big-sisterly thing she'd said to me in a long time. And yet, I wanted to call him. I wanted, more than anything, to hear his voice—to hear that he was doing okay. I wanted to hear that he missed me.

She wiped her hands on a dishtowel. "I heard you got a job offer."

I looked up. "Where?"

"When I ran into the bedroom to change, Sammy followed me in and pointed her finger at me and said, 'Mommy, she got a job offer. Be nice about it. Be nice!' "

I laughed. "I appreciate her support."

"What's this job?"

"Basically, it would be doing another show. Filmed here. All about starting over, finding my roots."

"Ah . . . redemption TV."

I nodded. "Yep. Pretty much."

She reached into the cabinet, started putting

the plates away. "How do you feel about it?"

"Great. And not so great."

Rain turned and looked at me as if considering whether to say something. "Do you know *Mrs. Beeton's Book of Household Management*?"

"Is that a book Sammy wants?"

"No, no. Isabella Beeton. She was like the original Martha Stewart, back in the 1800s. *Mrs. Beeton's Book of Cookery and Household Management* was the definitive book on cooking and keeping your house together."

"How do you know that?"

"How do you *not* know that? Next time you take on a role, you should do a little research."

I smiled.

"I read about her years ago, and of course I thought of you, 'cause, apparently, this Beeton lady didn't write any of her own recipes either. She literally copied recipes from other people, going as far back as the Restoration. And then she would add the list of ingredients to the front of every recipe. So it would look different from the original. So she could sell it as her own."

"Seriously?"

Rain nodded. "This is the best part. Even after she died, her husband pretended she was still alive and went on publishing more books. There's some real fraud!"

I shrugged. "It was easier back then."

"I just think it's kind of interesting. She did a

bad thing, right? But she also put the ingredients at the beginning. And now that's how every recipe is written. She did a bad thing *and* she was the first person to ever do that."

"So you're saying that's what I have to do? Put the ingredients at the beginning."

"Metaphorically speaking."

"That's your pep talk?"

She shrugged. "It's what I got."

I wanted to ask how we could know for sure that Mrs. Beeton was the person who came up with the ingredients idea, but I decided I was going to have a little faith that it was true. I was going to have faith in Mrs. Beeton, and—if Rain was bothering to be kind to me, to dredge up this story she'd been saving until I deserved it— maybe a little faith in myself.

My sister walked over to the bay windows, looked outside. "It is really freaky to be back in here."

I walked over to the windows, too, so we were side by side. "I've actually found it kind of comforting."

"*That's* even freakier."

I looked right at her, Rain's eyes still straight ahead. "I shouldn't have said what I did, about you and Dad," I said.

She flinched. "I'm not like him," she said.

"I know that."

"Do you?"

"If anyone's like him, it's me."

She turned and met my eyes. I nodded, wanting her to know she'd heard me correctly—that I meant it. I did. I knew it was the reason I'd had to leave Montauk. It was the reason I stayed away from my sister; because she knew it too.

I only understood it now—after *Sunshine* had taken such a terrible pivot, after Danny had outed me—and I was forced to face myself again. I had become my father's daughter. He'd had his rules. And I created my lies. And they served the same purpose at the end of the day. They let us live in alternative universes where we got to pretend that we were strong. Where we felt good enough.

Rain looked away, not sure what to say. I was sorry, and she knew it. I was trying to do better. If we had a different relationship, she could have taken my hand or touched me. But that wasn't who we were, not anymore.

She looked at me. "I'd like to go home now," she said.

I smiled, a little deflated. "Sure."

"And I would like you to come with me."

I nodded, my throat catching. She shrugged, playing it off.

"I guess that baby inside of you . . . he gets you some goodwill as far as I'm concerned."

"You think it's a he?" I said.

Rain started gathering up her things, doing a final sweep of the kitchen. "I just picked a pronoun."

50

Putting the ingredients up front. Here's how I planned to do it.

I called Julie, ready to take her up on her generous offer. There were many reasons to tell her yes after all. A new show would provide financial security, a career, a way to help take care of Sammy, to take care of my own kid, a way out of Montauk. A shot at redemption. No lies this time. And hadn't a version of this very thing been the goal?

Still, when I heard her voice on the phone, the word *yes* wouldn't come out of my mouth.

"So, are we going to do something great together?" she said.

"Can I ask you something first? Do you think there's a way to live in the public eye and be authentic? You work with all sorts of people. How do people do it?"

"Well, you don't lie about who you are. For starters."

I laughed. "I know, but even then . . . it seems tricky."

"Oh, jeez. I guess they don't take the whole thing so seriously," she said. "Or maybe they take it very seriously. I don't know. I think you're missing the point."

"Which is?"

"I'm offering you a second chance. And this time, there will be no pretending to be anything you're not. It will be the real you."

That stopped me. Because she couldn't promise that. That was the tricky part, wasn't it? That was Ethan's point. Danny had been able to hack me because I'd lied about who I was. But he was also able to do it because I'd put everything out there. I'd told the story about myself that I thought needed to be told. Until it had taken me so far away from myself that I couldn't even find it anymore. The truth. My truth. However large or small, however unimportant. However click-worthy.

Maybe that was all we had to hold on to. Our truth. Our thing. The thing that made us who we were. So the entire world wasn't suddenly for sale.

"Are you still there?" Julie said.

"I am," I said. "But I'm going to pass."

"No." She was firm. "Really?"

I almost didn't believe it myself. "Apparently."

"Come on. Why would you do that?"

It was a fair question. "I don't think it's right for me."

"Who knows what's right for them? Some days I want to move to Mexico, other days I'm scared of Zika. Do you get what I'm saying? I mean, you don't want to be a waitress forever."

"I'm on trash."

"I'm getting a headache."

"I think I just need a private life right now."

"Is the husband back?"

"No. I just don't want to put myself out there. At least until I know again what I'm putting out there."

"I'm not sure what that means. Though I hope you'll call me when you come to your senses."

Maybe I would. But I didn't think so. "Thank you for thinking it was a good idea."

"I'm thinking a little less so now," she said.

51

There is another thing you should know about "Moonlight Mile"—it was what I was trying to remember, what I was trying to hold on to again. The reason why Mick Jagger wrote the lyrics. The reason it spoke so eloquently to Mick Taylor. It was one of the few songs Jagger had written that showed his weariness of living life on the road, the pressure of keeping up appearances.

Jagger had always kept his public persona and his private feelings separate. So it was startling and incredible to hear him open up about his loneliness. To expose himself in that way.

As soon as I got off the phone with Julie, I turned on the song and—now that she didn't care anymore—I figured out a better answer to why I felt like I had to turn her down. I realized: It couldn't have happened that way today for Jagger, could it? If Jagger were coming up today, instead of listening to the most honest rock song ever written, we would see on his Facebook feed that life on the road was draining him. We would see on his Twitter, a few hours later, an apology for sounding ungrateful that life on the road was draining him. The world eager to chime right in with their judgments.

Was his apology sincere? Was it sincere enough?

And, really, it wasn't even about being famous—or famous in your corner of the world, like I'd been, for a moment.

I was still trying to figure out what we all lost in broadcasting our lives for everyone else's consumption. Before we took the time, you know, to figure out what we wanted our lives to add up to.

Something important, it seemed to me. Something like the chance to write the song.

52

That night, I told Chef I needed to talk with him.

I was still reeling a little from telling Julie no. I was reeling and trying to focus in on working things out with Z.

We were going over the trash, which was composed mainly of the whipped lardo and seaweed butter he served with the bread. It depended on the day of the week whether that rich, gooey lardo and the salty butter were spooned up or left behind. Saturdays, people drowned their fresh farm bread in both types of fat. But Sundays, they seemed to leave the lardo behind. Chef Z wasn't particularly interested—not in the bread, and not really in what I had to say.

Before I got a word out, he raised his hands, stopping me. "I already know what you're going to say," he said.

"You do?"

He motioned across the kitchen. "Douglas told me about your little fake TV show," he said. "When he was trying to get me to replace you with his nephew on trash."

"He did?"

Chef Z shrugged. "Headline is, I couldn't care

less. Cooking and television are two separate things. And one of them is idiotic."

"The show was actually just on the internet. Though when it came out that I couldn't cook, the Food Network did cancel my contract. I was going to host for them."

"Why do you do that?"

"Do what?"

"Think I care."

He shook his head, not interested in my part of this conversation, only in his.

"There is no way to make coq au vin in under thirty minutes and also to make it well. That's why you pay me to make it. Because you should not."

I smiled at him, feeling buoyed. I wanted to talk to Z about letting me work in food prep. I'd proven to have a good palate and I wanted to learn. I knew it was a long shot, but I couldn't help but think: Maybe this was where this roundabout road had taken me. I'd cook the kinds of food that I had learned to love at the restaurant—fresh, specific, thoughtful. And I wouldn't do it as a way to get a new show, a new shot at stardom, but as an end to itself. To actually be a great cook.

Putting the ingredients up front. Take two.

Chef Z was spooning the lardo into a plastic container. "Is there a reason you're staring at me or is this just the naturally awkward way you make people uncomfortable?" he said.

"I'm just happy to hear that you weren't irked by what happened." I paused. "I should say, by what I did."

I was learning to do it. Take responsibility.

"Fine," he said. Then he motioned toward the lardo. "Moving on."

"I was hoping to talk with you about pursuing cooking opportunities here at the restaurant," I said. "Under your tutelage."

"I don't like that word," he said. "*Tutelage.* Please don't use it again."

I nodded. "Okay."

"And, also, no."

53

So when I said put the ingredients on top, I didn't mean you should throw the baby out with the fucking bathwater."

Rain and I were sitting on the steps outside the front door, my belly starting to stick out.

"I did that when I was twenty-six, and it didn't work out."

"But this new show sounds like it would have been different."

I thought of what would be required. Social media and live television and Instagram updates sweeping me up, imploring me to let people into my world, into my experience, before I even knew what that experience was adding up to. Maybe I had been burned so badly I was officially a Luddite. I was certainly getting emotional during this pregnancy. But I now understood something about when I wanted to share myself. And why.

My sister shook her head, like I was crazy, though I could see she was also a little impressed.

"I guess it's a good thing you have job security," she said sarcastically.

I laughed. "I do have a proposition for you," I said.

"What's that?"

"It's a way for Sammy to go to that school."

"Maybe we should go back to you waiting outside until we fall asleep," she said.

I looked at her. "I almost took the show, just so I could get you guys set up in a nice apartment, make it so you didn't have to work. But I figured you wouldn't go for that anyway."

"You figured right."

"The school has a special weekend program. And I have some money from the apartment. Money I could stretch. I can't stay in Montauk anyway. What if I got a place in Harlem? Near the school? Sammy could stay with me on the weekends. That's one night away from you a week. And she'd get to do a bunch of nerdy kid things. It's just one night, but if it works out, we could revisit the full-time thing."

"No fucking way."

"Okay, we won't revisit. But the weekend thing, it'd be good for her. And maybe for you too."

She looked at me like she might yell. And like she might say yes. It could go either way. "I'll think about it," she said.

"You will? Really?"

"Yes."

It was a nice moment. No one reaching in to hug each other, no one offering anything definitive. But nice. At least it was until two headlights interrupted us. A guy drove down the driveway. And then got out of his car.

Danny. My heart skipped a beat, even at the

sight of him. His hands were in his jeans pockets, his uneven button-down, soft against his skin. He looked up and offered a small smile.

"Oh, brother," Rain said, shaking her head.

I wrapped my sweater around my small belly as he walked over to us. And I could feel it, my sister was steeling herself.

"Hey," Danny said.

"Hi," I said.

Rain shot him a look.

Danny nodded at her. "It's nice to see you, Rain," he said.

She pointed right in his face. "You did a shitty thing, *Danny,*" she said. "No, you did two shitty things, because now I'm in a position of having to stick up for my sister, and you know how much that pisses me off. You're not invited into the house."

"I'll stay out here," he said.

She stood up and looked at me.

"He's not going in the house," she said.

"I hear you."

She turned back to Danny. "And she's picking up my kid in fifteen minutes, so don't make her late," she said.

"I've got it," Danny said.

She gave him a last look.

Then she disappeared inside, and we were alone. He smiled, taking me in, not saying anything.

"You look good. Can I say that?"

I nodded. "I'm doing well."

Danny smiled—a real smile—like he could see it. Like that was enough for him. Fourteen years. He knew I was telling the truth.

Then he took in the property. "It's been so long since I've been here. It looks different."

I motioned toward the main house. "There used to be a lot more room."

He laughed. "Yeah, well. I remember the guesthouse being pretty cozy," he said.

I thought about it too. The first time I had brought him home with me from college, we'd stayed there. My father had liked Danny, so we ended up spending a little bit of time with him. Danny brought out the best of my father. It was almost enough to make me think it could be different between us. Danny had always had that power—how had I given it away?—the power to make anything feel possible.

He motioned toward the step where I sat. "May I?"

I shrugged. "You might as well."

Danny took the seat next to me, though he kept looking straight ahead, which was a good thing. I could feel the heat coming off of him, warming me, even from several inches away.

"So . . . I just wanted you to know that I pulled down the site. Ain't No Sunshine is no more."

"You do realize anyone can google me and they'll see everything, right?"

"They'll stop googling after a while. If they haven't already."

"Danny, if that's your idea of an apology . . ."

"It's not."

He focused on his hands, his wedding ring still there. I couldn't stop looking at it.

"I'm not here to apologize," he said. "And I'm not here to argue with you about whether I should."

"So why are you here?"

"I kept thinking that I had to do it, to help you, regardless of what it did to us. It's weird, I thought I wouldn't care if you hated me," he said. "Turns out I was wrong on that front."

He paused.

"Turns out I can't stop thinking about you."

I looked at him. It was the kindest thing he could say, but it wasn't enough. Fourteen years. I knew he wasn't willing to let go, maybe neither of us was. But that was different from knowing how to hold on. Neither of us knew if we could really do that—with so much negative stuff between us now. Except I couldn't feel the negative stuff. When I was with him, actually sitting there with him, he just felt like Danny. Maybe that wasn't enough either. But it felt like a good place to start.

"There was another way, Danny."

"Maybe. But this way worked."

It had worked.

"I'm pregnant."

Danny turned and looked at me. "Really?"

I nodded.

He turned away. "I'm going to need a minute to process that," he said.

I started counting in my head, but before I even got to ten, he reached out and held me to him.

54

You probably didn't think I was long for 28—
or maybe you did. Maybe, after I turned
Julie down (and Z turned me down), you thought
this story would end with Z changing his mind,
giving me a real job, a real shot at the restaurant.
It would have had a certain symmetry to it.
The man I had thought would be the way back
to my old life would instead lead the charge to
my new one.

After all, how often do you meet your opposite
self? Hadn't Chef Z been mine? Here was a
man completely uninterested in the very things
I had pursued—stardom, commercial success,
the praise of others. He had given them away a
long time ago. And even though they had found
their way to him again, he seemed to give them
the amount of time they deserved.

Very little.

There was a lesson in that, which Z had
taught me, about what we should pay attention
to instead. About taking a hard look at what we
are willing to throw away, about what we should
be letting it show us.

There was also a lesson in unmitigated honesty.

"Please get out of my face!" he said when I
found him in the wine cellar.

And how we should temper it.

I almost turned around and gave Lottie my notice instead. She also wouldn't have particularly cared, but she was a lot less scary.

But after I didn't run away, Z seemed mildly interested in what I wanted. "Speak, already," he said.

"I'm moving to New York," I said.

He sighed, not turning from his bottle search. "I thought you wanted a promotion."

"You said no. Plus, I'm having a baby. And the father is in New York. And I hate it here. I mean, not here at the restaurant. Here in the Hamptons, though."

He shot me a look, like I had stepped on his face. "That was a longer answer than I was looking for."

"I don't have a job there," I said. "And I could use one."

"Could you?"

"If you know of anything."

"If I know of anything?"

It was a crazy thing to ask him for, and I knew it. And he knew it. But I didn't actually expect his help. I just thought it would give him an opportunity to say good-bye in his own Chef Z way.

And it did.

Chef Z smiled, like he was going to say he was going to help, like he was going to say he knew a guy, like he was going to say I'd become indispensable to him.

"The radishes are shit tonight," he said.

I smiled. "Is that right?"

He nodded. "Take a bucket of them. And go."

55

The morning I left for New York—to find an apartment, to begin the process of starting again—I found Ethan at the end of the driveway, getting out of his car.

He had been avoiding spending too much time with me, so I was surprised when I walked outside, bag in hand, and saw him walking toward the guesthouse.

"Don't get excited," he said. "I'm just going to see my friend."

"Are you?"

He shrugged. "Depends how this goes," he said.

I motioned toward the top step, and he motioned toward the bottom one.

"Meet you in the middle?" I said.

He smiled, and we both sat down.

He pointed at the bag I was holding in my hands. "What's in there?"

"Lunch," I said. "I'm taking the train to New York."

He looked at the bag, which was incredibly full: two sandwiches, a salad, a large iced tea.

"Are you sure that's enough? You'll be on the train for at least two hours. Maybe three."

"Very funny."

"What are you doing in New York?"

I touched my belly. "I'm going to find out if this is a girl or a boy."

"It's a girl."

"What makes you say that?"

"The old wives' tale. When you're having a boy, it gives you beauty. And when you're having a girl . . ."

I laughed. "Hey! Not friendly."

He shrugged. "You've looked better."

"You're right about that."

He smiled. "Is the husband going with you?"

"That's the plan."

"Good." He nodded. "That's good."

I started to agree, but that wouldn't have been the truth. Everything was different between Danny and me now—a little forced, fairly tense. I didn't want to volunteer that part either. Danny and I would either work it out or we wouldn't. And it was better for Ethan to think we would. It was probably better for all of us to think that, but how could we work it out?

After all, what would that story sound like? We had been married, and I had been unfaithful. And he had sold out our entire lives. And then, we worked it out. It wasn't a good story. It wasn't a story that sells. In the story that sells, he would have forgiven me before he knew I was pregnant. In the story that sells, there wouldn't have been infidelity and betrayal. There wouldn't be someone new sitting in front of me that I didn't want to say good-bye to. There would have been a pervasive love that wouldn't have allowed me to sell my husband out, even when my entire world was for sale.

Yet, maybe having the right story didn't matter. Maybe wanting everything to sound a certain way was how I'd ended up in this mess. Maybe all that mattered was that I was having dinner with Danny tonight, just the two of us, and the possibility of that made me happy.

I did, just, feel happy. And free. It was a weird moment to feel free—with a baby growing inside me. But I'd shed the skin of the wrong life. And there it was, handed to me like a prize. Happiness, freedom. A little bit of both.

Ethan smiled, kindly. "All right," he said. "Life's too short for the awkwardness. When you get back, let me know, we'll go drink cider or something."

"That sounds . . . awful," I said.

"What? I'm running out of nonalcoholic choices."

"Maybe you just want to give me a lift to the station instead?" I said. "We could catch up now."

"No," he said. "Thanks anyway. I've got plans with my friend."

I looked at my old home, his girlfriend inside. "You deserve so much better than that. And maybe I don't have the right to say it, but you do know that, right?"

"They're just plans," he said. "Let me know if I should break them."

Ethan started to walk toward his girlfriend's house. Then he turned back.

"Hey. It's probably a boy. You've never looked better."

"You are lying . . ."

He shrugged, turned back around. "Well, if anyone should know."

56

Here's the last thing I'm going to tell you, at least for now. I left my car out in Montauk and took the train back to New York for many reasons. The main one was so that Sammy would know I was coming back. We made a weekend plan, just the two of us, Rain and Thomas finally going away on their engagement weekend. If Rain knew something was up beyond a weekend away, she wasn't letting on. She casually said, *See you soon,* trusting me to come through for her. We had that, between us, again.

So I wasn't leaving Montauk that day for good, but I would have to leave soon. I would have to set up shop and get ready for the baby and find a job somewhere. Chef Z, in the end, did help a little with that. He put me in touch with a woman who owned a toy store, a few blocks from where I used to live. The woman was a frequent guest at 28. Her store was so sweet— she only sold wooden toys. Noah's Arks and train sets. Her husband was a woodworker and apparently made all the toys himself.

They were opening a second store down the street—this one a specialty food store, this one her dream. Featuring off-the-beaten-path foods: olive oils from northern Kentucky, pinot noir from West Sonoma County, ginger scones from a bakery in Big Sur.

Chef had Lottie call to tell me they needed someone to run the shop. *It sounds pretty great, actually, but it's only tangentially related to cooking,* I'd said. I could hear Z scream in the background, *So are you.*

Then Lottie hung up the phone.

"Excuse me?"

I looked up from my window seat on the train to see a blond girl, mid-twenties, staring down at me. Smiling. I turned off the music.

"Are you Sunshine Mackenzie? *The* Sunshine? Like . . . of *A Little Sunshine*?"

"Maybe."

"Maybe?" Her smile disappeared. "Well, either you are or you aren't."

It seemed like a smart thing to say, except it wasn't true. We are and we aren't. We try and we fail. We tell the truth and then we lie. We want to be a part of things so badly that we'll pretend to be anyone to get into the room. And pretend to be someone else just to stay there. We want to be seen and we want people to guess. We want them to understand. We want to be forgiven. We forgive ourselves. We start again.

"I just wanted a selfie for my Instagram," Blondie said. "Can we do it anyway? No one will know."

"You've got a lot of followers?"

"About fifty thousand."

"Seriously? What do you do that you have so many followers?"

I knew that I sounded about a thousand years old, but she smiled again, pleased that I thought she was important. "That's like barely any."

Then she bent down, posed, and waited for me to get camera-ready too.

So I did. On the local train—somewhere between New York and Montauk, somewhere between the old life and the new one—Sunshine Mackenzie covered her belly (that wasn't their business) and made the peace sign for fifty thousand people she didn't know.

The girl looked at the photograph, analyzing it. "Not bad," she said. "But maybe we should do another without you making a peace sign? No one does that anymore."

I shrugged. "Consider it a throwback to a different time."

She looked annoyed. "The sixties?"

Then she clicked a button as she walked away.

She didn't say *Thank you,* or *See you around.*

She wasn't interested.

If I were a betting woman, I'd say she posted the photograph anyway. Maybe I just like to think she did. People would send in comments asking if I was nice *(Totally!)*, if I had gotten fat *(A little . . . yes!!)*, and one person would ask who I was *(The fake cooking show, remember?)*.

Most of them would. Some of them wouldn't. The rest of them wouldn't care.

Which, you should know, was a great way for Sunshine to say good-bye.

ACKNOWLEDGMENTS

Suzanne Gluck and Marysue Rucci. You remain the dream team.

My gratitude to everyone who gave this novel a great publishing home, especially Carolyn Reidy, Jonathan Karp, Richard Rhorer, Elizabeth Breeden, Cary Goldstein, Zachary Knoll, Sarah Reidy, Clio Seraphim, and Kitty Dulin.

I owe so much to the people who provided insight into Sunshine's world. Several of you asked to remain anonymous, so I'll thank you in a different forum than this, but please know your insight and humor made researching Sunshine a treat.

I can't say thank you enough to Sylvie Rabineau, and to my early readers, whose feedback was invaluable.

Thank you to my parents, Rochelle and Andrew Dave, and the entire Dave and Singer families. And much love to my wonderful friends.

Finally, my son and my husband. I love you with all my heart.

Laura Dave is the international bestselling author of Eight Hundred Grapes, The First Husband, The Divorce Party, and London Is the Best City in America. Her work has been published in eighteen countries, and several of her novels have been optioned as major motion pictures. She resides in New York with her husband and their son.

Books are produced in the United States using U.S.-based materials

Books are printed using a revolutionary new process called THINKtech™ that lowers energy usage by 70% and increases overall quality

Books are durable and flexible because of smythe-sewing

Paper is sourced using environmentally responsible foresting methods and the paper is acid-free

Center Point Large Print
600 Brooks Road / PO Box 1
Thorndike, ME 04986-0001 USA

(207) 568-3717

US & Canada:
1 800 929-9108
www.centerpointlargeprint.com